MURDOCH
MYSTERIES
Let Darkness Bury the Dead

MAUREEN JENNINGS

TITAN BOOKS

Murdoch Mysteries: *Let Darkness Bury the Dead*
Print edition ISBN: 9781783294930
E-book edition ISBN: 9781783294947

Published by Titan Books
A division of Titan Publishing Group Ltd
144 Southwark St, London SE1 0UP

First Titan edition: November 2017
2 4 6 8 10 9 7 5 3 1

Printed and bound in Great Britain by CPI Group UK Ltd.

WHAT DID YOU THINK OF THIS BOOK? WE LOVE TO HEAR FROM OUR READERS.
Please email us at: readerfeedback@titanemail.com,
or write to us at the above address.
TO RECEIVE ADVANCE INFORMATION, NEWS, COMPETITIONS, AND EXCLUSIVE
offers online, please sign up for the Titan newsletter on our website: www.
titanbooks.com

To Iden, as always and forever. He unfailingly provides me with support and encouragement.

And to all the boys who never came home.

On being informed of the death of his son, Harry Percy, Northumberland goes into a frenzy, vowing to unleash terrible rage upon the perpetrators. He says:

> But let one spirit of the first-born Cain
> Reign in all bosoms, that, each heart being set
> On bloody courses, the rude scene may end,
> And darkness be the burier of the dead.
> —WILLIAM SHAKESPEARE,
> *HENRY IV, PART 2*, ACT 1, SCENE 1

THE GOLDEN AGE
Not for national or personal
aggrandizement are we to
combine—far be it from us! But we
need the invincible strength of union for
righteousness and peace, the sheltering

power under which no man need suffer wrong and the resources of great Empires may be developed for the good for all. . . .

The energy, the inventive genius, the self sacrifice and wealth of the world can surely be set to a better task than by perfecting the engines of war by which to crush out in agony our brother man? For war is no abstract term—it is the bloody holocaust of thousands of brave men . . . and the bitter heartbreak of more thousands of desolate women. . . .

And yet it can only be "By Mutual Consent." Peace and goodwill must be no veneer, but right through the heart of the nations and their rulers, before strong defence can be abandoned as a slur on the good friends and neighbours of any land.

—S.J.C., *ENGLAND'S WELCOME*
(ON THE CORONATION OF GEORGE V)

AUTHOR'S PREAMBLE

DETECTIVE WILLIAM H. MURDOCH CAME INTO BEING (fictionally, that is) in 1895. He was thirty-four, single, lonely, and focused on his job. Seven books later (fictional time 1896) he retired, as it were, to take up a life on television. At this point he had found love.

The TV world and the book world are often, as you can imagine, quite different. As a writer whose books are adapted, you hope they are not too different. I've been very lucky that way. *Murdoch Mysteries*, produced by Shaftesbury and shown for the last few years on the CBC in Canada, have been faithful to the characters that came out of my brain. Nevertheless, when I decided to write a new Murdoch book, I thought it might be confusing to new readers if I attempted to pick up where I'd left off. Besides which, I was already enthralled by the stories of World War I, both on the battlefield and on the home front. It has been some of the most fascinating exploration I've ever done. So in this book we meet an older Murdoch. The year is 1917. He is fifty-six years old, a senior detective now, still living in Toronto. He has a son, Jack, who is returning from the trenches.

Canada's participation in World War I was highly significant, and that is a major part of this story. I have tried to create a picture of the city of Toronto as it was at that time. A city that slept in sorrow. As for Murdoch, it is his job to maintain the law, even though it may be at a terrible personal cost.

PROLOGUE

THEY MARCH INTO PLACE IN FRONT OF THE CANVAS screen and the post that has been hammered into the ground. It's not yet dawn but the sky is greyer now, seeping down into the pocked, muddy field, one mirroring the other. As commanded, they ABOUT TURN so that their backs are to the place of execution. They face the black silhouettes of the skeletal trees.

The sergeant is a big man, and the cutting wind has reddened his face and the drizzling rain made droplets on his moustache. He starts to pace in front of the line. His gaze is fixed on a point over their heads.

"Listen to me, lads. I know some of you have tender hearts

and you might be tempted to feel sorry for this prisoner. I'm telling you: don't. He is a proven coward who left his unit in the lurch." The sergeant has a strong voice, hoarse at the edges, as if he has spent his life shouting into large spaces.

"I know what it's like to be scared. I'm not ashamed to admit it. We all know, but *we* deal with it like men. We don't muck our britches and run off to cower behind Mother's skirts. In this case, the enemy mounted an attack and the prisoner dropped his rifle and refused to go over the top. There were several casualties in the push. Others volunteered to bring in the wounded, at great risk to themselves. He would not do even that. He was needed and he let us all down. If we can't rely on our comrades, who can we rely on?"

Nobody answers. They're not expected to.

The sergeant halts and deliberately meets the eyes of each man in turn. His brown eyes are bloodshot.

"You've probably heard the story that one of these rifles has a blank, not a bullet. That may or may not be true. But if you're the sort with a woman's conscience, you can comfort yourself with that notion. You might not be one of those who shot the poor sod. Even if one of these rifles holds a blank, not even me knows which one is which. It's random. Up to the Almighty. And don't think you'll be able to tell the difference because you can't." He begins to pace again. "But *please*, all of you lads, don't think you'll be doing the prisoner a kindness by firing over his head. All that will do is prolong his misery. If he's not dead after the first volley it's left to me to finish him off." The sergeant wipes rain from his cheeks. Surely not tears, just rainwater. "Rumours to the contrary, I too have a soft heart and I don't fancy doing that if I don't have to."

At the end of the line, the sergeant reverses his path. Again, he fixes his gaze on a point above their heads.

"The prisoner will be seated on a box in front of the screen. His hands will be tied behind him and fastened to the post. Most likely he will not move but you never know. Some prisoners do manage to wriggle and squirm. Makes things harder for us. He might be shaking but don't let that deter you. It's nippy this morning. He's had a good tot of rum for breakfast. He will have a reversed gas mask hood covering his head. Apparently he wanted it off but that's never a good idea for all concerned so the request was refused. Now don't forget this prisoner has shown himself to be as much an enemy to us as any Hun in his trench. You might even say more so."

There is the sound of a motor car coming along the road.

"Right," says the sergeant. "Here's the ambulance. It'll take a minute to get him settled then I will give the command. You've all been picked because you are crack shots, but to make things easier for you, there will be a circle of white paper pinned to his chest. That is your target."

He stares off at something they can't see. Then he's back. He continues. Louder.

"There will be three commands. First: *About Turn*, which you will do smartly and without hesitation. Second: *Present Arms*. Third: *Aim, Fire*. One volley only. When your guns are discharged, I will give the *At Ease.* You will wait while I go and check on the condition of the prisoner. I will remove the paper and count the number of holes. I expect to see every bullet accounted for."

The motor car has stopped nearby. Doors open and then slam shut. Over the heads of the soldiers, the sergeant watches the proceedings. He seems satisfied by what he sees. He addresses the men.

"*About Turn . . . Present Arms . . . Aim . . . Fire.*"

CHAPTER ONE

The grey November day had seemed endless, filled with trivial pieces of police officialdom: a variety of fines, numerous licences, several detectives' schedules. Murdoch had to sign off on all of them. On days like this he wondered if his position as senior detective was really worth it. True, he had an extra half a day off, his own office, small as it was, and a slight increase in his wages. And he was responsible for supervising the eighteen detectives at headquarters, which he actually liked. One of the jobs he truly did *not* like, however, was acting as mediator between couples who had run into trouble with the law, usually for disturbing the peace. Chief Inspector Kennedy was supposed to handle these cases, but he hated this duty too and always found an opportunity to fob it off on Murdoch.

"You're very good at it," he said. "You can calm them down. Me, I just get aggravated."

Murdoch risked a glance at the clock, which he'd deliberately positioned high on the opposite wall out of sight of his visitors—he didn't want to give the impression that he didn't have time for their various plights. Today, however, he could barely contain his impatience. The train bringing the returning soldiers was due to arrive at five o'clock and it was now twenty minutes to the hour. He didn't want to be late.

The young couple sitting in front of his desk had sunk into a sullen silence. She was staring off to one side; he was looking at the floor, twisting his cap round and round in his big hands. They'd both obviously dressed in their best for this meeting. He was wearing a smart, new-looking Ulster, and she was decked out in a navy blue serge coat and matching felt hat. However, the wide brim could not conceal a nasty bruise on her cheek. Her husband had a livid scratch running down his jawline. He said she'd started the row: one of many, as it turned out. When she flew at him, he pushed her away, and she hit herself on the dresser. She agreed to that part but said she'd only been defending herself when, quite uncalled for, he'd gone on a rampage over a comment she'd made.

Murdoch removed his watch from his waistcoat pocket and consulted it ostentatiously.

"I'm afraid I'll have to draw this to a close very soon," he said.

The young woman looked up at him, her thin face dark with anger. "But we haven't come to an agreement yet."

"I realize that, but it might be good for you both to sleep on things. Mr. Aggett, you said your tribunal isn't until Friday. You have until then to reach a decision. We can meet again on Thursday."

"I don't see what good coming back will do," snapped Mrs. Aggett. "Arthur is obviously not going to change his mind."

Her husband sighed. He stopped spinning his hat.

"Lottie's right about that, sir. I don't see as I will. I've got to apply for an exemption or else I'll break my ma's heart."

"What about me?" his wife said. "What about my heart? I can't hold my head up anywhere. People think I'm married to a slacker. I'm beginning to think they're right."

She delved into her handbag and fished out a crumpled sheet of newspaper. "Look. This was in the *Evening Telegram* just last week."

She thrust it out to Murdoch.

TO THE WOMEN OF CANADA

BAR THOSE MEN WHO REFUSE TO FIGHT, YOU WOMEN. REFUSE their invitations, scorn their attentions. Tell them to come in uniform, no matter how soiled or ill fitting. Bar out the able bodied man who has no obligations, show that you despise him.

Such letters had become less frequent since reports from the battlefields had started coming through. A lot less glory than when the initial enthusiastic volunteers had marched off; a lot more tragedy. Still, these exhortations were obviously having some effect. Murdoch handed the sheet back to Lottie.

"I mean to say, what if the Krauts invaded Canada like they did poor little Belgium? What would happen to us women then?"

"I don't think there's much likelihood of the Germans invading us, Mrs. Aggett."

"You don't know, though, do you? The Belgiums probably thought the same way. It's only if our men act like men and are brave that we'll be safe."

Arthur shook his head vehemently. "I ain't a coward, sir. I'd go in a minute if I thought my mother could look after herself without me, but she can't." He paused. "My ma and Lottie just don't get along, you see. If anything were to happen to me I know Lottie wouldn't stay around and take care of things."

Murdoch regarded her. "Is that true, Mrs. Aggett?"

"In a manner of speaking," she said with a shrug.

"Why don't you get along?"

"I suppose you might say we're like chalk and cheese. His mother was never partial to me from the start. I've done my best but she won't have any of it. She's a widow, see, and she's always doted on him as the only child and the breadwinner. If she had any say in it, he'd be a bachelor for the rest of his life. But that's not natural, is it?"

Fortunately for Murdoch, she didn't wait for an answer.

"She just won't accept that marriage means the wife must come first."

"When did you get married?" Murdoch asked.

"Last year. We was all right until the new act came in. Now all is woe."

Murdoch hid his smile at her expression. "You're referring to the conscription act, I presume?"

"That's the one. Like I said, she wants him to put in for an exemption, but I don't."

"There are a lot of women who don't want their sons to go to war, Mrs. Aggett."

"Maybe so, but Arthur's ma isn't acting out of loving feelings, believe you me. She's afraid if he cops it she'll have nobody to fetch and carry for her any more."

Aggett seemed about to retort but he swallowed it and ducked his head.

Murdoch addressed him. "Any comment on that, Mr. Aggett?"

"Ma has never been strong, and I'm the only thing she has in the world. I daren't risk leaving her alone."

"When did your father die?" Murdoch asked.

The young man shifted uncomfortably. "We don't rightly know, sir. He left my ma when I was just a sprig. Never a word from him since."

"Did your mother attempt to find him?"

"Oh, yes sir. She reported it to the police, but he'd vanished. Never found hide nor hair of him."

"Can't blame him for scarpering," muttered Lottie.

Her husband flashed her a look of fury but he didn't speak.

Murdoch checked his watch again. "I can't do any more until we know what the tribunal decides to do with your application for exemption. We can talk about what to do when we know what's what." He regarded the young man, making his expression stern. "In the meantime, if I see your wife come in here with another bruise I'm going to charge you with assault. I won't care if it's an accident or who started what. You'll go to jail, and neither your wife nor your mother will benefit from that."

Aggett sighed. "I'm sorry, sir. It's just that . . ."

"Just that what?"

"Lottie tries my temper sore sometimes. She's always on at me to sign up. Not a moment's let-up. She's on one side, ma's going prostrate on the other. It's enough to drive a man mad between the two of them."

"Maybe so, but it's also a man's job to show some character and not lose his temper. Especially when the object of his anger is weaker than he is. Do I make myself clear, Mr. Aggett?"

The young man nodded. "Yes, sir."

Murdoch returned his watch to his pocket and stood up. "I'm calling this meeting to an end."

Ten minutes. He could just make it.

OFFICIAL POST CARD.

Nothing is to be written on this side except the date and signature of the sender. Sentences not required may be erased. <u>If anything else is added the post card will be destroyed.</u>

[Postage must be prepaid on any letter or post card addressed to the sender of this card]

I am quite well.

I have been admitted into hospital

　{sick} and am going on well.

　{wounded} and hope to be discharged soon. *XX*

I am being sent down to the base.

I have received your

　{letter dated _____}

　{telegram _____}

　{parcel _____}

Letter follows at first opportunity. *XX*

I have received no letter from you

    {lately _____}

    {for a long time _____}

SIGNATURE ONLY   *Jack Murdoch*

DATE.   *October 27 1917*

CHAPTER TWO

UNION STATION WAS NOT COMPLETELY FINISHED YET but showed promise of being grand. Some people grumbled about the time it was taking and the cost of it, but the city fathers were keen to have a railway station that would befit a city of Toronto's growing importance.

As Murdoch hurried down the stairs to the platform he could hear the skirl of bagpipes. A piper was marching up and down at one end. His kilt swished about his bare knees, his sporran bounced, and the tassels at the ends of the pipes danced. Murdoch knew it took a good pair of lungs to get even a squeak out of the bagpipes, and the piper also had to have breath enough to march. This man, older, with a weather-beaten face, had got the routine down to a fine art. He was moving in a way that looked effortless, as if he could walk for hours more and still create enough music to stir the soul.

Murdoch stopped to get his bearings. The piper began to play an old melody, "Highland Cathedral," and almost of their own accord Murdoch's feet moved. He grinned slightly. Amy had often teased him about his response to the sound of the bagpipes, "You're no different from a hound who picks up a scent and starts quivering." He'd always replied, "I'm from Nova Scotia, what do you expect?" When the war had continued to gobble up the country's young men, his son had decided to halt his university studies and enlist. Murdoch hadn't been happy about that but hoped that, at least, Jack would join the 48th Highlanders. Instead, his son had chosen the newly formed Princess Patricia's Canadian Light Infantry. "We'll create our own history," he'd said to Murdoch. Fair enough.

The platform was jammed with welcomers. The mayor, Thomas Church, and a couple of aldermen were the official greeting party, accompanied by several photographers, presumably from the city's main newspapers. Next to them, a smartly turned out young officer was standing beside a banner that proclaimed "YOUR COUNTRY NEEDS YOU. JOIN UP TODAY." He was handing out leaflets. The air all around was alive with excitement. No matter what, these soldiers were at least returning alive.

Suddenly Murdoch heard the sound of chanting behind him.

"NO MORE WAR. NO MORE WAR."

He turned to see a little group of women, all carrying placards, all shouting. They reached the bottom of the stairs and headed with great determination in the direction of the mayor's party.

"STOP THE WAR NOW. DON'T KILL OUR SONS AND BROTHERS."

The startled crowd gave way before them but the recruiting officer jumped forward, holding out his arms as a barrier in front of his table. The women seemed determined to sabotage the recruitment. One of the aldermen grabbed a woman in the group and tried to pull her away. She struggled violently to get free, shouting, "Murderers! You're all murderers!"

Her comrades waved their placards. "STOP THE WAR!"

An older woman in the crowd joined in the struggle, on the side of the alderman. She actually swung at the young woman with her handbag, and the protester fell to the ground. Her allies tried to come to her aid but now there were more people involved. Some of the onlookers were trying to seize the placards but the young women were hanging on determinedly. More women fell to the ground. The mayor was calling for calm but nobody was listening. In a moment, the mood of the crowd had changed from happiness to anger.

"Police. Let me through. Make way, please. Police." Murdoch pushed closer to the melee. One of the photographers snapped a picture.

Mayor Church tried to help a woman to her feet but she shrugged him off.

"Look," she yelled, and she waved her hand in the direction of the train that was slowly puffing into the station. "Talk to *them* about the noble cause. See if they agree with you."

By now Murdoch had reached the mayor. The woman had got to her feet and she linked arms with two of her compatriots. Another couple of protesters were grabbing at the leaflets and tearing them into shreds. One of them was a young man, slight of build, well dressed. The recruiting officer pounced on him and gave him a hard clip across the side of the head.

"Stop that. You're destroying government property." He began to shake the young man. "You're a bloody coward. You just pretend to have principles but you don't. You're a thorough slacker."

Murdoch had got close enough by now to catch the soldier by the arm. "I'm a police officer. I'll take care of this."

The soldier's face was suffused with anger. "He's nothing but a yellow-belly."

The young man shrank back but couldn't get away.

"Let him go!" Murdoch had to shout above the din from the skirmish going on behind him.

One of the protesters suddenly shoved her way over to them.

"He's half your size. It's you who's the coward," she said to the officer, who raised his hand, looking as if he was too incensed to remember the rules of chivalry. She stumbled backwards. Murdoch caught her before she fell to the ground.

He was never to know what might have transpired as they were all saved from further demonstrations by the shrill whistle of the train conductor.

"Train's coming in," he called.

The soldier relaxed his grip on the young demonstrator, but not before hissing, "Coward."

The girl reached out and pulled him out of harm's way. She put her arm around his shoulders and led him into the bosom of the group. For a moment it looked as if the soldier would follow them, but he must have seen the expression on Murdoch's face because he remained where he was.

The guard blew his whistle again and the onlookers shifted their attention to the oncoming train. The piper had stopped playing, but with a couple of squeezes he began again.

"Officers will alight first, then walking cases, then others," called the conductor. "Please don't press in on them. Make room."

To Murdoch's relief the crowd obeyed. As one, the mayor and his group moved forward, photographers at their heels. The demonstrators had fallen silent. Murdoch could see they were picking up their placards.

Suddenly the young woman who had been involved in the fracas with the recruiting officer dashed over to Murdoch.

"Mr. Murdoch. It's me, Fiona. Fiona Williams."

She must have seen in his face that he didn't recognize her, because she added, "I was at Sackville School the same time as Jack."

Suddenly Murdoch saw the girl she had been. Back then she had braided her long hair, but now she had a fashionable bob. Her fair skin, lightly freckled, and her lively brown eyes were unchanged.

"So you were. I remember now."

"Are you here to meet Jack? I saw in the newspaper that he was one of the wounded. I was going to write but . . ." Her voice tailed off. "How is he?"

"It could have been a lot worse," answered Murdoch. "He's suffered a bullet wound in his upper arm. Also got a whiff of gas."

The hissing train, blowing off steam like an overheated horse, had drawn to a halt. Every second coach was hung with a large banner with a red cross on it. Striking and unmistakable.

Fiona turned to the group of demonstrators, who seemed to be hovering uncertainly. "Come on. We've done what we came to do." She glanced over her shoulder at Murdoch. "Please tell Jack I said hello."

Murdoch watched as they all made their way back to the stairs. The sole young man appeared to be in need of succour, and one of the women had her arm around him. A few people scowled, one older woman hissed at them, but the rest of the crowd was now preoccupied by the train.

The piper blew a trill.

The conductor called out, "Stand clear, folks. They will all be getting out. Just give them some room."

The officers disembarked first; there was a shout of excitement as they pushed open the train doors and stepped down onto the platform.

Murdoch could see a familiar figure leaning out of a window in the second coach. *Jack.* He felt a moment of joy so intense everything else was blotted out. He was irresistibly pushed forward until he was directly in front of the carriage door. Jack saw him.

"Hello, Pa." He held up one hand. "Hold on." It took him several minutes to get to the door in the crush but finally he was there.

"Give me that," said Murdoch. He grabbed Jack's haversack and set it on the ground as his son climbed down to the platform. Jack's right arm was in a sling but they were able to clasp hands at least.

"How was the journey?"

Murdoch knew how banal and inadequate his question was, but at that moment he didn't trust himself to say anything else.

"Bit tiring. Glad it's over," answered Jack. His voice sounded hoarse and raspy. Murdoch had known to expect that effect of the gassing Jack had suffered, but it was nevertheless shocking. As was his son's appearance. Jack had lost a lot of weight. His army greatcoat hung on him, and his face was too pale, his cheeks and eye sockets hollowed.

He stood back and surveyed his father. "You didn't have this many grey hairs when I saw you last, surely?"

"It's your imagination. I couldn't have changed that much in a year," spluttered Murdoch. He flicked at his moustache. "Besides, it makes me look wiser."

"Pa, you always look wise. It's your most compelling feature."

Before Murdoch could think of a suitable response, Jack bent to pick up his haversack.

Murdoch forestalled him. "I'll get that." And he grabbed it

as if it held a fistful of jewels in danger of being stolen. Jack didn't protest.

They started to walk along the crowded platform. Jack had fallen silent again and was looking around as if he were a country boy come to the big city for the first time.

"My God, Jack," Murdoch burst out after a few moments. "You look like you could do with a good scrub. Not to mention some clean clothes."

"The boat didn't have the greatest of facilities, and they took us directly from the dock to the train." He gave a faint smile. "Sorry. Do I pong?"

"'Fraid so."

Jack indicated the slowly moving soldiers all around him. "Good thing we're all the same. Nobody notices." Suddenly he called out, "Hey, Percy. Over here. Hold on a sec, Pa. It's my chum. I wondered where the silly sod had got to."

He waved at a soldier leaning on a cane next to the coach from which Jack had disembarked. The fellow waved back enthusiastically and headed toward them. Murdoch noticed he had a strange, wavering sort of gait. As he got closer Murdoch could see a V-shaped scar, still raw and livid, between his eyebrows. It puckered his brow and had the disconcerting effect of making him seem to be in a constant state of bewilderment.

"This must be your father," he said when he reached them. "You look a lot alike."

"Pa, this is Percy McKinnon," said Jack. "We're in the same platoon. I wrote to you about him."

"So you did."

Percy held out his hand. "Good to meet you, Mr. Murdoch. Jack has talked a lot about you."

"All good, I hope."

"All exemplary."

They shook hands, and Murdoch was struck by how icy cold the other man's skin was.

"Is somebody meeting you?" he asked.

"No. My folks couldn't get in. Too far to come."

"Where are you staying?" Murdoch asked.

"At a boarding house for the time being."

"Where is it? I can drop you off. I've got a motor car."

His son gaped at him. "A motor car? We *are* going up in the world."

"Don't get your hopes up," said Murdoch. "It's borrowed."

"And you know how to drive it?"

"Obviously."

"Where's your wheel?"

"I could hardly give you a lift home on that."

"You used to. Often."

McKinnon laughed. "Thank you for the offer, sir, but I'm fine with walking. The place isn't far."

"It's cold out. Let us take you there."

Murdoch didn't miss the quick exchange of glances between Jack and his friend.

"He's all right, Pa," interjected Jack. "He needs the exercise. It's good for us, so the sawbones tell us. Speeds up the healing. Isn't that so, Percy?"

McKinnon gave Jack a mock salute. "Absolutely right, Corporal. We can't take too long to recover. We might have to go right back in a couple of months."

"Good Lord. I hope not," said Murdoch. "I hope the war's over before then."

Jack frowned. "Didn't look to me like it was going to end any time soon. Wouldn't you say, Percy?"

His chum nodded. "Fritz is a tough customer. They aren't giving up yet. But then neither are we."

Suddenly Jack froze. He was staring back toward the train, where the last of the injured soldiers were being lifted to the platform.

"Percy. Look. There's Tim."

His friend startled and looked in the same direction. He shook his head and said, quietly, "It's not Tim, Jack."

"Yes, it is. I have to speak to him." He took a step but Percy caught him by the arm.

"I tell you, it's not Tim, Jack. It *couldn't* be."

His voice was low and intense but Jack reacted as if he'd been doused with cold water. He shuddered.

"Course, it's not. Just looked like him for a second." He turned to Murdoch. "Let's see if we can get out of here. Pa, why don't you lead the way. You can clear a path for us."

Murdoch obeyed. Over his shoulder, he addressed McKinnon. "Come and have a meal with us as soon as you're settled."

"Thank you, sir. Perhaps later in the week. Tonight I intend to sleep for twenty-four hours straight. I've got a lot of catching up to do."

"We're actually on the telephone now so you can ring," said Murdoch. "Shall I give you the number?"

"My father's very proud of having all the latest modern conveniences," interjected Jack. "Don't worry about it, Percy. Sending a pigeon will be just as good."

"Right. Just give me some time to rest up."

There seemed to be an anxiety coming from the young man that Murdoch didn't quite understand. He had the strange sense it had to do with Murdoch himself. Perhaps Percy had had some trouble with officers of the law in the past.

There you go again. Always the suspicious mind of a policeman, seeing things that aren't there.

By now they had caught up with a woman walking slowly toward the exit beside a wheeled stretcher, which was being pushed by a Red Cross nurse. The man lying there was engulfed in bandages. His wrapped hands were outside the blanket; his head was a white, shapeless lump. There was a hole in the bandage, presumably for breathing and eating, but that was all. The woman, fashionably dressed, of middle age, had brought a small brown terrier with her and it trotted alongside. It was wearing a bright tartan coat against the cold.

Jack turned to his chum.

"Hey, Percy, do you remember that dog who came into the trench? It was shortly before the last push. Poor little beast was out of his mind with fear but when he saw we had food, he jumped down and started begging. He'd lost part of his tail but he was still wagging the bloody stump to beat the band. He was actually white but he was so caked with mud he seemed to be brown at first. Do you remember?"

"Of course. He was a pathetic little beast."

"There were a lot of stray dogs," said Jack to Murdoch. "They'd been left behind when the villagers evacuated. Some cats, too. They came to us."

"What happened to him?" Murdoch asked.

"He was blown to pieces. I saw the remnants in No Man's Land. He must have been trying to get home."

His voice sounded strange, and Murdoch saw to his dismay that Jack was fighting tears.

FROM *CANADA IN FLANDERS*
BY SIR MAX AITKEN, M.P.

. . . THE EXPEDITIONARY FORCE MARCHING FROM their billets towards the trenches—they had been at the front for months, yet they stepped as freshly as though they were just from home . . . Their faces shone with health; their eyes were as bright as those of a troop of schoolboys. . . . They whistled as they marched.

RETURN OF THE DEAD

The mind can't take in the absence right
  away.
You expect to see him any day.
And you do.
That's him there on the fire step,
Shoulders hunched, chin tucked.
But close up
You realize you're wrong.
Your flash of joy burns out.
You could shout in anger
But you don't.
What's the use?
The moon shines then
And you spy him down the line.
Sitting among weary men.
Eyes closed. All asleep.
And you wake him and say,
Hey, comrade. Friend.
Aren't you supposed to be dead?
Captain saw you get it.
"Blown to bits," he said.
Right by my side.
He was grey as the coming day,
When he spoke
As if he was close to death himself.
But in all that smoke.

It's easy to make a mistake.
Could have been some other bloke.
Went to glory.
So you still expect to see him
Walk out of the fog that's on the hill.
And you'll tell him the story.
He'll shrug.
He'll say.
Blood and bone and brain
All look the same don't they?

CHAPTER THREE

Murdoch led the way upstairs. "Needless to say, I've put you in your old room."

"You didn't change anything, did you, Pa? Didn't think it needed new wallpaper or new furniture or anything like that?"

"Nope. I did consider leaving the dust undisturbed but Miss Dorsett wouldn't stand for it."

They entered the room and Murdoch put Jack's haversack on the chair by the bed.

"There. Just as if you'd never left."

"Thanks, Pa."

"I wish I'd known about your chum earlier. I could have made up the spare room. He could have stayed here."

Jack shook his head. "Percy got a bit scrambled when we were over there. He isn't very sociable at the moment. He'd prefer to be on his own."

"How did he get wounded?"

Jack walked over to the window and looked out.

"Can we have a moratorium on war stories for a little while, Pa?"

"Just asking. You haven't even said what happened to you exactly. You get the prize for short letters."

Jack shrugged. "I will talk about it sometime, I promise. Just not now." He leaned his forehead against the windowpane. "The street looks just the same as it did when I left, except the Andersons have painted their trim. It used to be green. Can't say I like the new colour as much."

"Don't you? I quite like it myself. Ours needs doing too but I haven't got around to it yet."

Jack turned back, yawning. "I'm bushed, Pa. I didn't get much sleep last night, what with one thing and another. Do you mind if I grab a bit of shut-eye?"

"Of course not. I didn't know if you'd be hungry or not so there's a stew we can heat up any time. And don't worry, I didn't make it, Miss Dorsett did."

"I'm sure anything will taste better than what I've been eating lately. Even the hospital rations left a lot to be desired."

Murdoch could feel himself hovering. He hated feeling so awkward in the presence of his own son but this tall, gaunt man seemed like a stranger. Twelve months ago, he'd marched off, chatty as ever, full of piss and vinegar, looking for *a chance to knock the Krauts off their pedestal*. Murdoch wished desperately Amy were still here. Surely she would have known what to do to erase that dreadful haunted expression from their son's face.

"Speaking of Miss Dorsett, she has been most faithful in writing to me. Not to mention sending food parcels. I understand she had to go to Windsor to look after her sister."

"That's right. Mrs. Philips is a widow on her own. Miss Dorsett always rushes down when called. Frankly, I think her sister suffers more from loneliness than anything."

Jack sat down on the edge of the bed. He'd taken off the sling and he gingerly rotated his shoulder joint. "You wouldn't happen to have a spot of liquor in the house, would you, Pa? Rum preferably. It's a good pick-me-up. To tell you the truth, I'm missing my daily tot."

"No rum but I've got some brandy. Will that do?"

"Much appreciated. And if you can find me a cig, I'd appreciate that as well."

"I bought you two packets of Sweet Caps."

"Thanks, Pa. You're a prince. By the way, the province going dry must be a pain in the backside. I suppose that's all you're dealing with these days."

"Not all, but enforcing the act is taking up time that could be better spent on less trivial misdemeanours."

"The policeman's lot. Don't think. Just do what you're told. Quite like the army, really. Ours not to reason why, Ours but to do or die, and all that."

At that moment, Jack was seized by a fit of coughing that made him clutch at his chest. Murdoch waited it out, forcing himself not to put his arms around his son. Finally it subsided.

"All right?"

"Good as can be, Pa. I'm told it will get better over time."

"Sure you want those cigarettes?"

"I'm sure."

Jack started to unwrap the wool puttees from his lower legs.

"Hey, let me do that," said Murdoch. He finished unwinding the puttees and then unlaced Jack's boots and pulled them off.

Jack accepted the help passively.

"While we're at it, let's get you right out of that uniform. You'll be more comfortable."

With Murdoch's assistance Jack took off his tunic, then slipped down his braces and undid the buttons of his trousers. Murdoch tugged them off.

"My Lord, they're not exactly satin soft, are they?"

He placed everything across the chair.

Jack grinned. "Makes me feel like a nipper again. I used to like it when you put me to bed, when dear old Mrs. Kitchen wasn't available. It didn't happen that often so it was special."

Murdoch nodded, not trusting himself to speak.

"You didn't always know what to do or where things were."

Murdoch winced. "Sorry about that."

"Oh, I didn't mind at all. Rather liked it, in fact. It made me feel quite smug that there was something I knew that you didn't."

With the uniform removed Jack's thinness was even more evident.

"Where did the bullet get you, exactly?" Murdoch asked.

Jack touched the under part of his arm above the elbow. "Right there."

"Whew. You were lucky it didn't break the bone."

"Yes, I suppose you might say that was my lucky day all round. Gassed but not as bad as many; wounded but not permanently. Definitely a lucky day."

The inflection of his voice betrayed no emotion, and his head was turned away so that Murdoch couldn't read his expression.

"How did it happen? Was it a sniper?"

"No, it wasn't. But war stories later, Pa. I promise."

Jack pushed up the sleeve of his combinations and scratched his arm. Murdoch saw the skin was covered with purplish red spots.

"Good heavens. What are those from?"

"Flea bites. They drive you nuts with the itching, but if you scratch they get infected quickly."

"I think we'd better get your things laundered."

"Thanks, Pa. We were deloused at the hospital but another round wouldn't be amiss."

"There are clean shirts and collars in the top drawer of the dresser. Underwear and socks in the second drawer. Your two winter suits are in the wardrobe. They'll hang on you but they'll have to do for now. We'll soon put some flesh back on your bones."

"Sounds like a good plan to me," said Jack. "I told Percy he could borrow some of my clothes if he needs to. He doesn't have any civvies with him. I hope you don't mind."

"Why should I? They're your things."

"Okay. Thanks."

"What do you want me to do with your haversack?"

"You can leave it for now. I'll empty it in the morning." Jack yawned, swung his feet onto the bed, and lay back. He coughed harshly for a few moments. Murdoch could do nothing but wait.

Jack must have seen the distress on his father's face.

"You couldn't always know where the gas was. It sank into the mud, and if you kicked that up the gas came with it. I'm told the cough will go away eventually. I should be doing my breathing exercises to strengthen my lungs but I keep forgetting."

"I'd better start reminding you, then," said Murdoch. Then wished he'd held his tongue. The last thing his son needed was a nagging father at his elbow.

Jack sighed. "Would it be possible to have a bath sometime soon?"

"Of course. Whenever you're ready."

Jack shifted his injured arm to a more comfortable position. "Sometimes in the trenches that's all you could think about. A hot bath that would wash it all off you. The mud, the lice, the blood."

He turned his head to look directly at his father.

"You said at the station that I had a pong?"

"I, er . . ."

"Is it the stink of death? I was in the mud, you see, and

boy does it smell. We don't have the chance to get everybody buried. Horses, mules, men. They have to lie where they fall. Pooee. Rotting corpses do give off a dreadful stink. Is that what you smelled?"

Murdoch was taken aback, both by the question and by the intensity of his son's voice.

"No, nothing like that. Just good old honest sweat. You'll be right as rain after your bath."

Jack closed his eyes.

"I'm a restless sleeper these days, Pa," he muttered. "Don't worry if you hear me prowling about in the night. I often find it's relaxing to walk about for a while. Best if you leave me be . . . Sleep is sweet at first . . ." His voice tailed off, and within a minute he was fast asleep. His mouth fell open and he started to snore softly.

Murdoch noticed the toes of both of his socks were neatly darned. He wondered if Jack had done that himself. There was no reason the sight of them should make him feel such a stab of sadness, but it did.

He took the quilt from the rack and gently covered him. In sleep, Jack's features softened, and he looked more like the boy Murdoch knew. He wanted to stroke his hair as he'd done when he was ill with some childish malady. But he didn't want to wake him up. Instead, he found himself making the sign of the cross. *May the Lord bless you.* Something he hadn't done in a long time.

He gathered up the discarded uniform and left the room.

TRENCH ORDERS.

#14: RUM

(a) Rum when authorized will be kept under the personal charge of the company commander.

(b) The best time for a rum issue is in the early morning.

(c) No issue of rum will be made, except in the presence of an officer.

(d) Men undergoing punishment for drunkenness will receive no issue of rum for fourteen days after the offence, unless it is necessary for medical reasons.

CHAPTER FOUR

JACK HAD AWOKEN WITH THE USUAL JOLT, PULSE RACING, breathing laboured. He lay staring up at the ceiling, willing his heart to stop pounding. He'd been told that inhaling deeply and slowly would help but all that did was stir up his cough. He thought briefly of getting up and going to his father's room, but he didn't want to give in. He wasn't a child, after all. This terror would pass. Besides, he'd seen the look in Murdoch's eyes when he'd greeted him at the station. He could tell his father was worried to death, but there was nothing he could do to help. Telling him what had happened would only shift the burden to him, and Jack couldn't bear that thought. He had always been aware of the deep sorrow his father carried within him. Once, when he was younger, he'd asked his father why he was so sad. Murdoch had seemed surprised. He'd obviously thought he had succeeded in hiding it. He'd brushed the question off. "I miss your mother, son. Sorry to be a wet blanket." And then he'd made a point of being cheery until, in an unguarded moment, Jack had caught him staring into the fire. Jack knew the sadness never really left him.

When Jack enlisted he'd been caught up in all the excitement of patriotic fervour and the unknowing exuberance of youth. But he knew that he had also wanted to make his father proud and, even if only briefly, bring light into his eyes.

Suddenly the man's face appeared on the ceiling. Jack knew it wasn't a dream because he wasn't asleep. He stared at the white, contorted face speckled with mud. The fluttering eyelids. The blue, bloodshot eyes. He lifted his arm to block out the image and shreds of blood-soaked cloth dripped off his sleeve. Then somebody walked past on the street outside. Two men talking to each other. He distinctly heard one of them say, "*Kamerad.*"

He pushed aside the quilt and got out of bed.

The bicycles were kept in a lean-to shed at the rear of the house. When Jack went to wheel his out, he discovered the front tire was flat as a pancake. There was nothing for it but to borrow his father's. He didn't think he'd mind a short-term loan, although the sturdy Ideal cycle was one of Murdoch's prized possessions.

The street lamps were sparse and made little dint on the darkness, but Jack was used to moving stealthily and the lack of light was not a hindrance. He mounted and rode to the corner before switching on the bicycle lamp, not wanting to attract attention from the neighbours or any workers trudging home from a night shift. The houses were all dark, all seemed deeply asleep, no restless women reading in the light of their bedside lamps while they tried not to think about their absent sons or husbands, trying not to imagine what news the morning papers would bring.

He'd composed a poem about that when he was on sentry duty one night. He called it "The City Sleeps in Sorrow." The next morning, feeling rather pleased with himself, he'd recited the poem to Percy McKinnon, who frowned comically.

"Well, Jocko, I don't know much about poetry. I suppose it's all right as poems go, although I like rhymes myself. What I don't like, though, is one of the last lines."

"What do you mean? What's wrong with it?"

"Well, you say *Lives ruined*, but that isn't true, is it? I mean to say, shirts are ruined if you sick all down them. Meat is ruined if a rat pisses on it. But lives . . . naw. No such thing. This friggin' war can shake you up. Shake you up very bad, as we know. But you've still got life, don't you? It's changed, yes, but you know what they say, where there's life, there's hope."

Jack didn't know whether to laugh or get angry. "So you're saying that even if you'd been made deaf and blind and you had no arms or legs and you were addled, you'd be all right with that because at least you're not dead?"

"That's right, that's what I'm saying."

"That's a load of horse plop. I don't believe you. I bet if something like that happened to you, you'd be begging to be put out of your misery."

"Not me, Jocko. I'll drink life to the dregs, no matter what."

THE CITY SLEEPS IN SORROW

The city sleeps in sorrow.
Come morning
Anxious eyes scan the lists.
Killed. Wounded. Gassed. Missing.
Each one, a husband, a brother, a son
All gone.
I knew him, says she, pointing at a name.
He lived nearby.
He was a good boy.
Always ready with a smile,
An offer to help if need be.
But not one of ours, says he.
Thank God.
We're not the ones weeping yet.
I'll bet you haven't checked the latest list.
It's called Lives Ruined.
And it is long.

CHAPTER FIVE

MURDOCH SAT UP BY THE FIRE UNTIL THE EMBERS WERE dying. There was no sound from Jack's bedroom. Finally, he banked the coals and went upstairs to bed. He didn't expect to fall asleep easily but he did, only to be awakened by the click of the front door closing. He squinted at the clock on the dresser. It was past midnight. Jack had said he liked to walk around sometimes so Murdoch supposed that was what he was doing. He lay and listened for what seemed like a long time, but Jack didn't return.

After a while Murdoch fell back to sleep.

It was only a ten-minute ride from Ontario Street to where Percy was boarding. When they had been sent to England to recover from their wounds, Percy had met a Chinaman named Chen. It turned out he had an uncle in Toronto who ran a laundry. Percy had let it be known that he wanted some place cheap and convenient to stay, and Chen had arranged for him to board with this uncle, Ghong Lee. What Percy did not reveal to Jack at the time was that Chen had also arranged for Ghong Lee to provide opium of the best quality. For a reasonable price, of course.

Elizabeth Street was in "the Ward," as the neighbourhood was commonly called. Initially the area had attracted a lot of new immigrants all wanting the familiar, and happy to reside in close proximity to shops selling food and goods they recognized from the Old Country. As with many such places, the Ward had compensated for a lack of visible affluence with a vibrant optimism and conviviality. Unfortunately, over the years this hope had been worn away by hardship and struggle. Too many people were crammed into too few small houses. Even in the year that Jack had been absent the houses seemed to have become poorer and more neglected.

The laundry was located in a two-storey house that was so ramshackle it looked as if it might collapse at any minute. The freshest thing about it was the characteristic red sign with white lettering: LAUNDRY. An adjoining shop pressed in close to its side, a sign over its door declaring it sold bicycles. If that was once true, it seemed no longer so. All the windows were boarded up, and the roof tilted crazily to one side. However, a bicycle rack remained in the front, and Jack pushed his wheel into place. Everywhere was silent and dark but he could see the merest sliver of light coming from the upstairs of the laundry.

He tapped lightly on the door. It seemed a long time before it opened slightly. A pair of brown eyes peered up at him.

"I'm a friend of Percy's," Jack whispered. "He told me I could drop by."

The eyes continued to stare at him.

"Sorry it's so late," continued Jack. "He said I could come at any time. Is he awake?"

The eyes disappeared abruptly and the door opened a little wider.

"Please enter," said his host, who turned out to be a young Chinese boy, perhaps not more than ten years old. He was dressed in a traditional black silk tunic and trousers with a round black cap atop long hair that was braided into a queue. He gave a look outside and, presumably satisfied that Jack was alone, he stepped back and closed the door behind them. For a moment the two of them stood close together in the pitch-darkness. Then the boy struck a match and lit a candle that was on a nearby ledge. He gave Jack a little bow.

"Come please, your friend upstairs."

He led the way through to a room at the rear that was jammed with washing paraphernalia. Jack could see huge metal vats on one side, and on the other, rows and rows of hanging ghostly white sheets that reached to the ceiling. The air was warm and moist. The boy opened another door at the far end and proceeded up narrow, uncarpeted stairs. Now Jack could hear muted voices and a sudden louder burst of laughter. A felt curtain hung at the top of the staircase and the boy pushed it aside, at the same time blowing out his candle.

Beyond the curtain was a large room lit with oil lamps turned low. The air here was smoky and pungent, and Jack had to struggle to suppress a cough. His child guide called out something in Chinese and four men standing around a table all turned to look at them. Whatever they had been doing, they stopped abruptly. Nobody moved or spoke. Jack saw Percy sprawled on a narrow cot in a shadowy corner. He was wearing only his army issue combination underwear. He was in the process of drawing smoke from an opium pipe. When he saw Jack he raised the pipe in a kind of salute.

"Jocko. I was hoping you would join me." He flapped his hand at the other men. "It's all right, friends. This is my friend Jack. He is a good man. Explain please, Mr. Lee."

There was a rapid exchange in Chinese among the men, then one of them stepped away from the table and came over to Jack. He was older than the others, and his thick, iron-grey hair was pulled back from his forehead and plaited into a long queue reaching to his waist. He put his hands together and bowed his head slightly.

"Welcome, sir. Please come in. My name is Ghong Lee. May I offer you some refreshment after your long journey?"

Other than the rather quaint expression, his English was good, only lightly accented. He waved his hand in the direction of a dresser behind him. It was lacquered black and beautifully embellished with gold inlay. The boy lifted a long, carved opium pipe out of a case.

"Don't take that unless you fancy a little trip to paradise," Percy called out. He was still lounging on the cot and he thrust out his arm and spread the fingers of his outstretched hand.

"Look, Jack. What do you notice?"

"You're not shaking."

"Bang on. That's the opium for you. No coughee, no shakee. Ghong and I have an arrangement. I will help his workers with their English and he will give me a pipe a day. More than that and I have to pay. Business is business."

The boy held out the pipe to Jack.

"Would you like to smoke, sir?" Ghong asked. "This one is complimentary."

Jack hesitated. "I, er . . . Perhaps another time."

Ghong nodded at the boy, who immediately returned the pipe to the dresser.

"In that case, you simply must try some *baijiu*. It is an ancient Chinese drink. Very popular with soldiers."

Percy propped himself up. "Be careful, Jack. That stuff will take the stitches out of your darning."

Before Jack could respond, Ghong again nodded at the boy, who picked up an amber-coloured ceramic bottle. He poured some clear liquid into a small handleless cup and gave it to Ghong, who in turn offered it to Jack.

"A sip at first is recommended. It is not accustomed to Western taste."

Jack looked over at his friend, who was grinning at him.

"What do you think, Percy? Shall I?"

"Why not? It's the best thing for chasing away melancholy I've yet encountered. Never mind what old Ghong says about taking sippee. Chug it down in one gulp."

Jack took the cup. The liquid had a slightly vinegary smell.

"One, two, three, down the hatch," chanted Percy.

Jack obeyed. My God, he felt as if he had just poured liquid fire down his throat! He started to cough violently.

"It's worse than being gassed," he spluttered.

"It'll feel better in a minute," answered his friend. "Give him another, Ghong. Put it on my bill."

Still coughing, Jack managed to wave away the second cup.

"No, thanks. I've just destroyed my stomach."

He could see that the Chinese men at the table were giggling behind their hands.

Percy pulled himself upright and put the opium pipe on the floor beside him. The boy picked it up immediately and returned it to the dresser.

"The fire in the belly will eventually subside and you will feel like Chinese tiger," said Ghong. "In the meantime, may I invite you to join us for a game of fan-tan? We can easily accommodate another person."

He spoke to one of the men, who moved to one side, indicating to Jack he could take his place.

Again Percy was the intermediary. "It's a good game, Jack. Better than Crown and Anchor, if you ask me. Less chance of being crooked."

"All right," said Jack, who could still hardly speak above a whisper after his encounter with the "ancient Chinese drink."

"Are you going to play too?" he asked Percy.

"Not this round. I'm out of money. I'll watch."

"Allow me the instructions," said Ghong. "At the table there is a simple square piece of cloth. The side closest to the wall is considered north, or number one; to the right is east or number two, opposite is west, number three, and below is south, number four. Very simple. You choose a side and place a wager. Whatever you wish."

Jack fished in his pocket and took out two quarters. The other man beside him pointed at the cloth and Jack put the money on the east side.

"That is to the value of two," said Ghong. "In other words, if two beans are left in the pile you will receive a return on your money of two to one."

"Less commission," called Percy. "Don't forget the 5 percent commission."

Ghong smiled. "Of course. But this first round we will forgo the commission. It is complimentary."

"Carry on," said Jack. "I still don't have a clue what you're doing but I'm in." His stomach and throat were now pleasantly warm. He felt ready for anything.

"Perhaps before we commence I should introduce the other players. They do not yet speak English but Mr. McKinnon has promised to correct that soon."

"Darn right," said Percy thickly. "And I'm going to learn Chinese."

Again Ghong smiled. Jack was starting to think him a most agreeable fellow.

"Immediately to your right is my number-one son, Hong Lee."

The young man made the hands-together polite bow. Jack bowed his own head in response. He was getting the hang of this quickly.

"I refer to them as my sons because they are essential to my well-being, but in fact we are not related by blood."

"Quite so," said Jack.

"At the head of the table is my number-two son, Gipkon Mak," continued Ghong. "And across from you is their cousin, Jiango Lee."

The Chinamen looked to be about Jack's age, though smaller, and all with the ubiquitous braid hanging down their backs.

Ghong beckoned to the boy. "Oh, I almost forgot my grandson, Ying. He is truly of my blood, and he understands some English."

There were what appeared to be some white beans on the table, and Ying took a curved bamboo stick and swept them up into a silver bowl. Ghong took both stick and bowl from him.

"Place your bets, if you please."

He gestured, and the three Chinamen immediately placed coins on the cloth. Ghong waited for a moment, then his grandson rang a tiny silver bell. The sweetness of the sound reminded Jack of the bells he'd rung at mass when he was an altar boy.

Jack winked at Percy. "This is my lucky night, I know it."

Ghong upended the bowl and a pile of beans spilled onto the cloth. Ying handed him a second, smaller bowl and he scooped up some of the beans into it. The remainder he pushed to the far end of the table. Moving very rapidly, he upended the second bowl and the beans tumbled out. Using the curved stick he first fanned them out and then, still moving with both grace and speed, he began to separate them, pushing them into straight lines.

"They are always in groups of four," he said to Jack. He repeated this action and, within minutes, the fan was diminished.

"Whatever number of beans remain is the winning number."

Before Ghong had completely finished, Jack could see that four beans remained. Ghong scooped them away.

"Ah, what a pity," said Ghong. "Nobody is winner this time. Nobody bet four number."

The other three men pushed the coins that they'd put on the table in Ghong's direction. He slipped them into a silk purse that was attached to his waist.

"So sorry, sir," he said to Jack. "But please let your money ride for another round. As I said previously, this one is complimentary."

"Watch it, Jack," called Percy from the cot. "You can get hooked on this game if you're not careful."

"Don't worry about me. I can hand . . . handle myself." His

words seemed to fall out of his mouth the way the beans had fallen out of the silver bowl. He had another couple of dimes in his jacket and he added them to his bet.

"And I'll take another cup of that ancient Chinese drink, if you don't mind, Mr. Lee."

Ying trotted over to the dresser and returned with a cup of the *baijiu*. Jack tossed it back, again to the covert smiles of the other Chinese men.

"Let's play, gentlemen. I'm quite capable of taking on a pile of beans."

CHAPTER SIX

IT WAS SEVEN O'CLOCK WHEN MURDOCH WOKE, AND A grey, thin light was just creeping in below the window blinds. He got out of bed, listening for any sound from the next bedroom. All was silent. Then he saw a note had been slipped under his door.

Hi, Pa. I seem to need to sleep. Just leave me. I'll be fit
for human company soon, I promise.
J.

Murdoch debated ignoring the request and waking his son but he knew that wasn't fair. It would only satisfy his own need, not Jack's. He dressed and went downstairs to the kitchen, where he wrote his own note.

There are some eggs and bacon in the icebox if you want them for your breakfast. Come over to the station if you feel up to it. Pa.

He propped the note against the cup he'd put out for Jack's morning tea and added the packets of cigarettes. He thought about putting out the bottle of brandy, too, but decided against it. He wished he could stay home, but two detectives were off on sick leave, and as senior detective it was his responsibility to make sure there were enough officers to handle the tasks of the day.

At the door, he paused, but there was still no sound from upstairs.

Outside a steady, chill rain was falling. He debated for a moment whether to walk to the station or to use his bicycle. There weren't many days, even in winter, when he didn't bike. Faster and easier. Bike it was.

When he opened the shed door, he noticed that not only was his bicycle not in its usual position, but the frame was flecked with globs of dried mud. He took a closer look at Jack's bike. Ah. That explained it. The front tire was absolutely flat.

Murdoch kept his bicycle outfits handy on a peg. On a rainy day like today, he didn't want to arrive at headquarters looking like a drowned rat, or to spend the entire day in damp discomfort. He'd acquired one of the rubber capes issued to the constables and he usually wore that. He took it off the peg. It was dry to the touch and clean. He added the serviceable

Persian lamb wedge cap, also police issue for the winter. He appreciated the way the flaps came down over his ears. Finally, his own acquisition, a pair of raccoon-skin mitts.

Feeling ready to tackle anything, he wheeled his own bicycle out to the street. Sodden leaves swirled around his feet; the bare trees tossed and shook in the wind. And as it was wont to do sometimes during his quiet morning rides, a memory assailed him.

His second child, a girl, had been born on just such a chill November morning seventeen years ago. The infant had survived for only four hours. And on that same day, his wife, Amy, had died. How many times had he relived those moments? He'd lost count. Jack had been sent to stay with a kindly neighbour down the street when Amy's labour began. When Miss Dorsett finally brought Jack home, his first question was where was his mother? Murdoch had no idea what to say to him. Miss Dorsett, a devout Baptist, said, "She's gone to be with Jesus."

"When is she coming back?"

"Your father can answer that, Jack."

The little boy frowned at Murdoch. "When is Mother coming home? We haven't finished the story we were reading."

Desperate, Murdoch answered, "I don't know when she'll be back, son. Probably not for a long time."

"She said I was going to have a little brother or sister. Have I?"

"Yes, a sister."

"Is that where Mother went? To fetch her?"

"Yes, yes, that's where she went."

"Where is she, then? Is she upstairs? Can I see her?"

"No, you cannot." Murdoch's voice was too sharp. His son flinched.

Miss Dorsett took the boy's hand. "Tell you what, Master Jack. Let's go back to my house. We won't bother your father right now. He has a lot on his mind."

"Will we come back home tomorrow?"

"Yes, we will."

"Will my mother be here, and my new sister?"

Again the woman looked to Murdoch for guidance.

He could not bear the knowledge that there would be no Amy, no new sister. "Perhaps they will, Jack. Let's see, shall we?"

And they had waited, both of them, until they'd finally accepted the fact that Amy and the baby he'd named, Suzanne, would never return.

CHAPTER SEVEN

A MOTOR CAR ZOOMED PAST MURDOCH ON ALBERT Street, flinging up a shower of muddy water from the gutter. His slicker protected him, but Murdoch was irritated and tempted to make an un-policeman-like gesture at the thoughtless driver. Motor vehicles had proliferated in the city in the last few years, and, despite the outcry from those of a more traditional point of view, Murdoch was sure they were here to stay. They were also the bane of the policeman's existence. Anyone who could afford a motor car was permitted to drive one, whether they had taken proper instruction or not. Reckless boys were forever stealing them and going for joyrides, frightening the horses that still trotted the streets. And splashing bicyclists.

Police headquarters were located in the northeast corner of the first floor of the magnificent city hall. The building housed all the departments necessary to run a bustling big city like Toronto. Sometimes the place reminded Murdoch of a railway station with all the comings and goings, although it usually lacked the excitement. Like all the other detectives, except the chiefs, Murdoch used the rear entrance. The chief inspector, Kennedy, had requested they do this. "Criminals are hanging around here all hours of the day, no reason they should become familiar with your faces. You can do better work if you're anonymous."

Murdoch was inclined to agree with him, and it suited him to get into his office without fanfare. He liked to arrive early and leave late.

He dismounted and parked the bicycle against the curb. Theft was not unknown but rare, especially this close to the august authority of the police department.

Murdoch headed inside. He took the stairs two at a time. Doing things like that kept him fit, and he was rather proud of the fact that he was only slightly breathless when he got to the second floor.

He stepped into the hall. To one side was the telephone desk. The constable on duty sat up straighter, stifling the yawn that was threatening to take over his head. Murdoch removed his cape and his hat, shaking them vigorously to get out the rain.

"Morning, sir."

"Morning, Wallace. How was the night? Any reports?"

The young constable whistled through his teeth. "Apparently it was very active, sir. There was a barney at a house over in the Ward. One of the neighbours fetched the beat constable, Mogg. Nothing seems to have developed further. Constable Mogg gave his report to Detectives Fenwell and Rubridge, who were on reserve."

"Where are they now?"

"Detective Rubridge left about half an hour ago as it's his day off. Detective Fenwell is in his office writing up his report. He was waiting for you to come in."

"I'll talk to him right away, then."

The constable reached underneath the desk and handed Murdoch a piece of paper.

"Here's Sergeant Allen's latest move, sir." He gave Murdoch a rather cheeky grin. "How's the game coming?"

"Early days yet, Wallace. Early days."

"I know you won't let us down, sir."

"I hope not. Allen's a sly fox."

Wallace lifted the barrier to the desk.

"I'll go and make you a pot of tea. I'm sure you could use one. It's right miserable out."

Murdoch hung his overcoat and hat and slicker on the coat tree by the door and proceeded down the hall. His office was at the far end. According to an unstated law of the universe, rank determined office size and order. The most important people got the largest, and the others diminished in size the farther down the hall they were. Murdoch was content with that. His faced onto James Street which meant he had a view, and although the room was hardly big enough to turn around in, it did have a door, which was more than his alcove at number four station had had.

Running the length of the opposite side of the hall was a three-quarter-height partition, topped with windows, which ran parallel to another, narrow inner hall; all the offices on that side belonged to the rank and file of the detectives. Supposedly the interior windows pulled in more light, but the partition also afforded privacy from the chiefs. Not to mention from any of the general populace who came to appeal fines or get licences and got trapped in the sticky web of bureaucracy.

Jack was awakened by the shrill ringing of the telephone. Still half asleep, heart jumping, he couldn't identify the strange sound at first. Where was he? He sat up. Yes, of course, he was at home, in his father's house, in his old bedroom. He could see the clock on the mantelpiece. It was just five minutes past nine. Morning? Yes, morning. Daylight was edging the window blind.

The telephone kept on ringing. He got out of bed, swaying for a moment as a wave of dizziness hit him. His arm throbbed and he pulled it in close to his side.

He went downstairs. The telephone, on the parlour sideboard, was still ringing. He lifted the receiver.

"Hello, Wilton 654."

The operator's pleasant voice came over the line. "I have a

collect call here from a Mr. McKinnon for Mr. Jack Murdoch. Will you accept the charges?"

"What? Oh yes, of course."

"Caller, you are now connected," said the unknown woman.

Percy came on the line. "Jack? Jack, is that you?"

"Of course it is. Who else were you expecting?"

"Has your father gone to work?"

"Yes, he has. Percy, what the hell's the matter with you?"

There was silence for a moment, then Percy said in a barely audible voice, "Jack, I think I've killed somebody."

CHAPTER EIGHT

TUCKED AWAY ON A TABLE IN THE CORNER OF Murdoch's office was his chess set, its carved wooden pieces set out mid-game. It had been a second anniversary present from Amy. They had played together often, and she checkmated him regularly. After she died, he'd put the set away, and it was only last year, when he moved to headquarters, that he had brought the board out again.

It wasn't that he was hiding the chessboard exactly, but other detectives coming in had the irritating habit of advising on the ongoing game he was playing with Sergeant Allen at number four station. He didn't want advice. He enjoyed the keen competition. They were communicating via wireless telegraphy and exchanged moves two or three times a week. So few other messages came over the wireless that Murdoch considered it a harmless use of the police line. Besides, the honour of the Headquarters Detective Division was at stake.

He looked at the note that Wallace had given him: "Bishop to c 8." Murdoch made the move. He clapped his hands and addressed his chessmen aloud, albeit quietly. "Ah. I think he's taken the bait."

Talking to oneself was an easy habit to fall into when you lived alone. He'd better watch out, especially about having conversations with the chess pieces. He didn't want his officers to think he was losing his wits. He tapped the knight on its glossy head. It looked as if it were ready to gallop off sideways. *I'd like to get going even if it is a strange trajectory I am compelled to follow. What other horse have you seen that goes one step on the diagonal, one forward?*

He already knew what his next move would be and he moved the restive knight to c 5. He wrote the move on a piece of paper. He'd hand it to Wallace to transmit in a couple of days. No reason to rush to Allen's downfall.

He had just squeezed in behind his desk when there was a tap on his door and Constable Madge Curnoe thrust her head in.

"I heard you arrive, Will. Shall I make a pot of tea before you get going on things?"

Madge and another woman, Miss Louise Trull, had been hired as police constables four years earlier. Positively revolutionary, but the timing had proven very prescient; the war had broken out soon afterward, taking many male officers away, some of whom would not return.

The chief constable had supported the new induction of the weaker vessel. "Got to move with the times," was how he put it. "Women can do some things better than any man. We need that softer side more than you think."

Louise had recently been seconded to the police department in Hamilton, so Madge was the sole representative in Toronto of "the softer side." Madge was generally referred to as "handsome"—the term usually applied to single women of a certain age. She was dark-haired with keen blue eyes, as tall as Murdoch, round at the edges, and as far as Murdoch was concerned, she brought the perfect balance of common sense and sensitivity to the cases they worked on together.

He smiled at her. "Wallace is bringing me a pot, but we can ask for more cups. I'm expecting Detective Fenwell to give me his report so we might as well include him."

"In here or the duty room?"

"In here, as long as you don't mind the squash."

"There's something here I wanted to show you." She handed him a copy of the *Toronto Daily Star*. She had circled one of the ads. It was short.

Available for adoption. Three-month-old boy. Healthy. Contact Star for information.

"I know some people have to give up their children for what they consider to be good reasons, the child's best interests and so forth, but it made me shiver. As if they wanted to sell a dog or a chest of drawers."

"Look into it please, Madge."

"I will. Oh, by the way, I almost forgot to offer my congratulations."

Murdoch raised his eyebrows. "For?"

"I see that Jack is to receive the Military Medal."

"Good Lord. He didn't tell me that."

"It's in the paper. The medals will be presented by the lieutenant-governor on Monday."

Murdoch was a little hurt that Jack hadn't informed him.

"How is he doing?" Madge asked.

Murdoch bit his lip. "Let's put it this way. It's obvious he's been through a dreadful ordeal. It's going to take a while before he's back to normal."

"I'm sure that's why he hasn't told you about the medal as yet."

"Possibly. I told him to drop in later. If he does, I'd like you to meet him."

"I'd love to."

She turned and almost collided with a detective in the doorway.

"I beg your pardon," he said, and stepped aside. Murdoch couldn't help but notice that the usually unflappable Madge looked flustered at the encounter. Oh dear, not another conquest for Peter Fenwell, surely?

Murdoch had to admit that his friend was a strikingly handsome man. He was getting close to fifty but he could have passed for forty. His light brown hair was thick, no sign of balding there. No grey hair, for that matter. As far as Murdoch knew, Fenwell didn't exercise a great deal, but he had a physique that always seemed fit and trim. Add to that regular features and keen blue eyes and you had a man that women fell for in droves. Fortunately, he was a devoted husband and father of three and never reciprocated, or even seemed much to notice, the attention directed his way.

"Morning, Will," he said. He plopped down on the chair in front of Murdoch's desk.

"I hear from Wallace there was a disturbance reported last night," said Murdoch.

Fenwell shrugged. "Nothing too serious, I'm glad to say. The beat constable took care of it. I didn't even have to go out."

Murdoch leaned forward. "You look exhausted."

"It wasn't just last night. I'm not sleeping too well these days."

"You and half the city. Maybe we should start an insomniacs club. We could get together in the early hours and discuss world issues."

Fenwell chuckled. "That would keep us awake, not calm us down."

"Shouldn't you have the day off today?"

"I should, but Crowther asked me to swap with him. He's got some important family business to take care of."

"Does he indeed? He should have let me know."

"I think it was all very last minute. We didn't think you would object."

"I don't, but I do like to keep informed as to what my detectives are doing."

"Of course, Will." Fenwell regarded Murdoch. "How's Jack? Did you settle him all right?"

"As well as can be expected, I suppose."

"I understand from Madge that he's up for a Military Medal. Congratulations."

"Thanks, Peter. I seem to be the last to know."

Fenwell eyed Murdoch sympathetically. "Just give him some time. It's probably a big adjustment for him, coming home."

"He doesn't want to talk about anything." Murdoch frowned. "I don't even know why he's being given a bloody medal."

"He'll tell you when he's good and ready."

"But surely it's something to be proud of?"

"Of course it is. Stop fretting. He's only been back for a night. Look, think yourself lucky he's here at all."

"All right. Enough said. What about your Eric? Heard from him yet?"

"No. In this case, no news is probably good news."

Three weeks earlier, Fenwell had received word that his oldest son had been taken prisoner. He was in a prisoner of war camp in Germany.

"I haven't had the chance to tell Jack. When he's more amenable, I'll ask him if he knows anything about those situations," said Murdoch. "Speaking of which, what's your opinion of how Rubridge is holding up?"

"He doesn't mention it at all," said Fenwell. "But I'd say he's still pretty devastated."

"That's certainly my impression. He insisted on coming back to work almost right away, as you know. Maybe I shouldn't have allowed him. It's only been a few weeks since he got the news."

"True."

"I suppose it doesn't help matters that he and Irma separated," added Murdoch. "There's probably not much comfort at home for him."

The door was pushed open again and Madge returned carrying a tea tray. Fenwell jumped up to help her clear a spot on the corner of the desk.

"Constable Wallace asked me to tell you there is a woman at the desk who wants to talk to you," she said to Murdoch. "She says her name is Aggett."

"Really? She's not supposed to come until tomorrow."

"Do you want me to tell her?"

"Would you mind? I'd like to get on with this report. Their appointment was for Thursday at eleven o'clock."

"I'll just be a jiffy." Her smile slid from Murdoch to Fenwell, who was busy looking over his notes and didn't notice. Murdoch felt a pang of what he had to own as jealousy. He'd grown to like Madge Curnoe a lot. Perhaps even allowed himself a few fantasies, such as asking her to go with him to the picture show, for instance.

He hadn't acted on that as yet.

Fenwell looked at him. "What's up, Will? You seem a bit despondent this morning."

"Do I? Damn war I suppose. It's getting me down. Seeing so many fine young men at the train station yesterday, damaged beyond repair some of them, was a sobering experience."

He reached into his desk drawer and took out his pipe and tobacco pouch. He smoked less these days than he used to, but every so often a pipe was comforting.

"If you're going to do that, I'll have a cigarette," said Fenwell.

They had both hardly finished sending plumes of smoke into the air when Madge returned. She flapped her hand in front of her face but didn't comment.

"She said it wasn't about a meeting. Her son hasn't been home all night and she's worried something's happened to him. She insists on talking to you."

"Her son?"

"This is the senior Mrs. Aggett."

"Is she by herself?"

"Yes, she is."

"Madge, would you mind running another errand? Would you tell her I'm tied up for at least another half an hour? Perhaps you could take down the particulars. We'll fill you in about this later."

She left, and Murdoch put his pipe in the dish on his desk.

"Go ahead, Peter, I'm all ears."

Fenwell consulted his notes. "We got a call at ten minutes past two from Constable Mogg. He'd been summoned to a disturbance on Chestnut Street. A man named Odacre said he had been woken up by the sound of shouting coming from next door." Fenwell looked over at Murdoch. "The house in question is owned by a Mrs. Bessie Schumacher. We suspect she's running a blind pig but so far we haven't had any solid evidence. Nobody wants to report and risk cutting off their own supply of booze. According to Mogg, he was on his regular beat when Odacre ran out and hailed him. Says there was a big barney happening on the street. Mogg says he could in fact hear loud shouts coming from Mrs. Schumacher's residence as he approached. He knocked—"

"Obviously an intelligent fellow," interrupted Murdoch with a grin. "Did he ascertain what was happening?"

"Not exactly. Mrs. Schumacher answered, and by this time all was dead quiet. She said she was merely having a late night with friends, discussing the state of the nation. She says things got a little heated but nothing serious."

"Mogg went in to have a look, I hope?"

"He did. There were two men sitting at a table. He asked them if they were all right and they answered in the affirmative. They had been discussing the state of the nation, just as she claimed. So he took down their names and left. He couldn't make a charge if nobody was a complainant."

"All right, let's keep Mrs. Schumacher and her house under observation."

Murdoch intensely disliked the new laws prohibiting the sale of alcohol. All they had done was send the making and selling of liquor underground, and they certainly added to the policeman's workload. More than likely Mrs. Schumacher was selling liquor, probably sneaked in from Quebec where there were no such restrictions.

Fenwell stood up. "By the way, Ruth wanted to know if you and Jack could have a meal with us soon."

"I'll ask him. I'm sure he'd like that."

Jack and Eric Fenwell had been childhood friends, and Jack had enjoyed spending time with the Fenwells. Ruth was a motherly sort, and after Amy died she had taken Jack under her wing.

There was a knock on the door and Madge popped her head in.

"Mrs. Aggett says she must talk to you, sir. She won't take no for an answer. She says it's urgent."

"All right, bring her in. We're done here for now."

Madge ushered Mrs. Aggett into the office as Fenwell left.

CHAPTER NINE

Arthur Aggett's mother was something of a surprise. Given her daughter-in-law's feelings about her, Murdoch had expected somebody frail and perhaps woebegone, but this was not the case. She was petite, true, but she entered the office with an air of brisk determination. Her grey hair was smoothed neatly under her hat. Her features were pleasant, but there was a firmness to the set of her mouth that made Murdoch think of schoolteachers he had known. She wouldn't brook any nonsense, as she perceived it, he was sure.

He got to his feet. "Mrs. Aggett, please take a seat. I understand you are concerned about your son."

She accepted the chair he offered, sitting ramrod straight on the edge.

"You don't mind if Constable Curnoe stays, do you, madam?"

"No. The more the better if it means you take some action right away."

Madge took up a position by the door.

Murdoch returned to his chair and pulled his notebook closer.

"You say Arthur is missing, Mrs. Aggett. Will you give me details? When did you see him last?"

"At ten o'clock last night. My daughter-in-law decided to visit her sister, who lives in Mimico. For the first time in weeks Arthur and I were able to spend a pleasant evening together. We enjoy reading to each other, you see, and did so regularly before he was married. He will read a verse or so of scripture and I will do likewise. His wife has no such interest. She prefers to play cards or go out to the picture show or the theatre."

Mrs. Aggett's voice was matter-of-fact but it was clear to Murdoch that Lottie's complaint about her mother-in-law not accepting her had some justification.

"I usually retire for the night about ten. Arthur said he was . . . er, he was going to use the privy and then go to bed himself. I told him I would prepare his favourite breakfast in the morning, waffles and bacon. His wife is no cook, and Arthur was delighted with the notion. I went to bed myself." She halted and her hands clenched tighter. "When I went to call him this morning, I received no answer. I looked into his room but his bed had not been slept in."

"What has made you think your son is missing?" Murdoch asked gently. "Perhaps he decided to go to Mimico to see his wife."

"How would he get there? We don't have a carriage or a motor car. There is no streetcar that runs to Mimico at that time of night." Another pause, and she glanced down at the hands clasped in her lap. "I know my son, Detective Murdoch. He would not have disappointed me and missed his breakfast. If there was an imperative reason for his absence, he would have left me a note." She looked back at Murdoch. "I am aware that you have met my son and his wife, Detective. I'm sure she told you I want my son all to myself and that I resent her."

She nodded as if Murdoch had answered.

"To some extent that is true. I did not and do not approve of this marriage, which was conducted in haste, only, I'm sure, to be repented at leisure. Arthur is a good man. He wants to make sure I am taken care of as he has always been my mainstay . . . I can say with absolute sincerity that I would joyfully accept as a daughter-in-law any young woman who was worthy of my son. But Lottie is a vain, silly girl who cares far too much for appearances. She is willing to cast Arthur into the maw of destruction if it means she will herself receive some of the reflected glory that comes to the wives of soldiers. I am *not* willing and will never be so."

There was another knock on the door. Madge opened it and stepped outside.

Murdoch turned to Mrs. Aggett. "I think we must wait . . ."

He didn't have the chance to finish his sentence. Madge returned to the room. He could see by the expression on her face that something serious had happened.

"Excuse me, sir. May I have a word with you?"

"My apologies, Mrs. Aggett," Murdoch said as he edged past her and followed Madge outside.

Keeping her voice low, Madge said, "We just had a telephone call from number two station. The body of a young man has been found in a laneway in the Ward. He was carrying calling cards in a silver case with the name Arthur Aggett. He was attacked."

"Good Lord. Did they give you a description of the victim?"

"About twenty years of age. Fair hair and moustache. Blue eyes. Wearing a grey mackinaw jacket and dark brown trousers."

Murdoch's heart sank. "Sounds like Arthur Aggett all right. Ring number two back right away. Say I'll be over as soon as possible. I assume they need the ambulance?"

"Yes, they do."

"Have Wallace send it out. And order the Ford for me, will you?"

"I'm so sorry about the boy, Will. The last thing we need is more young men dying."

Murdoch returned to his office, Madge again taking up a discreet position near the door. He hardly had time to sit down before Mrs. Aggett said, "You've found him haven't you?"

"It is possible we have, madam. We have just had a report that the body of a man has been discovered in a laneway not far from your home. The indications are that it is Arthur."

"What indications are those?"

"The deceased was carrying a silver card case. It held calling cards with your son's name on them."

Her face went even whiter. "He does indeed possess a silver case. It belonged to my father. But that proves nothing. It could have been stolen."

"That is true. However, the general description of the body, the age and colouring, does fit your son. About twenty years of age. Fair hair and moustache. Blue eyes. The man was wearing a grey mackinaw jacket and dark brown trousers."

"I see."

"Was Arthur wearing a mackinaw when you last saw him, Mrs. Aggett?"

"He was. But this does not make sense. He said he was going out to the privy. He took his jacket but he left his Ulster coat and his cap. Why would he do that if he intended to go any farther than the yard?"

Murdoch thought the most likely explanation was that Arthur didn't want his mother to know where he was going. He was a young man. A little cold night air wouldn't daunt him.

Mrs. Aggett got to her feet and stood, slightly unsteady but still straight. Murdoch thought back to what Arthur had said about his mother needing him to look after her. So far she had shown remarkable resilience.

"Let us go then, Detective."

"I can't take you to the scene of the crime, Mrs. Aggett.

I myself will be able to determine if this is indeed Arthur. I have met him, as you know. But there is a procedure we must follow. We will have to call in a physician to examine the circumstances of the death. I promise I will not leave you in suspense. I will get word to you as soon as possible, one way or the other."

"In that case, I shall remain here at the station."

Madge came forward to where Mrs. Aggett was sitting.

"Let's go into my office, then. It will be more comfortable." She offered her arm to the older woman.

Not for the first time, Murdoch was impressed by the constable's kind and steady manner.

"I'll just need a word with Constable Curnoe first," said Murdoch. He and Madge stepped back out into the hall.

Murdoch spoke quietly. "I'm going to take the police motor car. I'll ring you from the signal box on the beat."

"If it is her son, do you want me to tell Mrs. Aggett or wait until you get back?"

Murdoch knew that Madge could handle the situation, but he considered it his responsibility. Besides, he often found it useful to be present when news of a homicide was given to those concerned. All kinds of information had a way of spontaneously tumbling out.

"Wait for me."

"I must admit, I'm hoping against hope this is not Arthur Aggett. It would be devastating for her to lose her only child. And under circumstances such as these."

He knew what Madge was getting at. For bereaved mothers whose sons had made the ultimate sacrifice, there might be some consolation to think that they had died nobly.

CHAPTER TEN

Murdoch was glad when Peter Fenwell insisted he wasn't too tired to accompany him. He liked working with him.

"I almost forgot to mention," said Fenwell as they drove off. "I ran into George Crabtree at the curling rink. He asked me to pass along his regards."

"He was promoted to sergeant last year, I hear."

"That's right. He said he's counting the days until his retirement. And he told me he has two of his sons at the Front."

"Does he? I wish them all the best. I knew those boys when they were nippers."

"By the way, what happened to Inspector Brackenreid?"

Fenwell asked. "I hear he's living in England now."

Murdoch grinned. "He is. Apparently he's breeding hunting dogs. Trying to find the perfect cross between a spaniel and a retriever."

"He probably retired just in time. I'm sure he wouldn't have been too happy about having to enforce these temperance laws."

"I'd say you're right about that, Peter."

Murdoch pulled up at the end of the laneway, where Constable Mogg was keeping watch. He saluted the pair of detectives. He had been called back into service from retirement a few months earlier when the ranks of the police were being stripped by the demands of the war. He was a conscientious man, reliable and, if a bit slow, an asset, in Murdoch's opinion.

"Body's down there, sir," he said to Murdoch.

"I assume you were the one who found him?"

"Yes, sir. Didn't know what it was at first. Looked like a heap of discarded clothes. I went in closer and saw it was a body." He handed Murdoch a silver card case. "This was in his jacket, sir. I removed it for the purpose of identification."

Murdoch snapped open the case. The calling cards were on good stock, the printing elegant.

Arthur Aggett, Esquire

He showed Fenwell. "Fancy. Must have cost him a pretty penny."

"Was there anything else?" Murdoch asked Mogg.

"A few coins in the right-hand pocket of his trousers and a handkerchief in the left breast pocket of the jacket. I left them there."

"Good."

Murdoch removed his own handkerchief and wrapped the case carefully before stowing it inside his coat. Since his early days as a detective forensic science had advanced considerably, and fingerprints had become an accepted tool of investigation. The card case might yield something helpful.

He pointed down the laneway. "What's on the other side of that wall, Constable?"

"Just a patch of waste ground, sir."

"Did you find the weapon?"

"It's not in the immediate area but I haven't had the opportunity to mount a serious search. I thought I should wait for you."

"Thank you, Constable. Stay here please. Don't let anybody by."

A few curious passersby were already lingering around the motor car, trying to see what was going on.

Murdoch nodded at Fenwell. "Let's take a look. Keep to the side. If there are footprints, we don't want to trample on them."

As they approached the body, the shock of fair hair, currently blood soaked, and the tweed jacket confirmed what Murdoch had feared.

"It's Arthur Aggett all right."

He was lying on his left side, close to the wall. One arm was underneath his head, the other stretched out in front. The right side of his head was a bloody pulp.

"He was definitely attacked from behind," said Murdoch.

"Multiple blows, from the look of it. Delivered mostly from the right side. The fingers on that hand are smashed. He attempted to fend them off."

"What was he doing in the laneway? It doesn't seem to lead anywhere. The wall is too high to climb easily."

Murdoch bent over the body. "I'd say this is the answer." He pointed to the victim's trousers. "His buttons are undone. He must have come up here to relieve himself."

Carefully, he fished inside the pocket. There were several coins, which he took out and spread across his own palm: a couple of five- and ten-cent pieces and a few unfamiliar small coins.

"They look like English shillings," said Fenwell.

Murdoch flipped over one of the pieces. "This is a French sou. What do you make of it, Peter?"

"There's all sorts of foreign currency floating around nowadays. The soldiers bring it home. It's not legitimate but some people will accept it. They just pass it along."

"Give me your handkerchief. I'll take these back to the station with me."

Fenwell did so. "I wonder why he's not wearing a hat or an overcoat. It was nippy out last night."

"According to his mother, he stepped outside only to go to the privy in the yard. His overcoat and cap are still in the house."

"So either he was suddenly seized with the impulse to go walking or . . ."

"Or he wanted her to think the privy was the only place he

was going. I'd say whoever or whatever he encountered was fairly close to where he lived."

"Which was?"

"On Armoury Street. Probably just three or four minutes away."

CHAPTER ELEVEN

JACK GOT TO THE CHINESE LAUNDRY AS FAST AS HE could. Not many people were out in such dreary weather, but the shop was open and he went in. In the light of day, he could see that the walls were lined with shelves, all of them crammed with clean laundry wrapped in brown-paper packages. Ghong Lee himself was seated on a high stool behind the counter, writing in a big ledger. He greeted Jack.

"Your friend upstairs. He hurt hand. One of my sons treating it."

He picked up a bell from the counter and shook it. Immediately, the heavy curtains behind the counter parted and the boy, Ying, appeared.

"Carry Mr. Jack upstairs. Step lively."

He lifted the gate to the counter and Jack went through.

The rear room was hot and even steamier than it had been the night before. The two Chinamen he had met, both stripped to the waist, were standing over the huge vats of boiling water, stirring the sheets with long wooden tongs. They both gave Jack a brief nod but didn't stop working.

Ying led the way up the stairs and ushered Jack into the room where he'd been last night. Percy was lying on the same couch, and Jiango Lee was kneeling beside him. Percy was wearing a long, crimson silk robe, which he must have borrowed from his host. Incongruously, he was also wearing a grey woollen aviator cap that he'd brought back with him from the Front.

Percy called out to Jack as he entered.

"Hello, Jocko. I'm getting fixed up."

There was a small clay pot on the floor holding a plant with spiky leaves. Lee snapped off a piece and squeezed some of the juice onto Percy's hand.

"Hmm. Lovely," murmured Percy.

The Chinaman got to his feet and bowed toward Jack.

"Him be all right as rain. Very soon."

"What happened?"

"Him scalded hand."

Jack scowled at his friend. "How the hell did you do that, Perce?"

"Apparently I plunged my hand into the boiler. It was hot."

"Of course it was hot, you dolt. What were you thinking?"

"I'd say I wasn't . . . thinking, I mean. I must have been trying to get a clean shirt."

"When did you do it?"

"Some time last night, I believe. Woke up with much pain and a very red hand."

Percy blew on his skin.

"Good stuff. Chinamen make good medicine." He reached for the opium pipe that was lying on the bed beside him.

Jack caught hold of his arm. "Wait a minute, for Lord's sake. Do that later."

Jiango picked up the plant.

"I leave you now. More this night."

Jack waited until he'd left the room, then he pulled a chair close to the couch and sat down.

"All right, tell me what the hell's going on, Percy. You rang me and said, 'Jack, I think I've killed somebody.' What do you mean, you *think* you killed somebody?"

"When I woke up this morning, I had an image of a man lying on the ground. He was dead. Very bloody. I thought I must have been the one who killed him."

Jack groaned and put his head in his hands. "Come on, Percy. You were having a nightmare. I know what that's like. You don't even know you're dreaming at first."

Percy's eyes met Jack's. "Are you sure that's what it was?"

"Of course. And you got me out of bed for this?"

"I was scared, Jocko. It seemed so real. I thought I

remembered hitting somebody. And I had blood on my coat and on my hands."

"Where? Let me see."

"I can't. My clothes ended up in the boiler."

"*My* clothes you mean. That suit is probably ruined."

"Sorry, Jack. You'd better speak to Mr. Lee."

He pushed the aviator cap away from his forehead. The scar was livid.

"So? What's the verdict? Did I kill somebody or didn't I?"

Jack hesitated for a moment. "The war messes with our minds, Perce. It's hard to keep things straight."

"That's only saying the half of it, Jocko. Sometimes I think we'll never go back to being the way we used to be."

"It'll take time, but we will."

Percy closed his eyes. "Everything's so foggy in my mind. Maybe you can tell me what happened last night."

"If I can. It's not that much clearer in my mind. I do know we started off playing a few rounds of fan-tan. At least, I did. Then you said you were bored and you wanted to go out."

"Okay so far. I was getting fed up with fan-tan."

"We left here and went to a blind pig. Up on Chestnut Street. One of the fellows on the train told us about it, don't you remember?"

"No."

"Well, he did. There were some blokes in the establishment who were playing Crown and Anchor so we joined in. We also bought some liquor. Don't ask me what it was. Worse than

Chinese firewater, as I recall. Do you remember that?"

"Vaguely. It's all blurred together with the fan-tan game. They were cheating us. Not the Chinamen, the ones we met at the blind pig."

"I don't know they were. We were both so ape drunk that I don't think we were playing properly. You started to argue with one of the players. One thing led to another, I suppose. Got pretty heated."

"What were we arguing about?"

"The usual. Why were the soldiers being left high and dry over there? Did we need conscription?"

"Were they French Canadians?"

"No. Just fellows who'd got exemptions."

"Slackers, you mean."

"I suppose so."

"Did we come to blows?"

"You tried to but you weren't that steady on your feet. I thought discretion was the better part of valour and I got you out of there."

"Then what?"

"Then it gets really foggy for me too. But I do know you wanted to settle matters, as you put it. You wouldn't calm down."

"Sorry. I don't remember any of this."

"Somehow or other we managed to get back here to your digs."

"Did you put me to bed?"

"Not that I'm aware of. I just remember leaving you on the doorstep."

"Thanks a lot, pal."

"Oh, come on, Perce. We've slept in worse conditions. You survived."

Percy closed his eyes. After a moment he said softly, "You know what? I really and truly don't think it's worth it."

"What do you mean?"

"Going on."

As he was leaving, Jack checked with Ghong Lee. Had Percy returned last night with blood on him? The Chinaman shook his head. "I not aware of such thing. He put all clothes into boiler. We removed them soon and cleaned properly. They are in the wardrobe. Like new."

"Did he have blood on his hands?"

"I not see. His hand scalded. My son heal him with Chinese plant."

Jack slapped him on the shoulder. "We could use you people at the Front. We need a few healers."

Lee shrugged. "Thank you, sir, for compliment. I hope you not mind if I do not offer my services. Not likely they be accepted."

CHAPTER TWELVE

"You are telling me, Detective, that my son was murdered?"

Mrs. Aggett had gone so still she didn't seem to be breathing.

"I'm afraid it appears that way, madam."

"I don't understand. Why? By whom?"

"I can't say at the moment. We have not yet found the assailant."

"You said he was in a laneway?"

"Yes. The entrance is off Chestnut Street. He was at the far end."

"I don't mean to sound like a parrot, Detective, but I don't understand. What was Arthur doing in a laneway?"

"Most likely he was obeying a call of nature. By the look of things, his assailant came up behind him. We found some coins in his pocket that were not Canadian. Two English shillings and a French sou. Do you know why he had them in his possession?"

Mrs. Aggett looked at him blankly. "I have no idea. He certainly did not show them to me."

Murdoch caught Madge's eye. She stepped forward.

"Can I get you some tea, Mrs. Aggett?"

The other woman didn't turn. "No tea, but a glass of water would be appreciated. My mouth has gone dry."

Madge left at once.

"We should notify your son's wife, Mrs. Aggett," said Murdoch. "Can you tell me how to get in touch with her?"

"I have no desire to have her return, sir. She will only make matters worse, if that's possible. She is due to come back tomorrow. That will be soon enough for her to get the news."

Madge returned with a glass of water. She handed it to Mrs. Aggett and spoke very gently. "I understand how you feel, Mrs. Aggett, but is it fair to not impart this news at once?"

This suggestion seemed to bring some colour back into Mrs. Aggett's cheeks. "Fair? She has never been fair to me. Why should I be fair to her? She will no doubt become completely hysterical and it will all be hot air. She will relish the attention."

Rather bravely, Murdoch thought, Madge persisted.

"She was married to your son. She must have cared for him."

The other woman's mouth pursed. "Must she? You don't

have children, Miss Curnoe, otherwise you would understand. There is no love as powerful as that of a mother's . . . and no loss as deep." She looked at Murdoch. "When will I be able to bury my son, Detective?"

"In a few days. There will have to be an inquest, but usually the coroner acts quickly."

Mrs. Aggett stood up. "I'd like to go home now. There are arrangements to be made."

She swayed slightly and Madge took her elbow.

"Is there anybody we can fetch to be with you?" Madge asked.

"My neighbour is a good friend. If she is available I would rather like her company. She lost her only son last year at the Somme, so she will understand."

Mrs. Aggett's face was so grief-stricken Murdoch could hardly bear it.

"We will arrange for a motor car to take you home."

"Thank you."

She allowed Madge to guide her to the door. As she passed Murdoch, she bowed her head in acknowledgement.

"Thank you, Detective. You have been most kind."

After they left, Murdoch went and stood over his chess board. Victory was within his grasp.

Madge returned.

"She's gone. What on earth are we going to do about the daughter-in-law?"

"We'll have to get in touch with the police in Mimico. They'll need to track her down."

"I only hope it's not true that she'll make matters worse."

An image of the young woman he'd met only yesterday flashed into Murdoch's mind.

"From what I've seen so far, I'm afraid that may prove to be the case."

CHAPTER THIRTEEN

JACK LEFT PERCY TO THE SOLACE OF HIS OPIUM, AND ON impulse he turned and walked toward Agnes Street. A visit to the blind pig might be in order. He was pretty sure it was near the corner.

As he drew closer he saw a group of people gathered on the pavement. They were all gazing toward a laneway, the entrance to which seemed to be guarded by two constables.

Jack approached a rough-looking fellow on the fringe of the crowd.

"What's happened?" he asked.

"Don't know exactly," said the man. "Somebody copped it, apparently. Some time earlier this morning. Body's still in there.

They're waiting for the ambulance to cart it away. One of the constables said it was what they was calling a suspicious death."

"Really?"

"Yep, that's what he said. Means the bloke was probably offed. They took down all the names of us that live near here. Did we hear anything? See anybody suspicious?"

"And did you?"

"Not me. I was on the night shift at the foundry. Got off this morning. On my way home I seen the crowd here and came to have a look-see." The man gave Jack a rather sharp glance. "I don't recognize your face. Do you live round here?"

"No. I was just visiting a pal. Like you, I saw people hanging around and got curious."

"Bin a soldier, have you?"

"That's right. How'd you know?"

The man shrugged. "All you returning soldiers have a look about you."

"What sort of look would that be, my friend?"

"I dunno. Just a look. No offence. Me, I'd have signed up in a flash if I was ten years younger. Besides which I work at a foundry. We make horseshoes. Considered essential war work. I'd be exempted anyways."

Jack was prevented from commenting by the sound of the ambulance, bell clanging, roaring up Chestnut Street. The official police ambulances were all motorized now, horses long gone.

The older of the two constables moved forward and raised his arm.

"Step back now, folks. Let the men do their job."

The crowd reluctantly parted, allowing the ambulance to drive past them into the laneway. Jack felt a tug on his sleeve. He turned around and looked into the eyes of a young woman who was smiling at him.

"Hello, Jack."

She saw his hesitation.

"It's Fiona. Fiona Williams. Duncan's sister."

"Good heavens, so it is," said Jack, breaking into a grin. "You've grown up a lot since I last saw you."

"That was almost seven years ago."

"Was it really? Surely not that long."

Their attention was caught by the sound of the ambulance doors clanking open.

"What has happened?" Fiona asked.

"It seems there has been a homicide."

"Oh, Jack. You'd think there was enough killing going on without bringing it home."

"Quite so."

Jack strained to look over the heads of the people so he could catch a view of the body. The attendants had covered him with a blanket but Jack had seen enough. He recognized the blond hair, the big frame. It was one of the men who had been at the blind pig the night before.

"Is he somebody you know?" Fiona asked, her voice full of concern.

"No, not at all. Why do you ask?"

"Because you looked so shocked."

"It's always upsetting to see somebody whose life has been cut short too early, that's all."

She put her hand gently on his arm. "I'm sure you've experienced enough of that already."

Jack didn't trust himself to reply.

"Where are you heading?" Fiona asked.

"I was going to drop in on my father at police headquarters."

"I'm on my way to work. Eaton's telephone department," said Fiona. "It's on your way. Would you like to accompany me?"

"Love to," said Jack.

They heard the sound of the ambulance start up.

"Move aside now, folks," said the constable. "Let them come through."

The crowd shuffled away, murmuring among themselves. Jack could see the foundry worker was still keeping him in view. The ambulance drove slowly out of the laneway, turned, and, with a lurch, sped away. The bell started clanging again.

Jack grimaced. "I suppose there's really no longer any need for them to hurry, is there?"

He offered Fiona his arm. Jack felt in a turmoil but, in spite of everything, he was enjoying the feeling of a woman's body warm and close to him.

They walked for a while without speaking. As they approached the store entrance, Fiona disengaged her arm from Jack's. There was quite a press of customers entering the store.

"Looks busy," said Jack.

"It always is. Eaton's is one of the most popular stores in town. Guaranteed quality, fair prices, home delivery. What more could a woman ask for?"

Jack gazed down at her. "Do I detect a note of irony in your voice?"

"A little," she said with a shrug. "Mr. Eaton is very anxious to project an image of moral rectitude. It extends to his employees. Unless you are of demonstrably good character, he won't hire you. Any transgression and you're out on your ear."

"What is considered to be a transgression?"

"One girl was discovered having a cigarette in the washroom. Dismissed on the spot. Another had actually rouged her lips. Silly girl. She claimed it was her natural colour but they didn't believe it. Out she went." Fiona hesitated. "And no unpopular views are allowed."

"Unpopular?"

"You know. Unpatriotic. Anti-war, that sort of thing."

"And what sort of views do you hold, Miss Williams?"

She gave him an impish grin. "Well, I suppose you could ask your father."

"Really? How would he know?"

"He'll explain. But better still, why don't you find out for yourself? I'm part of a Red Cross fundraising event this Friday. It's at Shea's Theatre."

"I know where that is. I used to go there."

"Well, it still features lovely young ladies who will sing and dance. In skimpy clothing, of course."

"Is that what you're doing?"

"A little singing, no dancing, and I'm fully clothed. Actually, I do ventriloquism."

"No! You mean with a dummy, throwing your voice and all that?"

"That's right."

"One doesn't often find a woman in that line of entertainment."

"There isn't another woman in Ontario as far as I know. That's probably why they hired me. I'm a novelty! Good gracious, look at the time. I'm late. Employees enter by the rear door."

She walked away, then abruptly turned.

"It's wonderful to see you again, Jack. Do come to the show. Seven o'clock. I'm in the second half, so you can watch the lovely ladies dance and sing before I come on."

He beamed at her. "I will come, for sure."

"Bring a friend. I'll leave two free tickets at the door."

She strode off.

Jack watched her for a moment. His memories of Fiona as a girl were rather foggy; she had been lively and presentable, but just a child in his eyes. She certainly had grown into a most attractive young woman. Her presence had been a brief but welcome distraction from the sight of the murdered man.

Suddenly he felt exhausted. These depleted states came upon him regularly, and there wasn't much he could do about them. "It will take time" was the catchphrase of the army doctors.

But Jack had found that time was elastic. It seemed as if a long, long time had elapsed since he'd joined up. But the recovery from his wound felt agonizingly slow. "Be patient," said the last physician who'd examined him. "Your mind has to heal as well as your body."

Jack quickened his pace. You could rest your body; strengthen your body; exercise your body. But he had no idea how to do that with his mind.

CHAPTER FOURTEEN

MURDOCH MUSTERED THE CONSTABLES ON DUTY, organized them into teams, and sent them off to make door-to-door inquiries along the streets in the vicinity of the laneway.

"Don't intimidate the residents or they won't talk to you. They're wary enough as it is. Just see if anybody knew the young man in question. Or if they heard anything, or saw anything. He must have left his mother's house with the intention of going somewhere. It will help us if we knew where that was."

He beckoned to Fenwell. "Why don't we start by paying Mrs. Schumacher a visit. Her house isn't too far from where Arthur ended up. There was supposedly some kind of row happening last night outside her residence. Might be relevant."

"I had a thought about that foreign currency in Aggett's pocket," said Fenwell.

"He was gambling, don't you think?"

Fenwell smiled. "I expected you'd come to the same conclusion."

"It makes the most sense. It's not likely a shopkeeper would slip those coins to him. But on a gambling table, anything goes."

Mrs. Schumacher's house was nondescript, about as innocuous as it was possible for a house to be. Pale yellow brick, brown trim on the door and windows, lace curtains. The door was opened by the owner herself. She showed no reaction when Murdoch introduced himself and Detective Fenwell. She simply stepped back and ushered them in.

The small front room was dominated by a long table. Several chairs were lined up along the walls, and a bead curtain hung in a doorway at the rear. Paintings hung from the picture rail; all appeared to be of exotic birds. There was a strong odour of carbolic in the air and Murdoch spotted a bucket in a corner, a faint puff of steam drifting upward.

Mrs. Schumacher immediately sat down at the head of the table, in the centre of which sat an extravagant arrangement of dried flowers, and gestured to the two detectives that they should take a seat. She placed her hands flat on the table, which was covered with a sober brown cloth. A model of domestic respectability, if one ignored the unusual number of chairs.

Their hostess struck Murdoch as a formidable woman. It wasn't that she was large in the usual sense. She wasn't. She was of average height and weight, firmly held in by tight corsets. Her dark hair was pulled back in a smooth bun fastened with two tortoiseshell combs, and her grey silk dress was sober, adorned by only a single gold chain with a watch and fob. At first Murdoch couldn't understand why she seemed so intimidating. Then he realized several things: first, she never smiled, not in the slightest; second, she had piercing dark eyes; and third, she had a large nose. Her voice, when she spoke, was strong.

"I've already explained to one of your constables that some people were gathered here for a friendly game of whist last night. I do not serve alcohol, of course, as it is now against the law. We drank tea."

Fenwell answered. "A neighbour reported a disturbance in the early hours of the morning."

"Like any man born to woman, these men can get het up about delivering their own opinions. I wouldn't have called it a disturbance."

"What sort of opinions?"

"The usual these days. Should we force French Canadians into active service or not? I myself have no opinion either way. If they don't want to fight a war they consider is nothing to do with them, so be it. Throughout history, there have always been those who were only too willing to have another die for them if they can stay safe in their warm beds. Frankly, I despise slackers, no matter what language they speak."

This little speech was delivered in an unemotional voice, as if Mrs. Schumacher had been stating the price of potatoes.

"The constable took down the names of two men who were here when he arrived," said Murdoch. "They said they were Joseph Oliver and George Geary. Do those names sound familiar to you?"

"Good gracious. I never ask names. Different men come and go depending on their shifts."

"So you don't know a Joseph Oliver who says he lives at 16 Louisa Street, or a George Geary who lives at 101 Hayter?"

"I am not acquainted with those names."

"I'm surprised they don't ring a bell. Joseph Oliver was the thirty-fourth mayor of this city and George Geary the thirty-fifth. So unless the retired officials of Toronto have a predilection for tea and a late-night game of whist I can assume these are not the men's real names."

"That must be the case."

There was the tiniest pucker at the corner of her mouth, which Murdoch took for a touch of amusement.

"I wonder why they would give a false identity."

"Usually the urge for deception can be traced to a domestic issue."

"Was there another man here last night? Young, about twenty or so. Big fellow with fair hair. He was wearing a grey mackinaw. No overcoat or hat. If he did happen to give you his name, it was Arthur Aggett."

She furrowed her brow. "I don't know anybody by that name. Nor do I recall a guest of that description. I am curious as to why you are asking these questions, Detective."

"Because his body has been found not far from here. It is likely he was murdered."

If Murdoch had expected Mrs. Schumacher to evince some kind of shock, he was disappointed. She remained unemotional.

"Murdered in what way?"

"Until the investigation is completed, I'm not at liberty to say, madam. It would help if you could be more precise about your gathering last night. What time did the men leave the premises, for instance?"

He could see she was considering how much to reveal.

"I'd say it was about one o'clock but I can't say *precisely*."

"You don't have a clock?"

"I do but I don't consult it every minute."

"So did the gathering break up right after this lively difference of opinion?"

"Yes, I suppose it was shortly afterward."

The neighbour who'd reported the argument had put the time at a quarter past one, so in that at least she was telling the truth.

Murdoch nodded at Fenwell, who took over the questioning.

"Our witness reports seeing *several* men engaged in a loud argument on the street outside your premises. When the constable checked here, there were only two men present. Were there others who had perhaps left somewhat earlier?"

"Come to think of it, that may have been the case."

"If you don't mind, madam, we'll need descriptions of all of them."

"I have a dreadful memory for faces, Detective. I don't think I can be of much help. Besides, I was in the kitchen most of the time."

"Making tea, I assume?" interrupted Murdoch.

"Precisely."

He was getting irritated by this stalling but he doubted he was going to shake Mrs. Schumacher. Her livelihood probably depended on her complete discretion—and a bad memory.

"If you do happen to remember any details about your guests, however small, please let us know immediately." He and Fenwell stood up. "And I should warn you, Mrs. Schumacher, you and your establishment are considered to be under investigation until the case is solved."

She didn't respond, only stared at him with those piercing dark eyes.

"What do you think, Peter?" asked Murdoch once they were on the sidewalk again.

"There's no doubt she's lying. She probably has a lot to hide. But I don't think it's going to be easy to dislodge her."

"My sentiments exactly. I'd bet my boots young Aggett was here. She definitely runs a blind pig. She probably brews the liquor in the back. She was clever and prepared but you don't get rid of that smell quickly. Even with carbolic."

"Even if we assume that Aggett was here, with the two ex-mayors, I don't consider that qualifies as a group, do you? Four people?"

"No, I don't think so either."

"So there were more. And one of our ardent whist players was carrying foreign currency around with him that ended up in Arthur Aggett's pocket."

"The ones most likely to have shillings with them would be returning soldiers."

Fenwell had said the words and Murdoch was grateful. He couldn't go on avoiding the possibilities that presented themselves. It wasn't going to help anybody if he buried his head in the sand.

The first address, 101 Hayter, turned out to be boarded up. The roof had collapsed into the second floor and the front door was hanging on its hinges, and when Murdoch looked into the empty room he saw only bits of paper and dead leaves that had blown in. It was an eyesore, but the other cottages on the block were not much better. Corrugated iron was holding up two of them. Murdoch experienced his usual wave of irritation and indignation at the sight of these slums.

He complained on a regular basis to the Chief Constable, asking him to use his influence to force landlords to maintain the houses. He supposed Colonel Grasett's heart was in the right place but his response was tepid and nothing was done. Murdoch was hoping the latest scathing report by the city medical officer, Dr. Hastings, would bring results where there had been none before.

Louisa Street was not far from Hayter, and the houses there

improved slightly in appearance. The paint on the door of number 16 wasn't peeling and the lace curtains in the front windows looked fresh enough.

Murdoch knocked. After some time, an elderly woman, dressed in black velvet, opened the door. She was bent almost double, her eyes were milky, and she was holding up an old-fashioned ear trumpet.

"Yes?"

Murdoch tipped his hat. With the hearing aid in mind, he raised his voice.

"Good day, madam. I'm Detective William Murdoch, and this is my colleague, Detective Fenwell. We're inquiring as to the whereabouts of a man calling himself Joseph Oliver. I understand he lives here."

She appeared to have heard him. "There's nobody here by that name. My husband is Isaac Freedman. I'm Miriam. We live alone."

"Is the name familiar to you at all, Mrs. Freedman?"

"No. Our only son was named Moishe, but he is long gone."

"My condolences, madam."

"What?"

"I am sorry to hear of your loss," said Murdoch, more loudly.

She leaned in closer to him, almost as if she could pick up a scent. Then she gave a little smile.

"You misunderstand me, Detective. I meant he emigrated many years ago, to Australia. He couldn't stand the cold weather we get here. We do hear from him on a regular basis but it's lonely without him, I must admit. We don't get out very much, and you are the first visitors we've had since I don't know when."

Murdoch was at a loss as to what to say. "Are you able to manage?"

"Oh yes. My husband worked for the Toronto Street Railway Company and he gets a pension. Not a lot, but enough for us to live on. It is kind of you to ask, Detective."

Murdoch wondered if the pension would stop when her husband died. Probably. Then what?

She placed a tentative hand on his sleeve. "I don't suppose you have time to come inside and say hello to my husband. It would give him such pleasure."

"I'm afraid I don't, Mrs. Freedman. We're on duty at the moment."

"Yes, of course." She stepped back.

"I will call again, soon," he said. "Make sure you are managing."

"Thank you. By the way, you didn't say why you were looking for this man and why you thought he might live here."

"He may have been involved in an altercation. He gave this address to one of our constables when questioned."

"Is he a criminal?"

"He may be. We don't know for sure. Certainly we will charge him with issuing false information to a police officer, if we find him."

She flashed the little mischievous smile. "In that case, you must come back, Detective. Or somebody else from the police force. Perhaps the other detective?"

Fenwell tipped his hat but didn't say anything.

"If the man gave this address he may show up here," she continued. "We're not in danger, I hope."

"I don't believe so, madam. But of course, you must contact the police immediately if he does show up."

Murdoch took his leave. Fenwell did likewise. Mrs. Freedman didn't close the door right away but stood on the threshold, watching them walk away.

After a couple of minutes, Fenwell said, "Lord save me from old age and loneliness, Will."

Peter almost never made such personal statements, and Murdoch didn't quite know how to respond.

Murdoch had liked Mrs. Freedman. There was something about her that reminded him of his first landlady, Mrs. Kitchen.

"Perhaps she's more resilient than we think."

Fenwell grunted. "Let's hope so."

CHAPTER FIFTEEN

JACK WAS ON THE POINT OF HEADING UP THE CITY HALL steps when he almost collided with a man who was hurrying down them.

"Sorry," the man muttered. Then he stopped abruptly.

"Good heavens. You're Murdoch's lad, I'll wager!"

"That's right."

"You're the spitting image. I'd heard you had returned. Jack, isn't it?"

"That's right."

"I'm Roy Rubridge, one of the detectives here." And he thrust out his hand.

He was a husky man, with a wind-roughened face and a

119

bushy moustache. Jack noticed he was wearing a black arm band. He took the offered hand and they shook as heartily as possible considering Jack had to use his left.

"Caught one, did you?" Rubridge asked. "Sorry to see that."

"Thank you, I'm on the mend."

"Good lad."

"I see you have suffered a loss, sir. My condolences."

"Thank you." Rubridge touched the arm band as lightly as if it were covering a painful wound. "My son."

Jack expected Rubridge to elaborate but he didn't. Instead he shifted his attention back to Jack.

"Were you coming to see your father?"

"As a matter of fact, I was."

"He was called out to deal with a homicide in the Ward. He's probably still over there."

"That must have been what I saw on Chestnut Street," said Jack. "The ambulance was taking a body out of a laneway."

"That'd be the one."

"Any idea what happened?"

"Not yet. Just got reported."

"I think I'll get over there, see if I can catch him," said Jack.

Rubridge thrust out his hand again. "All right. I hope to see you before long."

They parted company at Albert Street and Jack proceeded up Chestnut. The laneway was on the west side, just above Armoury Street. Some people remained but they were silent now. The elderly constable Jack had seen before was still standing guard in front of the rope. His cohort had left. The police motor car was parked on the street and Murdoch was standing next to it. Jack walked up to him.

"Hello, Pa."

Murdoch turned and his face lit up.

"Hello, son. How'd you track me down?"

"I ran into Detective Rubridge at headquarters and he told me you'd be over here."

Peter Fenwell jumped out of the car, beaming too.

"Jack! Good to see you. How are you doing?"

"Mr. Fenwell. I'm coming along, thanks. And you?"

"All right I suppose."

"How's Eric?"

"I'm afraid we've had word that he's a prisoner of war. He's being kept at a camp in Germany."

"I'm so sorry to hear that."

Fenwell glanced around. "This isn't the place to talk but I sure would like to have a chat when you have the chance. We've got so little information."

"Of course."

"Tell you what. Your father's coming for dinner on Friday. Why don't you come as well? I know Mrs. Fenwell would love to see you."

"Great idea," Murdoch chipped in.

"Do you mind if I give you an answer later?" said Jack. "I'm not good company right now. Soon as I'm livelier, I would definitely love to see you both. So sorry about Eric, but I'm sure he'll be all right. Reports about the camps haven't been that bad."

"That's a relief to know," said Fenwell. "Of course, come when you can."

Jack addressed Murdoch. "I came past here not too long ago and saw the ambulance removing a body. What happened?"

"We're still getting to the bottom of that."

"He looked as if he'd been given a walloping."

"It appears that way."

Fenwell interjected, "Look, Will, why don't you drive Jack home? I'll take care of things here for now."

Jack shook his head. "Don't worry, Pa. I was just going over to have a visit with Percy. I'll see you when you're finished. Oh, by the way, don't bother with supper for me tonight. Percy says his landlord makes wonderful meals. I'll eat with him."

"All right. I'm going to be tied up with this case for a while, but let's plan to spend some time together soon."

"Sure will."

"Don't forget about the invitation to dinner on Friday," chipped in Fenwell. "I don't know if we can compete with the esteemed landlord but Mrs. Fenwell is a pretty good cook, as you know."

"She is indeed," said Jack. "I'd better be off."

He gave them a salute, and before Murdoch could say any more, he strode off down the road.

Both men watched him go for a moment, then Fenwell said, "I'm sorry, Will. I didn't know he was in such bad shape."

"It's hard to know what to say to him. I feel as if he's fending me off all the time."

"He is," said Fenwell. "Be patient is all I can say."

"I don't have much choice, do I?"

At Fenwell's insistence, Murdoch left him in charge and he made his way back to headquarters. He headed for his office, his personal sanctuary. He hoped the post-mortem report on Arthur wouldn't take long. There wasn't much he could do until they had gathered more evidence. Before he sat down, he took a peek at the chess board. He was ready to send off his move to Allen. He didn't think the sergeant stood a chance to escape checkmate but you never knew.

Murdoch had been in this office for two years now and he'd resisted adding any personal touches beyond a single photograph. He wasn't sure why, really. He liked the detectives, and the chief and his deputy would never dream of entering his domain; all meetings were conducted in one of their spacious offices or in the duty room. But with the exception of Peter Fenwell, Murdoch had been reluctant to share much of his private life with his colleagues here. Now he sat down and picked up the framed photograph of Amy that was on his desk. She was holding Jack on her lap. He was three years old. They'd had a hard time getting him to smile at the photographer and his chubby face was solemn.

Only a couple of hours before the appointment, he had fallen and scraped his knees on the pavement. He'd howled in pain at first, but Murdoch picked him up and held him close.

"Hush, Jack. Hush. Don't be a crybaby. Boys have to be brave."

Jack, with some difficulty, had swallowed his tears, and when they got home Amy cleaned his knees. There were bits of gravel embedded in the wound. He'd taken quite a tumble. But he didn't cry, although the salt water must have stung.

Murdoch had never seen his son cry after that, even when he hurt himself.

With a sigh, he returned the photograph to the desk.

OFFICERS' MANUAL.

PART III—GENERAL REMARKS

A platoon commander will have gone a long way toward having a well-trained platoon if he has gained the confidence of his N.C.O.s and the men and has established a high soldierly spirit in all ranks.

The confidence of the men can be gained by:—
. . . d) Enforcing strict discipline at all times. This must be a willing discipline not a sulky one. Be just but do not be soft—men despise softness.
. . . h) Being blood-thirsty and for ever thinking how to kill the enemy and helping his men to do so . . .

CHAPTER SIXTEEN

PERCY WAS ALONE, LYING ON HIS COUCH. THE EVER present opium pipe was across his chest. He raised his head.

"So, pal, what did you find out? Will I be hanged or not?"

"I'll hang you myself if you don't pull yourself together and stop those damn pipes."

Percy smiled. "I wish I could, Jack, but when the effect wears off I feel as if I just walked into Hell and all the demons are after me."

"All right. But try to cut back, at least. How's your hand?"

Percy waved his arm in the air. "Doesn't hurt at all. These Chinks have the best medicine going. Well, what's the news?"

"None at the moment, and that's good. The dead man was at the blind pig. I recognized him."

"Which one was he?"

"Big fellow. Blond hair."

"How was he killed?"

"Clubbed to death."

"What with?"

"They haven't found the weapon yet."

"Who did for him?"

"I don't know. A thief, maybe. Have you recalled anything more in the meantime?"

"Not a jot. Blank."

"Let's assume, then, that even though you were pie-eyed last night and upset with the fellow, I don't think you are, in fact, in your inner most self, capable of killing an unarmed man who is no threat to you."

Percy turned his head away. "Perhaps that was true a long time ago, Jack, but I wouldn't swear to it now."

"That was different. We were in a war."

"The flesh wasn't different. The blood wasn't different." He reached out and grasped Jack's hand. "What shall we do now, Jack?"

"I guess we'll have to wait."

"Should I turn myself in?"

"I'd say that wasn't necessary at this juncture. In the meantime, we'll carry on as usual."

"Whatever that is."

"Any day now, we'll remember."

"You know what I'd really like, Jack? Right now?"

"What?"

"I'd like to go to the City Baths. Ghong Lee told me that for five cents you can have a shower. Imagine that, Jack. All that lovely hot, clean water. As much as you want. It'll be ecstasy." Percy swung his legs over the side of the bed. "Can we?"

Jack paused. "I don't see why not."

Somewhat shakily, Percy straightened up. "By the way, I've got myself a chair."

"A chair? What are you talking about?"

"An invalid chair. Good Father Lee brought one for me. Who knows where he got it—he's got connections everywhere. It's downstairs."

"Ha. Well, don't think I'm going to push you anywhere, you lazybones. You can walk and you should walk. It'll do you good."

Percy grinned. "Why did I guess you'd take that attitude? But I get tired, Jack, I really do. And when I'm tired I cough. Most unpleasant. Takes me back to life in the trenches. Which is not what I want to think about. So the chair is perfect. I can wheel myself if necessary . . . although to tell the truth I was thinking I might find one of those sweet little Red Cross nurses and get her to help out. You'd be surprised how easy it is to win fair maidens when you're in a wheelchair."

"Percy, you are incorrigible. But the baths it is. Let's go."

"I'd like to make one stop on the way."

"Where?"

"My very own mademoiselle from Ontario. *Parlee-voo*."

"How did you manage that? We've only been here a day."

"Let's just say she was a previous acquaintance. Come on, it's not far from here. I won't linger, I promise."

Jack sighed. "McKinnon, you are incorrigible. But do me a favour, will you? Don't wear that ridiculous aviator cap."

"Why not? It's nice and warm."

"You look like a dope, that's why not."

"Besides, if I pull it down, it hides my scar."

"Oh, all right. By the way, I should tell you that my father is the detective in charge of the investigation."

Percy raised his eyebrows. "I presume that means it is in good hands."

"Yep. I'd say so. Very good hands."

CHAPTER SEVENTEEN

MURDOCH WAS WRITING UP AN OCCURRENCE REPORT about the death of Arthur Aggett. It was still woefully thin.

Madge Curnoe came in. "Any progress?" she asked.

"Not yet. How's Mrs. Aggett?"

"I was able to bring in her neighbour to stay with her. By luck, she brought up the question of the daughter-in-law. Mrs. Aggett would have none of it, but in private the neighbour told me Lottie's sister's name and where she lives. I rang the police station in Mimico and they're going to get hold of her. They said they could bring her back into the city by motor car. She should be here later today."

"The train would be faster."

"I know, but I think the duty sergeant fancied taking their motor car out for a spin. They told me they only got it a month ago."

The telephone on Murdoch's desk gave a shrill ring.

"Excuse me, Madge," he said, and picked up the receiver.

"Reception desk here, sir. We've just had a call from the alarm box on Centre Avenue. A Constable Handley. He was on his beat when he was called to the City Baths. Seems a young man has drowned."

"Isn't that in the jurisdiction of number two division?"

"It is, sir. But according to the constable, a detective needs to come and take a look."

"I'll go. Everybody's involved in the murder case. Is the Ford available?"

"Yes, sir. Do you want a driver?"

"No, no. I'll drive myself."

He hung up. Madge was looking at him inquiringly.

"There's been a drowning at the City Baths. Number two division say they need a detective on the scene. I've got to get over there, no one else is available."

"Do you need me to come, in case there is family to be notified?"

"Let me get the lie of the land first. I'd rather you start to follow up on that advertisement. I'll come back and get you later if need be."

The City Baths had been built in 1904. Everybody knew that a man with a clean and healthy body was likely to have a clean and healthy mind. The popularity of the baths in the midst of the steadily increasing squalor of the Ward had justified the initial expense. The City Council maintained the subsidy so that poor people could afford to go and scrub off the grime. Clean towels were rationed but at least they were available.

Like most public buildings created to take care of the needs of the lower classes, these baths were plain. There was no need for fancy gables or decorative brick around the lintels.

As soon as Murdoch drew up in front, an older man who'd been standing in a doorway rushed to the car. He looked frightened out of his wits.

"Thank God you're here, sir. Dreadful business. Dreadful." He was literally hopping in place. "And children around too." He flapped his hand in the general direction of a little knot of scruffy boys near the entrance. They were eying Murdoch and the Ford with great curiosity.

Murdoch put his hand on the man's arm. "Try to steady yourself, there's a good fellow. I'm Detective Murdoch. What is your name?"

"Joseph Steinberg. I work here. Seven years, and nothing like this has ever happened before."

"Where's the constable in charge?" Murdoch asked.

"He's keeping watch over the body. Good thing I hadn't let the next group in yet. They would have seen everything." He paused, obviously struggling to gain control. "Come with me, sir. I'll show you the way."

Steinberg went ahead through the double doors. He locked them as soon as they were both inside.

"I don't trust those kiddies not to try to sneak in. Free days are on Wednesdays and Saturdays only."

They were hit by the pervading smell of carbolic. It wasn't particularly warm inside, and Murdoch recalled coming to the baths with Jack years ago and how chilly it always seemed. The building was divided into two sections: the east side for boys and men; the west, with a separate entrance, for the girls and women. The pool was at the far end of the corridor. Murdoch knew that only males were permitted to use the pool, or the "dunk tank" as it was usually called.

"Seven years," muttered Steinberg. "Seven years and not a jot of trouble. And now . . ."

He pushed open a heavy door. The pool was still. A uniformed constable was standing just inside. He immediately came to attention.

"Good afternoon, sir. Constable Handley here." He pointed. "He's there," he said, rather unnecessarily.

The naked body of a young man was stretched out on a wooden bench. Already death's pallor had seized him. He was scrawny, more boy than man, his skin virtually hairless except for a thin, skimpy beard and dark pubic hair. He was circumcised. He might have been in his late teen years.

"Can you tell me what happened, Mr. Steinberg?"

"He took his own life, that's what. He committed suicide."

FROM "A FAREWELL ADDRESS TO THE FIRST
CONTINGENT" BY GENERAL SIR SAM HUGHES

What reck you whether your resting place be decked with
the golden lilies of France, or be admidst the vine-clad
hills of the Rhine; the principles for which you fought are
eternal.

CHAPTER EIGHTEEN

Murdoch sent the constable out to watch for the arrival of the ambulance and he led the attendant to a bench and had him sit down.

"Can we cover him up, sir? It's horrible to see him lying like that, all white and still."

"Of course. Stay where you are, Mr. Steinberg. I'll do it. If you feel faint, put your head between your knees."

The poor man was looking as pale as the corpse.

Murdoch went to a shelf and picked up a couple of towels and draped them over the body. He paused for a moment. A few years ago he would have murmured a prayer, but he hadn't done that for a long time.

He returned to the attendant, who had indeed put his head down.

"I realize what a dreadful shock this has been, Mr. Steinberg, but I do need to take a statement. All right?"

The attendant straightened up. "Go ahead. I'm better."

Murdoch took out his notebook and pencil. "First of all, why do you say he was a suicide?"

"Because nobody holds on to the drain in the pool unless they want to drown themselves."

"Are you sure that's what happened, Mr. Steinberg?"

"Absolutely sure. I could see him."

"It would take enormous determination to kill yourself in that way. It's contrary to every instinct for survival."

"There's no doubt, sir." The attendant looked as if he might break down again but he fought for control. "I was just about to open the entrance doors, see. The first shift was waiting outside but I won't let them in until they line up. They're the under-twelves, you see. You have to keep a keen eye on them or they'll try to sneak in without a ticket in the crush."

He paused. Murdoch waited, knowing he had to tell it in his own way.

"So there I am trying to get some order to prevail, when all of a sudden behind me I hear the crash of the shower room door. Somebody shouted. I don't know who. I turn to see what's the fuss and this young man comes rushing out. Before I could do anything about it, he runs down to the pool door. He's mother naked, and that's not allowed here, you have to wear a swimming costume. And it's an extra five cents to swim. I shout, but he could have been deaf for all the notice he took." Steinberg licked his dry lips. "I'm a touch aggravated, as you can imagine. I'm responsible for the proper running of this place and rules are rules. So, quick as a flash, I close the outside door to keep those children out. I lock it as a precaution and I go after him. He's gone through into the pool by then but I follow and go inside."

He stopped again, and Murdoch thought that in spite of his upset Mr. Steinberg was rather enjoying the drama of the situation and the attention it was bringing him.

"At first, I can't understand where on earth he's got to. There are no changing rooms in the pool area where he could be. Then I see he's at the bottom of the deep end." An expression of genuine horror came into the attendant's eyes. "He wasn't swimming at all. He was holding on to the drain." He shuddered. "There's a powerful suction from the drain which I've always been a bit nervous about. The kiddies sometimes like to dare each other and play with it. But it must have helped keep him there."

"Did you try to pull him out?" Murdoch asked. Steinberg's clothes were dry.

"I can't swim and I've got a withered arm, see?" He stretched out his arms so Murdoch could see the left was considerably shorter than the right. "From birth. Useless. So I run out to the corridor and start to call for help. Thank God another young man dashes out of the shower room. I can't even speak at this point so I just wave to the pool area. Must have been written all over my face that something bad had happened.

"He races down the corridor, me after him fast as I can. He opens the door and sizes up the situation at once. He dives in right away. He's only in his underwear, you see. The first fellow has let go of the grate by now and he's just drifting down there. The second chap has to go down a couple of times before he's able to bring up the body, but finally he does. Took both of us to drag him out of the water, what with me and my arm. We lay him out on his back and the chap tries doing artificial ventilation but it's not doing much good. He says to me to go and fetch a constable from the beat and bring him back immediately, so that's what I do. At first there's no officer in sight. Where are they when you need them, eh, Detective? Then just when I was about to give up one waltzes by. I tell him what's happened and bring him straight to the pool. The young fellow is still pumping but he looks like he's going to keel over. He don't look in the best of health himself. He's got one of them racking coughs. Could have been consumptive. Right away the constable has him move back and he checks out the body. 'He's a goner. Nothing more you can do,' says he."

"How long was the man trying the pumping?"

"From the time we pulled him out of the water and to the time I got back, it would be twenty or thirty minutes at least. The officer says he'll have to go and ring headquarters and get an ambulance to come. Says for us to stay with the body. So off he goes. The young fellow was dripping wet and he was shivering like all get out. 'I'm going to dry off and get dressed,' he says to me. So without another word, he leaves me with this corpse who's looking more and more like a dead fish. Fortunately, the constable doesn't take too long. He says he's rung headquarters and somebody will come right away. He'll take over now. He tells me to go outside and keep a watch for the police motor. Says to send everybody away who's wanting to come in. So I did just what he said and I put up the *Closed* sign."

"Good. Right thing to do."

"Thank you, sir. It's easy to lose your wits in a situation like this."

"Most definitely. Do you know what's happened to the would-be rescuer?"

"No, I don't. Maybe he went home, seeing as there was no more he could do."

"Did he give you his name?"

"No, he didn't, which is a shame because in my view he's a hero, even if he couldn't save the poor lad. It was extra hard for him because he'd got a bad arm."

"A bad arm?"

"Yes, sir. Not like me, but he was favouring it quite a bit. I heard him actually yelp when we lifted up the body. In fact, he and his friend both looked like they'd been in the wars."

"He was with another man?"

"They came in together and were chatting with each other so I assumed they was friends. The other fellow had the shakes. When he handed me his ticket he almost dropped it, and he had the most dreadful scar on his forehead. As if he'd been branded by the devil himself."

Murdoch stared at him for a moment. "But this friend didn't help with the attempted rescue?"

"No. I didn't see hide nor hair of him. Just the dark-haired one."

"You said you heard somebody shout just before the first fellow ran out of the shower room. Could you make out who it was and what he shouted?"

"No. It might have been the dead lad himself. But I couldn't make out what he said."

Before they could continue, there was a knock on the door and Constable Handley poked his head inside.

"Excuse me, sir. The ambulance is here. Shall I have them come down?"

"Right away." Murdoch gazed down at the body. Poor lad. He wondered what was so badly wrong in his life that he saw this as the way out.

He turned back to the attendant. "Where are his clothes?"

"They'll be in the change room I suspect."

"Let's take a look." Murdoch addressed Constable Handley now. "Have the body taken to the morgue. I'll come there as soon as I can."

Steinberg led the way down the corridor, the bunch of keys clipped to his belt jangling.

CHAPTER NINETEEN

THE AIR IN THE CHANGING ROOM WAS DANK, TINGED with the ubiquitous carbolic, but the smell from too many unwashed bodies and clothes overwhelmed the efforts to keep the place clean. The communal showers were at the far end behind a tiled partition that reached partway to the ceiling, not for reasons of privacy but to serve as a backsplash for the water from the half a dozen faucets attached to the wall. A battered sign on the partition declared "ENTRANCE ONLY." An arrow pointed in the correct direction. Next to that was another sign: "NO SPITTING ALLOWED. IF CAUGHT YOU WILL BE BARRED." And beside that: "USE THE URINALS IN THE TOILET ROOM. DO NOT USE THE SHOWER." There were shelves with rows of wire baskets along all four walls, and wooden benches in front of them.

"The men put their clothes in the baskets while they are taking a shower," said Steinberg. "If they are going to the dunk tank they have to wear a regulation bathing costume. Those are loaned out free of charge."

"Do you have a problem with theft?" asked Murdoch. He could see no way to secure the contents of the baskets.

"I'm happy to say we do not. Too many observant eyes. Most of our patrons live by the 'Don't do unto others what you don't want them to do unto you' motto. You don't steal my things and neither will I steal yours. Besides, in most cases you would be exchanging rags for rags."

"Those must belong to our fellow," said Murdoch, pointing to the only basket that wasn't empty. He removed it from the shelf and placed it on the bench.

Contrary to Mr. Steinberg's comment about rags, the clothes were decent enough, if on the shabby side. A brown overcoat, relatively new, was on the top; under it was a grey woollen jacket, patched at the elbows, and a pair of black trousers, also patched. A thin white shirt; the collar had been turned not too long ago. Darned socks. A pair of worn black boots were tucked underneath the clothes. Underneath them was a brown envelope.

The name on the front gave him a jolt: "*To Miss Fiona Williams.*"

He turned the envelope over in his hands. There was a

name and address written on the back in the same immaculate handwriting: "*D. Samuels, 10A Hagerman Street.*"

The flap of the envelope hadn't stuck properly, and, carefully, Murdoch tugged it open.

There was a slim red book inside. *Canada In Flanders*, by Sir Max Aitken. Murdoch knew it well. It had been published the previous year and had sold like hotcakes. He had bought himself a copy, eager to study the maps of the battles that had occurred since the war began. By then Jack had already been sent to the Front, and he wanted to understand as much as he could about what his son might be facing.

"*D. Samuels*" had signed and dated the front page, "*May 15, 1916.*" Murdoch turned to the back. There was the same neat signature and address. But this time, in the lower corner of the page, was another date, "*Sept. 1915,*" and underneath it a series of what looked like ink scratches. The ink and handwriting were identical to that of the signature and address above. Murdoch knew enough to recognize this was in fact Pitman shorthand. Clerks and secretaries used it to transcribe verbatim what an employer was dictating. But what the shorthand message said, Murdoch had no idea.

He was about to replace the book in the envelope when he noticed there was something pressed between the pages. It was a small white feather.

"Oh dear me. I wonder who gave him that?" said Steinberg, who had been watching keenly.

Murdoch knew that some young women earlier in the war

had got into the deplorable habit of handing young men who weren't in uniform a white feather, a symbol of cowardice. He hadn't seen it lately, thank goodness, as it had become increasingly obvious that the war ministry couldn't snatch up every possible young man—someone had to keep things going at home. He wondered who had given it to Samuels and how it had affected him, if it had anything to do with his suicide.

He returned the feather to the book and tucked it inside his own jacket. The envelope he returned to the basket. The attendant was watching him anxiously.

"Bad business, what's happening in the world these days."

"Indeed it is," said Murdoch. He could feel his eyes starting to burn with the amount of carbolic in the air. "Is there somewhere more comfortable we can go to talk?"

"There's a room at the end of the corridor. The attendant on duty is permitted to use it for his tea."

"Let's go there, then. Can we lock this door?"

"Yes, sir."

Steinberg selected a key from the bunch at his waist and locked the door.

The door to the pool room was open. The body had been removed. The pool was still, no ripples disturbed the surface.

The tea room was more like a cubbyhole than a room and it reminded Murdoch of his first so-called office at number four station. At least this room had a door. He'd had to rely on a bead curtain in his old office.

There was space for two wooden chairs, a standing cupboard,

and a tiny oil stove with two rings. No sink, but a water jug and bowl on a washstand.

"Don't suppose you'd want a cup of tea, would you, sir?" asked Steinberg.

"Not right now, but make one for yourself if you like."

The attendant busied himself with filling the kettle and preparing the teapot. He was quite adept, despite being effectively one-armed.

He poured some weak-looking tea that was barely steaming, carried his cup over to the other chair, and sat down. He took a gulp of the brew.

"Thank goodness I remembered to put up the *CLOSED* sign." He glanced over the rim of his cup at Murdoch for approbation. Murdoch nodded.

"Let's go over what happened again. If anything else comes to you, just add it."

Murdoch forced himself to concentrate. The description of the young man who had tried to save Samuels fit Jack to a T. And the scarred pal was certainly Percy McKinnon.

What had the shout been all about? What had so distressed Samuels that he had rushed to take his own life?

FROM *CANADA IN FLANDERS*

WHEN DOMINION DAY CAME THEY REMEMBERED WITH PRIDE that they were the Army of a Nation, and those who were in the trenches displayed the Dominion flag, decorated with flowers of France, to the annoyance of the barbarians, who riddled it with bullets. . . .

BUT THE SHOUTING BASEBALL TEAMS AND MINSTREL shows, with their outrageous personal allusions, the skirl of the pipes and the choruses of well-known ragtimes, moved men to the depths of their souls. For this was the first Dominion Day that Canada had spent with the red sword in her hand.

CHAPTER TWENTY

Madge finished typing her report, rolled out the sheet of paper, and read over what she'd written. She took pride in her reports, which were concise and well presented. This particular incident had given her a lot of satisfaction. Another con artist, a man claiming to be raising money for wounded soldiers. He was leaning on crutches holding a basket and he was soliciting on Yonge Street. He fell into Madge's trap when she pretended to be a grief-stricken mother.

"Will the money go to the Lakeview Convalescence Home for soldiers?" she asked.

"Every cent, ma'am," was the reply.

"You're sure? I mean the place on King Street in the west end."

"I'm certain. I shall deliver any donations myself."

But there was no such place as Lakeview. She then identified herself as a police officer and was about to charge him. Foolish man might have got away with a protest of simple mistake, but instead, he abandoned his crutches and made a run for it. Madge caught him easily. He surrendered without further struggle. And all of that without any male help.

She stowed the paper in the file folder, ready to be handed to Murdoch.

She enjoyed her work with the police force but she particularly liked the "tougher" tasks that came her way. She was being assigned more and more of these as the war continued. A troubling number of discharged soldiers seemed unable to settle into the responsibilities of family life. They drifted aimlessly, didn't make their child support payments, vanished from the city without a trace. She had to track them down. Those men she could have some sympathy for. The ones she despised were the cheats who preyed on the vulnerable. Lately, many so-called fundraisers had appeared, like toadstools after a rain. Some were like the man she had nabbed on Monday. Others typically went from door to door in the better neighbourhoods claiming to be soliciting for the Red Cross. The gullible or the guilty handed over money. Over the past month, Madge had been given the responsibility for catching such cheats. Knowing that Jarvis Street had been targeted, Madge had spent a couple of hours strolling up and down the streets in the area. The houses were large, grand, staffed with servants, easy pickings for the smooth-tongued con artists.

Her first confrontation had been with a young man who had obtained money from an elderly householder on Sherbourne Street. Madge had witnessed the entire transaction, and as the young man was walking away, actually counting his money, she identified herself. Unlike the other fellow, he didn't succumb. He pushed her violently to the ground, cursing and swearing, and ran off. He wasn't caught, and Maud's back and shoulder were bruised. After that, mortified that he hadn't been more careful of her welfare, Murdoch had insisted she always be accompanied by a detective, and he'd assigned Roy Rubridge to be her partner.

From the beginning, Madge wished she could be paired with somebody else. Rubridge made too many personal comments. Her hair was "luscious," her dress "becoming"; "a nice armful" he'd called her once. His overly attentive manner made her uncomfortable. She also strongly suspected he was an inebriate. The new temperance laws didn't seem to impede him, however, and when he arrived on morning duty he had the pained, slow movements of a man who had imbibed too much the previous night. Madge had been reluctant to speak to Murdoch about this but she would probably have to, sooner or later. She was glad today was Rubridge's day off and she could deal with the child for adoption advertisement on her own.

She was on the point of seeking out Murdoch to learn what had transpired at the City Baths when he came in.

"I need you to come with me. It seems certain it was a

suicide. We have some identification and I have to notify the family."

"Right. I'll get my things."

They headed down the hall, and Murdoch checked in with Wallace.

"If anybody comes in with information on the Aggett case, tell them I don't expect to be too long."

To Madge, he said, "We're only going over to Hagerman but we'll drive. It's miserable out."

They went downstairs to the rear courtyard where the motor car was parked.

"You said you had some identification on the suicide?"

"I believe so, but it's not absolutely positive so I'll have to tread carefully. I don't want to give an unnecessary shock to a family that has no connection with the dead lad."

Murdoch opened the passenger door. He handed her the little red book.

"This was with the dead man's belongings. I'm assuming he is, or rather was, the 'D. Samuels' who signed it."

He got in the driver's side and started the engine. He shifted into gear with a jolt and they drove noisily out to the street.

"Before too long, I hope they will design a motor car that runs a bit quieter," said Murdoch. He made a cautious right turn onto Terauley Street. You could hardly describe the Ford as responsive. It was like aiming a battleship.

"Anyway, Madge, take a look at the back page. See, there's a notation in the corner. You don't happen to have a knowledge of shorthand in your considerable arsenal of skills, do you?"

"This is Pitman's. I learned Gregg's. Quite different, I'm afraid."

"There's a white feather shoved in between the pages."

Madge pursed her lips. "So there is. Poor fellow. Do you think it had anything to do with his killing himself?"

"Might. The book was being sent to a certain Fiona Williams. By coincidence, I encountered said Miss Williams at the train station yesterday. She was one of a group of young women with strident placards protesting against the war."

"*Strident* placards?"

"You know what I mean. Caused a ruckus. The last thing most of those present needed at that moment. The sight of the casualties was bad enough."

"I suppose we don't know the connection between Mr. Samuels and Miss Williams?"

"No."

"I can't believe she would be the one to give him a white feather if, as you say, she's so anti-war."

"My thoughts exactly. The little message and the feather might not be connected. Not everybody knows shorthand. It's as good as writing in code."

He slowed down in order to pass a plodding dray. The bony horse looked as if it could care less about a noisy motor going by, but the driver leaned over to peer balefully at Murdoch. He crawled past before accelerating.

Madge peered out the window. "This is near where I was going, to look into that advertisement about the baby boy. I telephoned the *Star* and was able to obtain the address of the person who placed the advertisement. Her name is Mrs. Henrietta Payne and she lives at 82 Louisa Street. Interested parties are instructed to apply in person."

"Shall I drop you off after?"

"No. I'll need to go back to the station. I've got to get into my costume."

"Wealthy matron?"

"That's right. I'm getting quite attached to the role."

Murdoch drew up in front of a row of houses. The house at number 10 had such a desolate appearance that it could have been abandoned. He turned off the engine.

"Before we go in, Madge, I just want to get your opinion on something."

"Go ahead."

"It's not to do with work, it's personal."

"Really, Detective! I didn't know you had a personal life."

Murdoch smiled ruefully. "That sounds like a reproach."

"I didn't mean it to be, Will. It's just that . . . well, I think there have been times when I've nattered on to you about my life. About Gran, for instance. Emigrating."

"I'm glad you did. I found it most interesting."

"And I'm sure I'd find your life interesting as well. But back to the matter at hand. You wanted my opinion?"

He recounted what Steinberg had told him about a young man coming out of the shower room and his attempt to rescue the drowning boy.

"From his description, I'm positive that person was Jack. I believe he was there with his pal, Percy."

She frowned. "Why is that troubling, Will? It sounds more as if what he tried to do was heroic."

"Why didn't he stick around and give his name? Why did he even go to the City Baths? We have a perfectly decent bathroom in the house. I had it installed right after Amy and I got married. Jack actually asked me yesterday if he could take a bath."

"Will, I think you're making a mountain out of a molehill. Nothing nefarious seems to have taken place. Surely Jack and his pal couldn't have forced Samuels to take his own life? What reason could they have had? Besides, Jack tried to save him."

"I don't know. The only connection among them that I can see is Fiona Williams."

"How so?"

"She and Jack went to the same school. Her brother and he were chums."

"That doesn't seem significant to me."

"Probably not. It's just that . . ." He paused.

"Just that what?"

"Jack doesn't seem himself at all. He won't talk about what's bothering him and he's avoiding me. It is so odd that he wouldn't mention he's been awarded a medal. Won't even explain how he was wounded."

Madge's words echoed Fenwell's. "Give him time. He's only just got home."

Murdoch drew in a deep breath. "All right, let's go inside. Oh, and thanks for listening, Madge."

"Any time."

CHAPTER TWENTY-ONE

NUMBER 10A HAGERMAN STREET TURNED OUT TO BE AT the rear of the row of houses. They entered a small, desolate courtyard by way of a narrow laneway. The stench from the decrepit privy in the corner was pungent. Five houses backed onto the courtyard and Murdoch assumed that, as was typical of these slums, all the families had to share it.

"I'm wondering if we've got the right person," said Murdoch. "That handwriting was exquisitely neat. I'd say Samuels had been trained as a clerk. Why would he be living here?"

Stepping carefully around something foul on the ground they approached number 10A. Murdoch knocked.

The door was opened almost immediately by a woman

wrapped in an overcoat and a shawl that rendered her almost shapeless. A checkered head scarf was tied tightly underneath her chin. At first Murdoch thought he was looking at a woman close in age to the elderly Mrs. Freedman, but then he noticed that the hair that showed around her scarf was dark brown with no grey. It wasn't years alone that had etched the lines on her face.

She had started to smile, but her expression changed when she saw Murdoch and Madge.

"Sorry. I thought you customer. What can I do, sir, madam?"

She had a thick Yiddish accent. Her eyes were wary.

"Am I speaking to Mrs. Samuels?" Murdoch asked with a tip of his hat.

"Yes. That is me."

"I am Detective Murdoch and this is Constable Curnoe. May we come in, Mrs. Samuels? I have come about your son."

"Daniel? Why?"

"I'd rather speak inside if you don't mind, madam. Is Mr. Samuels at home? It is better if I talk to you both."

"My husband, he working."

A door across the courtyard banged open and a woman, also wrapped in a shawl, hurried to the privy. Mrs. Samuels shrank back in the doorway and the two women did not exchange greetings.

"Come in, quick," she said to Murdoch, and he and Madge stepped into the house.

When he thought about it later, he decided angrily that it

didn't deserve the title of house. It was one room with a low ceiling and bare plank floorboards. A bed took up a lot of the space. There was a cot at the foot, which Murdoch assumed was Daniel's. Two worn chairs were drawn up in front of a minuscule fireplace. The room was spartan indeed, but he could see how neat it was and how there had been attempts to make it homey—a multicoloured quilt on the bed, crocheted cushions on the chairs. There was a menorah and a single framed photograph on the mantelpiece.

The moribund fire was giving off the merest suggestion of heat. A man, also well wrapped, was sitting as close to it as he could get, surrounded by a collection of pots and pans in various states of disrepair. He was tapping out dints in a large pot. He didn't look up.

"My husband," said Mrs. Samuels. She spoke to him in their own language. He got to his feet with some difficulty; there was a strangely vacant look to his eyes.

"He not understand English well," said his wife. "He shot by a Cossack when we run from the pogrom. Not same again." She spoke in a cool, matter-of-fact way but Murdoch was jolted. He could only guess at the experiences they had already endured, and now he had to heap the greatest of sorrows on their backs. He had no doubt the boy who had drowned himself was their son. The photograph on the mantel was a younger version but clearly Daniel. And he resembled his father.

There was a trickle of mucous running from Mr. Samuels's nose, but he seemed oblivious to it. His wife stepped forward and wiped it away with a corner of her shawl as tenderly as if he were a child.

Somehow it was that gesture in particular that made Murdoch's heart sink. He straightened his shoulders. There was nothing for it but to tell them what had happened.

They didn't stay long at the Samuels'. There wasn't very much to say. Other than declaring Daniel to have been a high-strung boy, his mother could offer no insight into his suicide. She didn't know anybody by the name of Fiona Williams and didn't know why her son would be sending her a book. Murdoch showed her the strange little inscription at the back. That she was able to shed some light on. Daniel had saved his money and taken a special course at a secretarial college on Yonge Street. He had become very good at shorthand and typing, she said with pride. He showed her his work all the time. At Murdoch's request, she gave him the school's address.

Rather reluctantly, Murdoch showed her the white feather. She looked very upset seeing it. He wanted to go to war, she said, but he was exempt because of their circumstances. She was not aware somebody had given him a white feather. It was likely this could have bothered him. It seemed clear to Murdoch that no matter how much Mrs. Samuels had cherished her son, she had not been privy to his inner thoughts and feelings.

Murdoch asked permission to inspect Daniel's effects and she directed him to a wooden box by the cot. Not much in there except his exercise books from the college and a notebook, which Murdoch received permission to borrow. He agreed to contact Mrs. Samuels after the post mortem, which he promised to hurry through so that she would be able to bury her son as soon as possible.

When they returned to the motor car, Madge pulled out a handkerchief and wiped at her eyes. "Sorry, Will."

"Don't apologize. We've had to deal with two major losses in a short space of time."

"What are you going to do now?"

"I think I'll drop in on the secretarial school Mrs. Samuels mentioned. I'd still like to know what that inscription means. It's possible it might give us an insight into why Daniel succumbed to despair."

"Why don't you go ahead. I'll walk back. Give me time to think."

"About anything in particular?"

"Just the usual minor concerns. You know, death, life, love, loss. That sort of thing."

"If you reach any conclusions, let me know."

"I certainly will."

"All right. I'll see you later. Maybe the meeting with Mrs. Payne will be less tragic."

"Why do I have an uneasy feeling that isn't going to be the case?"

CHAPTER TWENTY-TWO

HE PROCEEDED ON HIS OWN TO THE COLLEGE, WHICH was in the Yonge Street Arcade just north of Queen Street. When it was first built, more than twenty years earlier, the Arcade had been considered an architectural gem to make Torontonians proud. The years had nibbled away at the facade but it was still impressive. The two-storey, ornate, arched entrance would have done justice to a church. The interior gallery, where the shops and offices were located, was covered by a glass roof, which let in light and gave protection against inclement weather. Today there were many shoppers strolling about, happy to avoid the intermittent cold rain. The electric lights that hung from the ceiling brought warmth and cheer. A balustrade ran around the circumference of the second floor and there were more shops up there, but fewer people going in and out. These shops had much smaller frontage and were less desirable.

The secretarial college was on the third floor, its entrance sandwiched between two second-storey shops. On one side was Lynette's Confectionery, on the other Wilson's Cigarette and Sheet Music.

Union Jacks were hung around the window of the confectioner's and a couple of open wicker baskets stood just inside the doorway with a sign: "Our boys will appreciate these for Christmas. We will donate five cents to the Red Cross for every dollar spent." The baskets were brimming with oranges and packets of biscuits. A box of chocolates sported a large red-white-and-blue ribbon. Murdoch paused. He decided that, on his way out, he'd buy some sweets for Jack. He liked toffees.

Not to be outdone on the patriotic front, Wilson's advertised discounts for all those in uniform or who had somebody serving overseas. Hmm. Maybe he should get more cigarettes?

He turned his attention back to the matter at hand. On the door that led upstairs was a neatly printed sign: "MISS WILDIN'S SECRETARIAL COLLEGE FOR YOUNG LADIES AND GENTLEMEN." Below that, in smaller letters: "REASONABLE RATES." An arrow pointed upward. "COME STRAIGHT UP."

Murdoch pushed open the door, heard a bell tinkle from on the upper level, and climbed a rather steep flight of uncarpeted stairs to the third floor. There were several doors leading off the landing but the only one with a sign identifying it was for the college. This time he was instructed to "PLEASE KNOCK," so he did.

"Come in," called a woman.

He did that, too.

He entered a spacious room with deep windows along one wall. It was no doubt usually bright and airy but today the grey skies permeated everything, sucking any sunlight away. There were about a dozen desks lined up in neat rows facing the blackboard at the far end, each bearing a typewriter. Just inside the doorway was a larger desk. A shaded lamp cast a greenish light across the face of the woman who was seated there. She was of indeterminate age, thin and angular. Her hair, streaked with grey, was pulled back into a tight bun that would have been severe except for the frizz of curls at her forehead. Everything about her said "professional." And efficient. In a totally different way from Bessie Schumacher, she too was somewhat intimidating. Her black silk blouse was unadorned except for a silver chain from which dangled what appeared to be a small propelling pencil, also silver. Murdoch almost expected her to bring out a notebook and begin taking dictation the second he started to speak.

"May I help you?" she inquired. Her voice was pleasant.

"I'm Detective William Murdoch, madam. Do I have the honour of speaking to Miss Wildin?"

Even to his own ears he sounded old-fashioned and

stilted, but the classroom and the woman had that effect.

"I am she," she replied. She raised her neatly trimmed eyebrows. "Are you here in a professional capacity or are you interested in our courses?"

"I am afraid I am conducting an investigation into the death of a young man. He was enrolled as a night student at this college."

"Oh dear. Who was it?"

"His name is Daniel Samuels."

Miss Wildin's hand flew to her firm bosom. "Mr. Samuels. How dreadful. He was here to see me only two days ago. What happened?"

"I regret to say he took his own life."

She turned and gazed out the window for a moment. "I am most sorry to hear that. He was one of my best pupils. I awarded him a first-class certificate upon graduation, which I don't do very often."

"You say he came to see you recently. Did he seem despondent at all?"

She twisted the pencil in her fingers. "Daniel was a quiet young man. Reserved. I cannot say if he was despondent. He was distressed, however, because he had just lost his position." Her eyes met Murdoch's.

"My students are always in demand. Employers search my graduation lists for good candidates. With such an excellent examination result, Daniel was offered a position right away. Unfortunately, his employment was terminated a few days ago."

"Why was that?"

She reached into her desk and took out a bundle of papers, riffled through them, and pulled one out to show Murdoch. "You may read this. I always request a report from the employer if my student is not satisfactory."

Murdoch unfolded the letter.

WARDELL'S MONUMENTAL WORKS
The Home of Classy Monuments

Dear Miss Wildin,

As requested, I am herewith forwarding my report on <u>Daniel Samuels</u>, who was taken into my employ on October 10 of this year. Mr. Samuels came with excellent credentials but I have been forced to terminate his position as of November 20. His office work was quite satisfactory, but part of his job was to deal with our customers. When they have made their choice of monuments they then proceed to the clerk, who must take down pertinent information. Mr. Samuels's performance in this regard left much to be desired.

In fairness I should say that was not entirely his fault. Many of the bereaved are purchasing monuments for sons, brothers or even husbands who have lost their lives abroad. As we tell them, "Their corporeal remains may be in a foreign land but their souls are here in their homeland and we can attest to their bravery with a splendid marker." However, when questioned why, as a healthy young man, he was not in active service, Mr. Samuels seemed unable to give a satisfactory answer. As I am aware, he was given an exemption on account of the ill health of his father and the need of his mother for support. He would inevitably become agitated when this was raised. I cannot afford to alienate my valued customers and this was rapidly becoming a bone of contention between him and I.

In addition, he is of the Jewish persuasion. My customers are entirely Christian. He would be better to apply for a position with somebody of his own faith within his own community.

I am your most obedient servant,
C.W. Wardell, Mgr.

Murdoch returned the letter to Miss Wildin.

"I only wish Mr. Wardell had thought about these matters before he accepted Daniel." She touched her eyes with a lace handkerchief as if to wipe away a tear. There was none visible, but Murdoch thought her distress was genuine nonetheless. "Daniel did confess to me that he had not yet informed his mother about this turn of events. For the last two days he was simply leaving the house as if going to work as usual. He was most anxious about bringing in wages. I assured him he would soon find another place. I would give him a very good testimonial." She put the letter in the desk.

Murdoch removed the red book from his coat.

"This was among his effects. Sir Max Aitken's account of the Canadian Expeditionary Force to date. It appears that Daniel was about to send it to a Miss Fiona Williams. Is that name familiar to you?"

Miss Wildin frowned. "Yes, it is. She too was a student here, at the same time as Mr. Samuels. Unfortunately she and I both soon realized that she is not temperamentally suited for secretarial work. She is a most intelligent young woman but restless in spirit. She reached a certain level of accomplishment but decided that spending her life taking dictation, as she put it, was not for her."

"Was she a friend of Mr. Samuels's?"

"I suppose she was. She tried to bring him out of his shell. She is an attractive young woman and Daniel was quite taken with her."

"There was a white feather in the book. I assume you are aware of the significance?"

"I am."

"Do you think Miss Williams gave it to him?"

"I would very much doubt that. She made no bones about her anti-war sentiments." Miss Wildin's lips tightened. "I myself am not in favour of trying to shame young men into enlisting, but we here in Canada are committed to a war that we must win. We cannot allow evil to triumph."

"Do you think somebody else in the class may have given him the white feather?"

"I think it highly unlikely. The topic of the war did come up once in a while but frankly I discouraged it as being too distracting. I did not witness any particular interaction between the other pupils and Mr. Samuels. They were more likely to take exception to some of Miss Williams's statements. If any discussion ensued it was more likely to be in that quarter."

"There is a note in the back that appears to be written in Pitman's shorthand. I wonder if you could translate it for me."

She fixed a pair of pince-nez on her nose, took the book, and turned to the back page. There was no hesitation in her response.

"It says, '*Tried to enlist but*' . . . the next symbol is not clear but I believe he meant to say '*two objected. Several of my chums went overseas.*'" She regarded Murdoch over the top of the pince-nez. "The tone of the note is apologetic. Perhaps he wanted to justify himself and the fact that he wasn't in the army. He makes such a point of declaring he did try to enlist. Clearly it was very much on his mind."

Murdoch was of the same opinion. Perhaps the hateful white feather had tipped the balance.

"Will you tell his mother and father that he had been dismissed?" asked Miss Wildin.

"Frankly, I'm not sure. I have no desire to cause them any more grief. Mrs. Samuels was very proud of him. On the other hand, according to Mr. Wardell, a reason for his dismissal was his inability to deal with the criticism levelled against him. More than likely the two who 'objected' to him joining up were his parents. I would hate to have his mother feel responsible for his despair."

"I do not envy you your task, Detective. I am truly sorry about Daniel. He was a gentle soul. May he rest in peace."

Murdoch took his leave. And on his way out, he stopped at

the second floor to buy toffees and cigarettes for Jack. And a box of chocolates for Madge Curnoe.

CHAPTER TWENTY-THREE

Madge took the hat from the clothes cupboard in the tea room and pinned it on firmly with a sparkling hatpin. It was a wide-brimmed, elegant affair that she wore only on these assignments, when she was impersonating a well-to-do woman. The same with the gabardine Ulster, which cost as much as she earned in a week. She still hadn't got used to the smooth feel and smart cut of the coat. Finally, she took out a cardboard box that held the *pièce de résistance*, a silver fox fur muff. She slipped her hands inside. How silky and warm the fur was. All articles were considered police property.

Oops. She'd almost forgotten the wedding ring. Murdoch had offered to put in a requisition to pay for the cost of a ring but she'd refused. She wanted to use her mother's. It was a thin band of white gold, a little modest for the affluent matron she was pretending to be, but she liked wearing it. It made her feel that her mother, who had died when she was a child, was watching over her. She kept it locked in a special box on her desk. She took it out, put it on her finger, and stepped back. Done. *Hello, Mrs. McIvor.*

She checked herself in the mirror on the wall. Her hair was neatly tucked up under the hat. The walk in the cold air had brought colour to her cheeks and a sparkle to her blue eyes. For a moment, her thoughts jumped back to the visit to the Samuels. It never ceased to impress her how kind Murdoch could be to the bereaved. She was also touched that he had confided in her about his son. Madge allowed herself a little smile. Maybe she could invite him to the picture show. She could always say she'd been intending to take her Gran but she wasn't available. She supposed that was being a little forward, but it was all in the name of friendship. Wasn't it?

Louisa Street was a brisk fifteen-minute walk from headquarters. The wind was icy and Madge was grateful for the warm coat and the muff. A hansom cab went past and the driver slowed down to see if she wanted to get in. He scrutinized her as if he were puzzled, and she realized she should indeed have hired a cab given her pretense of affluence. She certainly hadn't noticed any other well-dressed women travelling on foot. However, it was too late now, and she waved him off and proceeded on her way.

Number 82 was one of a ramshackle row built close to the road. The narrow houses seemed to be leaning on each other as if they had barely been caught from toppling over. The Payne house was on the end.

Madge knocked hard on the door. No answer. She was aware that the curtains had twitched in the window of the house at the opposite end of the row. She knocked again, and this time the door was opened a crack. A girl whom she could hardly see was peering around the doorframe. She didn't speak.

Madge smiled. "I've come about the advertisement in the newspaper."

The girl's expression was so blank, Madge wondered if she was in fact a deaf-mute.

"I've come to see the baby," said Madge more loudly.

A woman appeared behind the girl. She smiled, revealing a distressing absence of teeth.

"Good afternoon," said Madge. "I've come about the advertisement. A baby boy is available for adoption?"

The woman eased the girl to one side and opened the door wider.

"Come inside, madam," she said, pleasantly enough. "It's perishing out there."

Madge was only too glad to obey.

The house was warmer than she'd expected and smelled like singed linen. There was no hall, and the front door opened directly into the main room. Madge could see why it smelled the way it did. There were two ironing boards near the wall and an older girl was tending to the irons themselves, heating them on the small coal fire. Two young boys were sitting under a quilt on a bed in one corner. At first Madge thought they might be ill but she noticed there were two pairs of trousers hung on a line in front of the fire. The boys most likely had only one pair each and were waiting until they dried. None of the children said a word.

The woman moved a cane chair forward. "Have a seat, Mrs. . . . ?"

"McIvor. Elinor McIvor," said Madge. "And you must be Mrs. Payne?"

"That's right." She lapsed into silence. The girl continued with her ironing, her back to Madge.

"My husband and I have not been blessed with children, and when I saw the advertisement, my heart leaped. Perhaps this is what we've been waiting for."

Madge wasn't too happy about saying such outright lies but she hoped the ends would justify the means.

"May I see the child?"

"Of course."

As if on cue there was a thin wail from a wooden apple box next to the fire.

"Winnie, deal with the baby," the woman said sharply to the girl at the ironing board. A sullen expression on her face, the girl put down the iron and went over to the makeshift cradle. The infant was crying in earnest now. Winnie picked him up and rocked him back and forth. Madge thought she was rough.

"Let Mrs. McIvor hold him," ordered her mother.

It was only when she came closer that Madge got a good look at the girl, whom she had thought to be about twelve years old. Her arms and bare legs were emaciated but, whatever age she actually was, it was obvious she had the full breasts of a woman who had given birth. The baby was nuzzling at her.

"He seems to be hungry," said Madge.

"He's all right," said Mrs. Payne. "Boys are always more demanding. Why don't you hold him?"

The child was bellowing his lungs out, his little face scarlet with pain and need. Madge held her hands firmly in her lap.

"And how old is he?"

"Just three months."

"Mrs. Payne, it is as plain as a pikestaff that Winnie here is the baby's mother. Please allow her to feed him before we go any further."

Mrs. Payne looked as if she were going to protest but then simply nodded at Winnie, who went to a stool in the corner. She turned her back and fiddled with her blouse. The baby stopped crying and Madge could hear suckling noises. Winnie didn't speak.

"Perhaps you could explain what happened, Mrs. Payne."

"Like I stated in the advertisement, the babe is healthy as a horse. You can see what an appetite he has. I already have too many mouths to feed. I thought he would have a better chance at life if he was adopted by a good family."

"That's all very well," said Madge, making her tone hard,

"but it is your daughter who has given birth. She is very young and I assume she is not married."

Mrs. Payne scowled. "She was taken advantage of."

"By whom?"

"Winnie, tell the lady what you told me."

The girl didn't move but addressed the wall in front of her.

"He's a soldier. He said he'd take care of me if anything happened but I ain't seen him since. He's gone overseas most like."

"Do you know his regiment? We can follow it up."

"No, I don't, missus."

Winnie lifted the infant to her shoulder and patted his back.

"Do you at least know his name?" asked Madge.

Winnie shrugged. "He said it was John."

She got up and returned the now drowsy baby to his cradle.

"John what? What is his surname?"

"He said he wasn't allowed to tell me because of the war."

An expression of exasperation crossed Mrs. Payne's face.

"I raised my Winnie to be a good girl. She's too trusting. She didn't know what was happening. He took advantage of her."

"How old is she?"

"She just turned sixteen."

"Seduction of an underage girl is a criminal offence, Mrs. Payne. You can have the man prosecuted."

The woman slumped a little in her chair. "If we could find him. There's dozens of soldiers doing things they shouldn't. Who knows where this one is. Damage is done now. We have to deal with it best we can."

Madge glanced around the room. The dirt, the untidiness were quite different from the Samuels' house, where Mrs. Samuels had made such an effort to create a home. The walls here were bare of any kind of decoration, the plaster cracked and peeling. Damp patches stained the corners. The small, silent girl who had opened the door had joined her brothers in the bed and the three of them watched the proceedings.

Madge smiled at them and got a tiny response from the younger boy.

She did a quick calculation in her head. If the baby was indeed three months, Winnie had conceived sometime late last year. And where the heck had she had connections? Not in this room, surely.

"Where did you meet the baby's father, Winnie?" Madge asked.

The girl had returned to the ironing board and now began to stretch out a man's shirt. She didn't answer.

"Winnie," said her mother sharply. "Mrs. McIvor asked you a question."

"I, er, well it was down in the Beaches. Ma had given me the day off and I went for some fresh air by the lake. I was strolling on the boardwalk when he went past. He stopped to say hello and what a nice day it was and all. We got chatting. He asked if he could walk further with me and I agreed."

Mrs. Payne interrupted. "See? I told you she is too trusting."

"Was he in his uniform?" asked Madge.

Winnie nodded.

"By himself or with some pals?"

"By himself."

"Where did you go then?"

"Nowhere, we just walked up and down."

"And it was after this encounter that you had connections and he promised to look after you?"

The girl slapped the hot iron hard on the shirt. "That's right."

"And where was that, Winnie? Where did you have connections with this man?"

"I don't see the need to know that," interrupted Mrs. Payne again. "What does it matter?"

"It might help us to track down this person," answered Madge. "I mean, for instance, did he take her to a hotel? His home? Or did they just lie on the grass and do it in public?"

"Really, madam," spluttered Mrs. Payne. "Watch what you say. There are children here."

"And if I or anybody else is going to proceed with this adoption, we will need to know much more about this supposed father. I would want his medical history, for instance. And a statement of character from his commanding officer. Likewise for your daughter. We can't risk any inherited taint."

"You have no need to fear that from my Winnie, madam. As for the father, I'm sure he's also a decent lad. Just got carried away. Isn't that right, Winnie?"

"You didn't answer my question," Madge said to the girl. "Where did you have connections with this young man?"

"We went to a hotel."

"Where?"

"I don't remember exactly. It was dark. It was on Queen Street."

"The same day when you first met?"

Winnie nodded.

"How on earth did you convince them you were man and wife?" Madge asked.

"Er, we didn't. John had a room there, and he went in first and I followed a few minutes later."

"How long did you stay at this hotel?"

"Only a couple of hours. I had to get back home."

Madge addressed Mrs. Payne. "Did you suspect what your daughter had been up to?"

"No, I did not. It was only when she missed her monthly flow that she told me."

"And you made no attempt to find the soldier who had seduced her?"

"You heard her. He was going overseas."

"Winnie, did you meet this John person more than once?"

"Three more times."

"Always at the hotel?"

"Yes. Then he said he was leaving but he'd write to me, and when he came back we could walk out together."

"Has he written?"

"No." She rubbed at her eyes but Madge hadn't seen evidence of tears. She was beginning to think she was dealing with a consummate actress. Two consummate actresses, for that matter.

"Winnie, did this soldier give you any gifts?"

Madge didn't miss the glance that shot between mother and daughter.

"What do you mean, gifts?"

"Jewellery, for instance? A bracelet, perhaps? A necklace?"

"No. Nothing like that. He said he'd bring me back something from France."

"How kind," said Madge, not bothering to hide the sarcasm. She had a feeling Winnie's story was much more sordid than the innocent first love she had presented.

Madge started to gather together her bag and gloves. "I'm sure you can understand, Mrs. Payne, that if we are to continue with any arrangements about adoption I will need to gather a lot more information. I will need a certificate from a physician attesting to the baby's health."

Mrs. Payne scowled. "That costs money. And money is not what I have. My husband died two years ago leaving me with these four to bring up on my own."

"Surely you can get relief from the city?"

"Ha. It's not nearly enough to keep us fed and clothed. If I didn't work my fingers to the bone, I'd be in the poorhouse and this lot in an orphanage."

Madge glanced over at the three children in the bed. Their thin faces were impassive. This was clearly a refrain they'd heard before.

"You say you don't have children, Mrs. McIvor," continued Mrs. Payne. "Perhaps that's why you don't understand how much it costs to raise them. We owe money all over the place, but it was borrow or starve." She lowered her eyes. "I was hoping that anybody who took this lovely little baby for their own would help us out."

Now they were getting to the nub of the issue.

"How much would you need to pay your debts?"

"About seventy dollars."

"That's a lot."

"But look what you're getting." Suddenly she raised her voice. "Winnie. Bring him over. Let the lady hold him."

Winnie put down the iron and went to the box again. She picked up the baby and brought him to Madge, who had no choice but to take him. How light his little body was in her arms. He woke up as he was taken from his box and he scrunched his eyes and flailed his fists in the air. He had soft, dark hair, his cheeks were plump, and for a moment his dark blue eyes seemed to stare into hers. Madge began to rock him back and forth almost in spite of herself, making clucking noises as Winnie had done.

"See, he feels right at home with you," said Mrs. Payne. "He's settled right down."

"Does he have a name?" Madge asked.

"We just call him Baby. We thought his new mother would like to name him."

Madge addressed Winnie, who was still standing in front of her. Milk stained the front of her cotton frock. "He's very bonny," she said.

"Are you taking him now?" the girl asked.

"No. There are a lot of details to be taken care of."

Madge felt as if, given half a chance, she would turn on her heel, Baby in her arms, and run from this miserable hovel. But she couldn't raise a child on her own, an unmarried woman, no husband in sight. Could she?

She got to her feet and held out the baby, who was now squirming in earnest.

"I must get going."

Winnie took the child, who immediately shifted his head in the direction of her breast.

"When will you come back?" Mrs. Payne asked. "You can't wait too long. There have already been other people interested in him."

"I'll return in one or two days," Madge answered.

"Do you have a calling card?"

Madge pretended to look in her handbag. "My goodness. I'm sorry. I rushed out without them."

Not giving the woman a chance to continue, Madge swept off to the door. She couldn't resist touching a finger to the baby's soft cheek as she passed.

"He really is very bonny."

As she closed the door behind herself, she heard the infant wail. Nobody seemed to be comforting him.

She hurried away, nodding briefly as she passed an older woman with a cane who had just left her own small house.

CHAPTER TWENTY-FOUR

ALL THREE OF THE POLICE CHIEFS HAD THEIR DOORS closed. Murdoch would have to fill them in on the deaths soon, but he knew they were all tied up organizing the arrival of an important dignitary who was to address people at the Masonic Hall later this week. Pump up recruitment and so on. His identity had not yet been revealed, but everybody wanted the event to throw credit on the city. Rumour had it that it was Theodore Roosevelt, the former president of the United States. Murdoch did know that the private order was to "move along" any protesters: that meant arrest them and throw them in jail, out of sight, at least until the event was over. He wondered whether Fiona Williams and her friends were planning to stage a protest at the event. He liked the girl and didn't want her to come to harm.

He picked up the notebook that he'd taken from Daniel's box. A date was written neatly at the top of each page, and below that, a series of notations. The most recent page said "WEDNESDAY NOVEMBER 21." He must have written it before he went to the City Baths.

"*In 22 throws: Cr. 5x; Anchor 7x; Heart 2x; Diamond 1x; Club 3x; Spade 4x. Won 75 c.*"

It looked as if the boy had been gambling. He was noting plays in the game of Crown and Anchor, keeping track of what came up and what didn't.

Murdoch turned back to the first set of notations: "OCTOBER 31." Daniel had also written down an address, 48 Chestnut Street. Well, well. It seemed as if he had been a regular visitor to Mrs. Schumacher's tea-and-chat establishment. And whist was not the game he'd played. Murdoch wondered if that was where he'd been given the white feather. By Arthur Aggett, perhaps? If so, had he been provoked to retaliate? How far can a lad described as shy and quiet be pushed before he commits an act of violence? And having committed such an act, had remorse caused him to take his own life? And where did Jack, almost hero of the hour, come into the picture? The most likely person to be carrying foreign money was a man who had been overseas. Such as Jack.

"Will, have you got a minute?" Peter Fenwell was standing in the doorway.

"Of course. Come in. Have a seat."

Murdoch cleared a chair where he'd piled the latest newspapers. He had a tendency to use any available surface as a storage area. Probably a holdover from his days at number four station, where all he'd had was the alcove.

"Let me just do one thing," he said to Fenwell, and he picked up the telephone that connected him with the reception desk.

"Wallace, I want you to ring Elias Rogers. Order two sacks of coal to be delivered to 10A Hagerman Street, a Mrs. Samuels. Have them bill me."

He hung up.

"You know that's just a drop in the bucket," said Fenwell. "Are you personally going to feed and warm all of the paupers in the city?"

Murdoch shrugged. "This family has been dealt a particularly hard blow. Why add a cold winter to their misery?" Murdoch couldn't get rid of the image of that single freezing room and the two people swaddled into almost unrecognizable shapes.

The clock chimed the quarter hour.

"Good gracious, the office meeting is in fifteen minutes. Did you want to talk to me about something before it starts?"

"Yes, I did. I'm afraid it's rather delicate."

"In that case, I'd better have a smoke." Murdoch fished out his pipe from his desk and, taking a twist of tobacco, he filled the bowl. A couple of draws got him going.

"I think one of our detectives has stepped out of bounds," said Fenwell. "He's buying illegal liquor."

"Damn. Who is it?"

"I don't know yet. But you know that nab we did last week on Parliament Street? Used to be the John O'Neill Tavern?"

Murdoch nodded. "I know it well. They were supposed to be closed down. I must say, I feel sorry for the tavern owners. How are they going to make a living now? But we didn't find anything on that raid."

"More than likely they were tipped off we were coming. Clean as a whistle when we got there. Just a group of sober men drinking tea and playing whist."

"That seems to have become the game of choice across the city," said Murdoch.

"We couldn't really lay any charges that would stick. There was a man working there, said he was a janitor. He came in to the station yesterday. Turns out he'd been caught a couple of weeks ago dispensing extract of ginger. About to make 80-per-cent-proof ginger beer I suppose. Said if I reduced his fine, he'd give me valuable information concerning one of our officers."

Fenwell paused.

"And?" said Murdoch.

"I wasn't about to get into that kind of bargaining. I said it was his duty to tell me if one of our men was doing something illegal. He gave me what I'd call a nasty look and clammed up. I couldn't get anything else out of him."

"Do you believe it's true, what he said?"

"I doubt he would have brought it up if it wasn't. I'm afraid it's pointing at Roy Rubridge."

"Right."

"You're not surprised?"

"No. Poor blighter. I think he might have come back to work too soon."

"I mean the fact that he's had something to drink isn't against the law. As you know, a doctor can prescribe alcohol if he thinks it necessary for a person's health."

Murdoch grimaced. "The number of people who suddenly need a bottle of whisky for their lumbago has increased dramatically."

Murdoch's telephone rang. It was Wallace.

"Everybody's in the duty room, sir. And Dr. Vaux is on the line, sir. He says he has some preliminary post-mortem results on Arthur Aggett and Daniel Samuels. Do you want to take the call now or later?"

"Now. Have him hold on."

Murdoch covered the mouthpiece of the telephone. "Peter, would you mind telling everybody I'll be there in a few minutes? I'd like to talk to Dr. Vaux before we start. And we'll talk more about that other matter. I want to proceed carefully."

Fenwell left.

"Put me through please, Wallace."

CHAPTER TWENTY-FIVE

DR. RAYMOND VAUX WAS THE SON OF A PHYSICIAN Murdoch had worked with many years ago. He was very meticulous about his work and cautious about what he said to the living. Murdoch liked both qualities.

The doctor's deep, rumbly voice came on the line. "I've done preliminary post mortems on both young men. I'll run some further tests, blood analysis, stomach contents, and so on, but I don't expect to find anything unusual, and I thought you'd like to know sooner rather than later what I've determined."

"I appreciate that."

"I'll start with the suicide case first, then. There is no doubt that the cause of death was drowning. His lungs were filled with water. He was basically a healthy young fellow, a bit on the thin side but not undernourished. His teeth were good. Any idea why he chose to kill himself, Murdoch?"

"Nothing definitive, I'm still investigating."

"All right, then. The homicide. Arthur Aggett. The cause of death was multiple blows to the cranium. I would say he was struck at least four or five times with great force. I would say the weapon was metal. Not sharp but with a smooth, rigid edge."

"Any ideas as to what it might be?"

"I really don't know. I haven't seen anything like it before now. There was a scratch on his face but I don't believe it was recent. There were no abrasions anywhere else on his body, but his fingers were badly bruised. One knuckle was broken. He must have put up his hand to defend himself. There was a considerable amount of alcohol in his stomach. Food partially digested indicates a meat dish consumed several hours before he died."

"Would the assailant have blood on his person?"

"Not necessarily. There were no arteries severed. He might have some on his hands, depending on how close he was to the victim's head. That's about it. Not a lot to go on, I'm afraid."

"Thank you, Doctor."

"Good luck with your investigation, Detective. Terrible waste of life. They both might have been serving their country."

They hung up.

Murdoch clicked the receiver to reconnect with the clerk on the desk.

"Wallace. Do me a favour, will you? Ring my home, see if you can get hold of my son. If he does answer, tell him I'd like to talk to him. Come and get me. I'll be in the meeting."

Murdoch picked up his notes and went to join the other detectives.

There were eighteen detectives stationed at headquarters, including Murdoch. Their average age must have been about a half century; all detectives were expected to have first served at least six years on the beat and two as acting detective at one of the other stations. Murdoch had been promoted to the rank of senior detective a year ago, and as far as he was concerned, the challenge of melding such a disparate group of personalities into a cohesive and efficient team never ended. On the one hand, there was the earnest, dogged Baldy Watson. He'd acquired his nickname for obvious reasons, but the smooth pate gave him a professorial air that had proved on many an occasion to be completely misleading. At the other end of the spectrum was the newest member of the team, Herb Maurer. He was originally Swiss and had a command of four languages. Not only was he the youngest in the department, he was the most keenly ambitious. He and his partner, Stephen Hess, were in charge of the alien section. Lately they had been very busy dealing with war tribunals and cases of disenfranchisement. Mistrust and suspicion flew from neighbour to neighbour with not a lot to contain it.

The duty room was already thick with tobacco smoke, and

the detectives were enjoying a joke when Murdoch entered. Timothy Lennox was reading from the *Toronto Daily Star*. He was relatively new to the department and had already set himself up as the wit of the group.

"Listen to this, chaps. It's choice. 'Canon Dixon (major) roundly denied the appeal of J.F. Rutherford who said he suffered from flat feet and wasn't fit to fight. "I'd say he suffers from cold feet not flat feet. Appeal denied."' Lordy, the reasons some of these slackers come up with to get an exemption are completely ridiculous."

Lennox was strongly pro-war and both his sons had enlisted early on. So far they were safe. He read excerpts from their many letters home at every opportunity. He also smoked like a chimney and was currently adding to the fug with an appallingly smelly pipe.

The men fell silent as Murdoch took his place at the table near the front of the room. There was a chalkboard behind him, which he'd brought in from the nearby school. He knew that the others made fun of his schoolmaster-ish tools, but Murdoch found it useful to use the board when he needed to illustrate something.

"All right, gentlemen. Can I have your undivided attention? You're all probably getting hungry so we'll make this meeting short." He turned to Peter Fenwell. "Peter, would you be so good as to write down the agenda for today?"

Fenwell went over to the board.

"The major item is the murder of Arthur Aggett," continued

Murdoch. "For those of you who don't know, the body of this young man was discovered in a laneway off Chestnut Street early this morning. The time of discovery was eight o'clock but he died some hours earlier. The body was found by the constable on the beat, Constable Mogg. The coroner has been most prompt and he has already telephoned to give me his preliminary report."

All of the men were paying attention, except for Jim Archibald, who seemed to have gone into some kind of fugue state.

"Jim. Are you with me?" Murdoch called to him.

"Sorry. I'm a bit under the weather. Hot and shivery all at the same time."

"You're probably coming down with the flu," interjected his partner. Donald Rawlings was a lanky, sallow-faced man who was perpetually worried about contagion. Their specialty was lodging houses and pool rooms, and Murdoch knew that Rawlings's wife nagged him to move to a different section. After a house inspection, Rawlings had already carried home bedbugs.

"Take care, Jim," continued Murdoch. "Book off if you need to. All right, back to the post-mortem report."

He relayed what Dr. Vaux had told him.

"The amount of alcohol in his system possibly explains why he doesn't appear to have defended himself except by putting his hand to his head. The laneway is dark. He was relieving himself against the wall, so his assailant would have been able to come up from behind and take him by surprise. If he was already stupefied, he was probably not too alert."

"I wonder what the killer hit him with," said Watson. "I gather no weapon has yet been found."

Murdoch shook his head. "We've conducted a search in the vicinity but we've found nothing to date. Dr. Vaux didn't have an opinion other than that the point of contact was metal with a smooth edge. Assuming the murderer carried the weapon away with him, I realize we're probably looking for a needle in a haystack. It could be anywhere, including in the lake, but we'd better have another search around the vicinity with that in mind."

Murdoch looked over at the men. No detective wore a uniform but they were expected to present a respectable image to the public. All of them were wearing sober suits, quiet ties. Not for the first time, he thought the uniformity of their apparel actually made them distinctive. You could always tell when it was a detective at your door.

He continued. "It's already getting dark. We won't be able to resume the search until daylight. Peter, anything you can tell us from the canvassing?"

"I'm afraid not. Nobody saw the young man. Nobody heard anything untoward. The only disturbance reported was the one at Mrs. Schumacher's, which we have already investigated."

"Do you think that's where he was?" asked Archibald. "She's been on my list for a while now. Probably running a blind pig."

"It's likely. Her house isn't too far from where he was found. And it's minutes from where he lived. He wasn't wearing an overcoat or a hat although it was a cold night. As far as his mother knew he had only stepped out to use the privy in the courtyard."

A couple of the men exchanged grins. They knew the situation. Probably grown up with similar facilities.

"Probably he didn't put on his hat and coat because he didn't want to let on where he was going to his mother," said Murdoch. "There were other men at Mrs. Schumacher's but at the moment we don't know who they were. Some, at least, were there until the early hours of the morning, so let's operate on the premise that they had jobs that didn't require them to be up early and alert. They might have come off a late shift. These days a lot of necessary work is running around the clock. They had some money, or thought they did. But don't get blinkers on. Could be anybody." He turned to Archibald. "It's your area. If you hear the slightest whisper about Mrs. Schumacher, let me know."

Archibald nodded.

"All right then," Murdoch continued. "Let's move on. Call out your items to Peter. We'll deal with them, then you can all go and get some supper."

Fenwell began to write on the blackboard as instructed.

"Two youths, one white, one coloured, have escaped from Mimico Industrial School. They appear to have stolen two bikes."

"A resident on King Street arrested for being drunk and disorderly has been sent to hospital from the effects of tincture of ginger. Dangerously ill. We need to follow up on the source of the ginger."

"A motor car collided with a horse and wagon at the corner of Parliament Street and Wilton. An investigation is underway."

And so on.

CHAPTER TWENTY-SIX

"Fiona, supper's on the table in ten minutes," Molly Williams called up to her daughter.

"Thanks, mam. I'll be right there."

Fiona turned to the dummy sitting on her lap. "Are you ready for your debut, Miss Happ?"

She pulled the lever that was fixed to a shaft inside the dummy's back and moved the head in her direction. Another lever on the same shaft moved the jaw up and down.

"Quite ready, Miss Williams."

Fiona had been practising her dummy voice but she wasn't satisfied. There was nothing distinctive about it. What would make people laugh? French Canadian? "*May wee. I am quite reddee.*" No, that wouldn't work. French Canadians weren't popular in the rest of the country. She wanted her audience to chuckle at Miss Happ's wit, not dislike her. She'd learned that from her teacher, Mr. Kelehan.

"Your dummy has to have a distinct personality. You're just the foil. You can be on the cheeky side but not crude. Never be vulgar. Audiences don't like to see women being crude. And don't be too satiric, Miss Williams. Make fun of the objects that most people like to see ridiculed. Soft humour is always best."

Fiona looked at herself in the dresser mirror. Keeping her lips slightly parted as if she were smiling she projected her voice.

"Quite ready, Miss Williams."

Darn, that wasn't any good. She'd moved her lips too much, it was obvious. She tried again. Smile. That was better with the movements. Turn your head slightly downward to disguise what you are doing.

She twisted the dummy's head and moved the jaw open and closed.

"How do I look? This hat is one of Mr. Eaton's specials. I bought it two years ago and every year I add to it myself."

Fiona dropped the head to one side. She wanted to find a way to knock the ridiculous hat sideways but she hadn't figured out how to do it yet.

Her mother's voice sounded again from the kitchen.

"Lassie, get ye down *now*."

Fiona's parents had emigrated from Edinburgh at the turn of the century. When her father had died in a streetcar accident two years later, her mother, Molly, had been able to squeeze a good settlement from the Toronto Street Railway and she remained in Toronto to raise her two young children. However, her ties to the Auld Sod remained as strong as her brogue.

Fiona stared at her own image again. Harry Lauder had made an entire career out of being Scottish, and he was one of the most famous vaudevillians in the world. Maybe Miss Happ should have a Scottish accent, like her mother did.

"And what do you do for a living, Miss Happ?" she said, looking down at the dummy.

"I write a column for the newspaper."

"How splendid. What is it called?"

Keep your eyes on the dummy. The audience will look where you are looking.

She turned Miss Happ's head so she seemed to be gazing upward.

"I call it 'Don't Worry.'"

"That's an intriguing title. Do you get many people asking for advice?"

"Many, many letters. Ye'd think the whole world was worried."

Hmm. That was better. Quite funny if she exaggerated the rolling of the *r*: *wurrried*.

Fiona stood up and laid the dummy on the bed. It was about the size of a four-year-old, and she had made it herself. The head was papier mâché, which she'd painted. The large eyes were glass and she'd bought them from a man on Yonge Street who was making artificial eyes for blinded soldiers. They had cost a small fortune but they were worth it. She had also purchased a grey wig, which had almost wiped out her savings. But she was proud of the look of the doll. After much thought, she had decided to dress Miss Happ as a rather frumpy matron with delusions of youth and beauty. Rouged cheeks and lips, false eyelashes. The body was made from old sacking stuffed with horsehair, and she'd sewn the clothes herself—an ugly brown walking suit, and a felt hat with a wide brim that was loaded down with false fruit and feathers.

"Fiona. Last call. If ye don't come now I'm going to give your supper to the cat."

Fiona wished she had more time to practise her act.

"I thought you were against the war," her mother had said when she'd heard about the engagement.

"I most definitely am, but that doesn't mean I don't pity the soldier's lot. Look at the letters Duncan has been sending. He said the comfort boxes make the unbearable bearable."

"Well, it's your funeral, Fee. Let's hope they don't pelt ye with rotten eggs."

"They'll be too well bred for that, mam. The worst they can do is boo me. And you never know, they might even laugh."

At the door she called, "Five minutes, mam. I've just got to do one more thing."

She returned to the bed and picked up the dummy.

"Miss Happ. I need your advice."

"Of course, lassie. That's what I'm here for. It's my specialty, advising people."

"What I would like to know is . . . how long can somebody hold a torch for somebody else?"

Fiona moved Miss Happ's mouth and rolled her eyes.

"Ah. That is not an easy question to answer, lassie. Look at Orpheus. He loved his wife for his entire life. Risked everything. And then there's Othello, I suppose. And Leontes. And don't forget Ophelia."

Fiona held her hand around the puppet's mouth. "Stop. Don't show off."

Miss Happ shook her head. "No need to get rough. You are speaking of yourself, I presume?"

"Of course I am."

"And we both know what you are referring to."

Fiona giggled. "Well, if I know, you must know also." She gave the puppet a shake. "Come on. Answer my question. What if a girl hasn't seen this man since they were children? What if her original feelings were those of a little child?"

She forgot to move the dummy's mouth, and Miss Happ sat slumped forward.

"And then," continued Fiona, "and then she sees this same person again and she feels just the same as she ever did. She thinks he is the handsomest, most charming fellow she has ever met. But it's clear he has suffered. And he still suffers."

She jerked the dummy up. "What is your answer, Miss Happ?"

"Give me the question again?"

"I want to know how long I will feel this way."

"For the rest of your life, I would say, lassie. A man who is both handsome and nobly suffering is irresistible to a woman."

Fiona rolled Miss Happ's eyes. "I can't believe I said that."

She threw the dummy to the floor.

CHAPTER TWENTY-SEVEN

BOTH JACK AND PERCY WERE SPRAWLED ON THE couches, each smoking an opium pipe. They had returned to the laundry from the City Baths, and Ghong Lee had poured them each a glass of hot *baijiu*.

"You have look to your faces," he said. "Drink down, then I make you up a pipe. You feel much better."

"Maybe there are some things that we shouldn't feel better about, Mr. Lee," said Jack. But he tossed back the drink and sank down on one of the couches.

Percy was by then already well into his pipe. Several minutes elapsed while the Chinaman and his grandson set up Jack.

When they left the room to go downstairs, Percy said, "No

use being angry with me, Jack. It wasn't my fault."

"Wasn't it? You were the one who got into a row."

"He was a slacker. I could tell."

"You knew nothing about him."

"He didn't deny it either, if you noticed. It's not my fault if he was a yellow-belly."

The silence sat heavy between them. Jack laid the pipe on the table beside him.

"What should we do now?" Percy asked.

"We should go about life as usual."

Percy screwed up his face. "What the hell is that, Jack? Life as usual. It is beyond my comprehension. *Usual* is wading in icy mud up to your knees. *Usual* is being cold and hungry every hour of the day. *Usual* is seeing the bloke in front of you getting his eyes gouged out by a piece of shrapnel. *Usual* is wiping his brains off your face. You were there too. You know what I'm talking about."

Jack glared at him. "I do, but unlike you I'm not wallowing in it."

"I'm not wallowing. I just can't shake it off. The stench is the worst. It's in my nostrils no matter what's around."

His face was so full of misery, Jack relented. He got up, went over to the cabinet, and poured out two more glasses of *baijiu*. He handed one to Percy.

"Here. It'll make you feel better." He held out his own glass in salute. "*Ganbei*. Bottoms up."

They both gulped down the potent drink.

"You don't have to understand, Perce. Just act. We'll take it one day at a time."

"Okay. As long as you won't stop me from playing fan-tan."

"The Chinamen will skin you alive, but if that's what you want to do, go ahead. Just don't overdo it."

Percy raised his empty glass. "Another, please."

Jack obliged but didn't fill his own.

"I think I'll head home now, Perce. I've not spent much time with my old man since we got back."

"Has he said anything about the murdered chap found in the laneway?"

"He's not going to tell me much while he's still investigating."

Percy took a gulp of the *baijiu*. "It probably wasn't me that killed him."

Jack shrugged. "Let's hope not."

"Like you said, I was getting all mixed up."

"You were."

"But if I didn't, then who did?"

"I don't know, Percy," Jack snapped. "Who the hell knows who's prowling the streets these days."

"Maybe it was one of those chaps at the blind pig. Might have been one of them."

"Possibly."

"Are you going to tell your father we were there?"

"Only if it comes up."

"What about us being at the baths when the Jew boy did a diver?"

"Only if it comes up."

Percy put down the glass. "I guess I'll see you tomorrow, then?"

"Sure. I don't have anything planned, except I might go to Mass. At my old church."

"What on earth for? Don't tell me you still believe in that load of horse plop. The *God on our side* rot. *Good boys go to Heaven.*"

"I don't know what I believe any more, so I thought a visit to St. Paul's might be worth making. Clarify some things."

"Ha. Good luck with that."

Percy suddenly reached under the cot and pulled out a piece of newspaper.

"This makes more sense than any Bible." He shook it in Jack's direction. "*The Wipers Times*. Listen to this one."

"Read it to me later. I've got to go."

"No, wait. It's a good one. It's called 'A Poet's Dedication.'" He held out the newspaper and recited.

> O Motive Force, that makes a soldier move
> Great mountains of oppression from his soul;
> Let others sing about the varied goal
> Of Great Ambition, Women, War and Love . . .

Jack shifted.

"Hold on," called Percy. "Listen to the next line."

Such plaudits always leave me cold and dumb,
Only your charms, I praise, o Tot o' Rum.

"Very funny." He stood up. "Don't forget, we're going to Shea's Theatre Friday night."

Percy wagged his finger. "Come on, 'fess up. Are you sweet on her?"

"Who?"

"You know who. Fiona Williams. Are you falling for her?"

"Don't be ridiculous. I've known her since she was seven years old. She's a child."

"May I remind you, children have a way of growing up."

Jack shrugged. "I've seen her once. She seemed like a good sort."

"Do we have to go?"

"It'll be fun. I told her I'd come. She's leaving tickets for us."

"You said it was a fundraiser. There'll be lots of rich women who want to know how we are, whether life in the trenches is as bad as it's made out. They'll practically salivate to know all the gory details." Percy adopted a falsetto voice. "*Young man, how many arms did you lose, would you say?*—Just the two I was born with, ma'am."

"Oh come on, Perce. They won't be like that. Most of them are decent, concerned people."

"You're being soft, Jack. If they don't want gore they want examples of bravery and self-sacrifice and honour. Set their hearts aflutter."

"Give them that, then. They happen as well."

"I'll tell them about you, shall I?"

"No."

"I will. I'll tell them how you dragged me back to the trench across No Man's Land although bullets were dancing all around us." He made zinging noises. "*Buzz! Whish!* Bullets to the right of us. Bullets to the left of us." He made his voice deep and solemn. "My best friend saved my life. He should have got a medal. Oops. Wait a minute. He *did* get a medal."

"I'm thinking of throwing it into the lake."

"Don't be ridiculous. You deserve the Victoria Cross as far as I'm concerned."

"I didn't do anything different from what a hundred other chaps did."

"Yes you did, Jack."

"Besides, I don't think I was in my right mind."

Percy nodded. "Who was? It was us or them."

"Was it? I wish I could be sure of that."

"Well, you have to admit that the other incident was above and beyond. No doubt about that."

Jack got to his feet. "Let's not talk about it, Percy. The poor chump would likely have survived if it weren't for me. I can't accept any glory for that."

"Whatever you say." Percy raised himself on his elbow. "One question before you go, Jack."

"Yes?"

"You don't despise me, do you?"

"Don't be a dope. Of course I don't."

"Just to let you know . . . I wouldn't blame you if you did."

Jack left him, and as the cold outside air hit his face, he realized that, for all his protestations, he hadn't been really truthful. Especially concerning the now grown-up Fiona Williams.

He must have been lying there for almost an hour, waiting for a lull in the barrage so he could take his chance and get back to the trench. The cold was biting; the vile stench of the mud and water in which he was half submerged made his gorge rise. But the worst was the incessant banging of the artillery shells. They shook his skull, threatened to shatter his eardrums. If the devil himself had appeared and offered to stop the noise in return for his immortal soul, he would have made the bargain.

Then, suddenly, through the mist and smoke that was hanging in the air, another soldier half slid, half tumbled over the rim of the shell crater and flopped beside him. He'd lost his helmet, and a deep cut across the tip of his nose had bled into his moustache, turning the once blond hair a bright red. It was almost comical. Worse was his other injury. He'd been hit in his abdomen, and a glistening piece of intestine was protruding through the shredded trousers. He was trying to push back his innards with one hand and hold on to his rifle with the other. When he realized the shell crater was already occupied he tried to lift the rifle but he had no strength left.

"Kamerad . . ."

CHAPTER TWENTY-EIGHT

MADGE CURNOE LIVED WITH HER GRANDMOTHER IN A tiny house on Elm Street. It was old and in need of repair but Madge loved it. She'd scrimped and saved to get the down payment and, six months ago, she'd taken possession.

"Going cheap, just needs some fixing up," the agent had told her. That proved to be an understatement, but Madge was as handy as any man with a hammer and nails, and the house was soon snug and cozy. Just in time for winter.

Although it was almost midnight she was waiting up for her grandmother, who had been called away to tend to a neighbour.

Madge's wages were decent but by no means extravagant, and when she could, her grandmother, Harriet Cooke, supplemented their income by laying out the dead, an occupation she had followed all the years they had lived in the city. These days, Toronto's bereaved were more likely to have their deceased picked up by a funeral home, such as Humphrey's, who took care of arrangements for them. But when there was insufficient money, Mrs. Cooke's skill was in demand. There were still those who preferred to take care of their beloved dead in the traditional way.

Madge had made up the fire and a kettle was at the simmer on the hob, ready for the strong tea her grandmother loved. She leaned back in the rocking chair, her feet propped on the fender. She was starting to drift into sleep when the clock on the mantelpiece dinged out twelve strokes. Midnight already. Madge felt a twinge of fear. She hoped nothing was amiss. Her Gran was a sturdy woman with grit to spare, but she was over seventy. Madge had tentatively brought up the suggestion of retirement, but Gran would have none of it. "What would I do all day long? I'd kick off from sheer boredom. No thank you, I'll keep going until I can't do it any more."

Madge couldn't imagine what life would be like without her Gran. She was really all the family she'd ever known. Her mother was a shadowy figure who'd died when Madge was eight years old. Her Gran hadn't been forthcoming about the cause of death, which she'd called "chest trouble." As for her father, he had walked out one snowy winter's day and never returned, when Madge was a mere babe in arms. Gran wouldn't talk much about him either, except to say he was handsome and a devil both. That left Madge and her Gran, who had been a widow long before Madge was born. They'd coped pretty well in the ensuing years.

Just sometimes, Madge pined for a family of her own. A husband to love and to cherish.

She heard the sound of the front door opening and her Gran's step in the hall. She went out to greet her.

"Madge, you shouldn't have waited up," said Harriet.

"Nonsense. How would I know whether you'd got home safely?"

"I was only a few houses down," answered her grandmother, but Madge could see she too was spent.

"Sit down," said Madge. "Your boots are soaked. Let's get them off you."

"Will you stop fussing and fretting? I'm not an invalid. And I'm not decrepit yet."

"You will be if you don't get out of those wet boots. Come on, the front room's nice and warm. Do you want some tea?"

"Of course I do. When I don't want tea you can start worrying."

Not until she heard the familiar sigh of pleasure as Gran sipped her tea was Madge able to relax.

"How did you get on with Mrs. Turnbull?" she asked her.

"She had a long life and a peaceful death. Her oldest daughter, who is no spring chicken herself, helped me lift her when needed." Harriet took another sip. She looked over at her granddaughter with a twinkle in her eye. "Poor woman. When we were turning Mrs. Turnbull onto her side, doesn't she emit the most awful moan. Scared the living daylights out of the daughter. 'Dear God, Mama's still alive!' says she. 'No, she's not,' says I, 'that's just the lungs letting go of any air they were holding. When a person dies, everything lets go,' I adds, just to prepare her in case of a sudden stink. But it didn't happen. I'd stuffed cotton down Mrs. Turnbull's throat and up her nose so no fluids could escape. We didn't have to suffer that."

Madge couldn't help but laugh. "That's one small mercy."

"They're waiting for one of the sons to come in from Nova Scotia so she won't be buried for four days. I promised I'd look in daily. Make sure the corpse isn't decomposing too rapidly. Should last in this weather if they keep the windows open."

Harriet put her teacup on the tray beside her.

"So that's my news. What about you, Madge? You look utterly wrung out. Shall we chat in the morning or now?"

"Do you think you can stay up a bit longer?"

"Of course I can."

Madge related what had happened to Arthur Aggett and then to Daniel Samuels. To her dismay, she found her eyes filled with tears.

"Mrs. Turnbull died at the end of her life of natural causes, but I can't get these two young men off my mind."

Harriet sighed. "I can understand why. But God moves in mysterious ways. I suppose he had a purpose for taking those young lives."

Harriet Cooke was a pious woman, a Methodist by

persuasion and a devout churchgoer. She and Madge didn't always see eye to eye on religious matters but long ago had agreed to differ.

Madge stifled a yawn and her grandmother wagged a finger at her.

"Get up that wooden hill, Madge Curnoe. I'll be right after you as soon as I've finished my tea."

"All right. I'll warm up the bed."

Madge wasn't ready to go into an account of the visit to Mrs. Payne's. Harriet could be fierce in her condemnation of women she termed "fallen." Especially *young* women. But for Madge, the feelings Winnie's baby had aroused in her seemed too tender to share just yet, even though normally she told Gran everything.

She stood up and gave her grandmother a kiss on the cheek. "Night night." Suddenly she halted. "I almost forgot. Detective Murdoch gave me a box of chocolates. I've put them in the kitchen cupboard. They're Cadbury's. I've had three already. Don't worry, I left you the creams. Help yourself."

"Chocolates? What was that in aid of?"

Madge shrugged. "I think he knew a little sweetness today wouldn't be amiss."

"Oh, I see. Just general thoughtfulness, was it?"

"Yes, Gran. That's all it was."

CHAPTER TWENTY-NINE

IT WAS HALF PAST SIX WHEN THE TELEPHONE RANG. Murdoch got to it as fast as he could, a flood of alarm serving to wake him instantly. One of the detectives on reserve was on the other end.

"Lennox here, sir. There's been another attack. A young lad again."

"Fatal?"

"No. But close to it. Apparently it's touch and go. He has suffered a severe blow to the head. His father was the one who discovered him. He was lying in front of the family shop on Centre Avenue. The boy is in the Toronto General."

"I'll be right there. Stay by the telephone. I'll ring you

from the hospital."

Murdoch hurried back upstairs but stopped at Jack's door. He was muttering in his sleep. "Come on. Quick. *Quick.*"

Murdoch had got home later than usual and found the expected note propped up against the teapot.

Sorry. Wanted to wait up for you but got too tired. I'll see you in the morning.

Murdoch had been tempted to go and wake Jack up and talk to him then and there but had decided to wait until morning. Damn. Now he wasn't going to have the opportunity. He scribbled his own note to say he'd been called away. It was ironic that Jack and he were under the same roof now, but they were still communicating by writing letters.

He got to the hospital quickly on his bicycle and the night matron met him immediately. She had a kind face, but there was an air of fatigue that sat on her shoulders like a mantle. Not enough staff, too many cases now. She introduced herself as Miss Gillespie.

"The young man is not yet out of the operating room," she said. "Dr. Howitt is the physician in charge. He should be available to speak to you within the hour."

"I understand this was an attack."

"Apparently so. He had a severe blow to the head. His father and a constable brought him in. I have been asked to relay a message to you from the constable. He says he has returned to the scene of the attack to make sure no evidence is disturbed." She furrowed her brow. "I hope I have stated that correctly."

"Indeed you have."

"I've put the patient's father in my office for the time being."

"Is the lad likely to recover?" Murdoch asked.

Her eyes met his. "Frankly, it might be for the best if he did not, er, did not continue. I've seen such head injuries before, and the damage to the brain can be so extensive, life thereafter is drastically reduced."

She was simply being realistic, but Murdoch felt a surge of irrational anger.

"Let's not give up just yet, Matron. We should hear the results of the surgery first."

She turned pink. His tone had been sharper than he'd intended.

"Of course, Detective. Young men never cease to surprise us, do they? Dr. Howitt is very skilled, and if anybody can save the boy, he can." She gestured to the hall. "My office is down here. Please follow me."

Murdoch regretted his outburst, but it was too late to take back his words.

She ushered him in. An older man was seated in a chair by the window. He was bearded, with long, grizzled hair and the weather-beaten face of somebody who spent a lot of his time outdoors. He jumped to his feet.

"Any word, Matron?"

In spite of her pessimistic statement to Murdoch earlier,

Miss Gillespie gave the man a cheery smile.

"Not yet, Mr. Swartz. But he's a strong, healthy young man and that goes a long way."

"Not that strong, ma'am. He's had weak lungs from a child. He had bronchitis. That's why he was turned down for active service. He'd never make it in those trenches. The tribunal board knew that. He just received his exemption."

Miss Gillespie indicated Murdoch. "This is Detective Murdoch, Mr. Swartz. He would like to ask you some questions."

Swartz nodded. "Sir, you got to find who did this to my lad."

The matron left, not looking at Murdoch. It would take a while for him to get back in her good graces.

Swartz resumed his seat, and Murdoch took out his notebook.

"Tell me what happened, sir."

"I own a grocery shop over on Centre Avenue. Number 77. Morris—that's my son—always goes over early before the shop opens so he can sweep up, trim the vegetables, and so on. Then we're all ready for the customers."

"What time does that take place?"

"Always the same. Morris gets there at five. Myself by six o'clock. We live down the road, not far to go."

There was the sound of talking outside in the hall and Swartz stopped to listen. Nobody came in and the voices faded, but he remained poised, watching the door like a creature on the alert.

"Please go on, sir," said Murdoch.

"When I get to shop I see Morris lying across the doorway.

His head is bleeding. I think he is dead for a minute but then I see he is breathing. Deep rattling breaths." The memory caused Mr. Swartz to stop. Murdoch made a sympathetic murmur.

"I start to shout for help," continued Swartz. "Nobody come. There is barrow there. Vegetable barrow. I manage to pull Morris on to it. I am running fast as I can to the hospital. At the corner of street I meet constable. He takes one look and grabs the handles of the barrow. 'Follow me,' says he, 'fast as you can.'" Again Mr. Swartz paused. "I've heard tales of soldiers getting strength that surpasses that of ordinary humans when they're out there on the line. Now I understand. The constable took over but I could have run all the way to the hospital even if my heart would have burst. I don't know if you understand that, Detective."

"I believe I do, Mr. Swartz."

Swartz glanced up at the clock on the wall. "That was almost an hour ago. Nobody's come out yet to tell me what's happening. Morris wasn't looking good, sir. I don't know if he's going to make it."

"You acted very promptly. That will make a difference."

"We shall see."

"Mr. Swartz, do you have any idea who might have attacked your son? Did you notice anybody in the vicinity, for instance?"

"It was still dark. I suppose such a person could have been hiding for all I'd see him. I didn't hear no footsteps or nobody running away or anything like that."

"Did Morris have any enemies that you know of? Would he have quarrelled with anybody?"

The familiarity of the words made them sound oddly hollow to Murdoch's ears. How many more times was he going to have to ask the same questions? Swartz's answer was also familiar.

"He isn't what you call a quarrelsome sort, my Morris. Very good boy."

"Was the shop broken into?"

"I think it was not. Morris was in the doorway. He hadn't opened up as yet."

"Did your son ever mention the name Arthur Aggett to you?"

"Never. Why do you ask?"

"He was attacked also. Tuesday night."

Swartz bit his lip. "Does he live?"

"I'm afraid he was already dead when his body was discovered."

"Who did it?"

"We don't know yet."

Abruptly, Swartz lowered his head. "I don't understand, Detective. We do nobody any harm. Never. We live quiet. This will break his mother's heart if he does not pull through. She doesn't know yet. She thinks we're both at the shop."

"I can have somebody fetch her to the hospital."

"Thank you, sir. That would be a good thing." Swartz regarded Murdoch. His face was full of sorrow. "I'm not interested in revenge, sir. That belongs to God. It does not change the situation. On the other hand, when you find the culprit, I would like to have a chance to meet him face to face. I want to see what shape the devil can take when he chooses to."

Suddenly he tapped himself on the forehead. "How could I forget? There was a strange thing. Somebody drew a cross on Morris's back. It was this big." He held his hands about six inches apart. "Yellow chalk. You can check yourself. The nurse has his clothes."

"You say that your son had no enemies that you know of, but might this attack have been more general? Aimed at your family, for instance?"

"I know what you imply, Detective, but we live among children of Israel." He allowed himself a wry smile. "And Italians. We get along very well."

Before Murdoch could answer, Miss Gillespie came in.

"Your son is out of surgery, Mr. Swartz, and he is being transferred to a special care ward. You may see him. For a few minutes only."

Swartz caught her by the hand.

"Will he live?"

She pulled away gently. "The doctor is optimistic. The next twenty-four hours are critical."

"I'll go right away."

Swartz was practically out of the door as he was speaking.

"He's not conscious yet, Mr. Swartz."

"I don't care about that. He will know I'm there. He will live for me."

CHAPTER THIRTY

Dr howitt's room was simply furnished with a desk, a couple of comfortable armchairs, and a couch long enough to stretch out on. The desk was littered with papers, but otherwise the office was neat and tidy. There were several framed diplomas on the walls and Murdoch had a look at them while he waited. James Howitt had accomplished a lot, by all accounts.

The doctor arrived with the matron. He looked younger than Murdoch had expected, about his own age most likely. He had a shining bald dome balanced by a neatly trimmed beard, streaked with grey. Like the matron, he gave the impression of somebody in need of a holiday.

Greetings accomplished, they sat down, and Miss Gillespie bustled off to get some refreshment.

"We did all we could," Howitt said to Murdoch. "He has sustained a blow to the head that fractured his cranium. There was copious bleeding but we transfused him." He gave his head a stroke. "It is a rather sad truth about we humans that some of our better developments in the field of medicine have been in step, hand in hand as it were, with developments in the machinery of warfare. We can kill more men than ever before with our guns and then save more of them by such things as transfusions."

Murdoch didn't have a chance to comment before Miss Gillespie re-entered wheeling the tea trolley. The cups and pot were china and the cloth on the tray was pristine linen. There was a plate with buns.

"I'm afraid I have to leave you to serve the tea yourself, Doctor. I have to deal with something on the ward."

"I think I am capable of doing that, Miss Gillespie. If not, I'm sure our detective here would be proficient."

His tone was devoid of any sarcasm, affectionate really, and the matron beamed.

Howitt was reminding Murdoch of Peter Fenwell and his effect on women. He thought he should perhaps take pointers.

Miss Gillespie left and Murdoch accepted the offer of a cup of tea and a currant bun. His stomach was rumbling.

"Could you determine what kind of weapon was used, Doctor?" he asked.

Howitt dabbed at his mouth with one of the linen napkins. "The cut was jagged. I found several splinters of brick. Reddish colour. It was wielded with great force. The blow struck the head quite in the middle of the skull, which suggests the attacker was not striking downward, or upward, for that matter. He would have been on a level with the victim. The young man is almost six feet tall so his assailant might be about the same height."

"Or he could have been standing on a higher elevation."

"You're right. It could be that. I was getting carried away. Perhaps the post mortem will reveal more."

Murdoch blinked at him. "Post mortem? You don't think the lad will survive, then?"

"Most unlikely, I'm afraid."

Tea and civility dispensed with, Murdoch was conducted to the recovery room where Morris had been taken.

"Don't expect too much from him," said Howitt before they entered. "He's been heavily sedated."

Mr. Swartz was sitting beside the bed.

Dr. Howitt beckoned to him. "Let's wait over here, sir. The detective needs to talk to your son."

Swartz offered no protest and moved to the door. Murdoch went to the bed and leaned very close to the young man's head, which was swathed in bandages.

"Morris. This is Detective Murdoch. Can you hear me?"

A barely perceptible flicker of his eyes. He seemed to be scarcely breathing, and his lips were dry and caked.

Murdoch raised his voice. "You've been wounded. Don't give up. You're going to be fine."

He wished he truly believed that.

MEMORANDUM ON THE TREATMENT
OF INJURIES IN WAR, BASED ON EXPERIENCE OF
THE PRESENT CAMPAIGN

ON THE FILLING UP OF TALLIES.

Much trouble has been caused on the arrival of cases in the casualty clearing stations, stationary and general hospitals by the incompleteness of the details inscribed on the tallies. Observances of the following rules will much facilitate the work of the hospitals to which the patient is transferred.

All tallies should bear—

1. The stamp of the Unit through which the case has been passed.
2. An *accurate* description of the injury, for example— "Compound fracture of skull," *not* "G.S.W. head." "Compound fracture of femur," *not* "Shrapnel wound of leg."
3. Time of last dressing.
4. Concise account of the operation performed.
5. Amount of tetanus antitoxin injected.
6. Whether morphia has been administered and in what amount.

CHAPTER THIRTY-ONE

MURDOCH WENT TO THE MATRON'S OFFICE, WHERE HE was able to ring the station. He had hoped to send Madge to fetch Mrs. Swartz but she wasn't in yet. Wallace himself had just arrived. Murdoch gave him instructions to convey the directive to Detective Herb Crowther, who was on reserve. He thought Crowther would be more inclined to be sympathetic and tactful toward Mrs. Swartz than his partner, Lennox.

"I'd like to call an emergency meeting at nine o'clock. Gather as many of the detectives as you can. No. Better make that half past nine. Give them time to wake up. I'll be there within the hour."

He hung up, and requested Morris's clothes from the nurse

waiting discreetly by the door. Miss Gillespie herself brought them to him. They'd been neatly folded into a cardboard box.

The cap and wool overcoat were heavily bloodstained. As Mr. Swartz had said, there was a yellow cross chalked on the back of the coat. It was about six inches long and about half an inch wide. Murdoch tested the chalk with his finger. It was powdery. No smell. As far as he could tell it was ordinary school chalk. He examined the rest of the garments carefully but there were no other marks.

He returned the clothes to the box. He sincerely hoped Morris Swartz would get to wear them again.

Murdoch left the hospital to find a city coming awake; people were going about their business. A weak sun was even struggling to come through. As he bicycled down Centre Avenue he had to stop suddenly at the corner of Edward Street to allow a woman to cross. She was wheeling a perambulator, and from her dress he guessed she was a nursery maid out with her charge. He'd been so preoccupied he'd almost sailed right past her. She flashed him an indignant look and he tipped his hat apologetically.

What he couldn't get out of his mind was Mr. Swartz's comment about his son. And how he had rushed to the bedside. *He will know I'm there. He will live for me.*

While Amy was dying, Murdoch hadn't left her side for an instant. Between one intake of breath and the other, her life had stopped as abruptly as if an electric light had been switched off. Afterward he was forever grateful he had been present at that moment of separation between body and soul. Ironically, just days before she died, Amy had received word that a former colleague was seriously ill and she had gone to visit him. When she returned, she had been in a strange mood. "I thought he was dead. He looked like a corpse and he wouldn't wake up. I thought he was sailing off to that unknown bourne. The nurse sent for his wife. She came in, didn't seem perturbed. We said we couldn't wake him. 'He will for me,' she said, and then she called his name softly in his ear. Sure enough, he started to wake up."

Amy had put her arms around Murdoch. "Is that what love is, Will? Is the beloved the one you'll always come back for?"

Constable Fairbairn was standing outside the Swartz grocery store. As Murdoch approached, Fairbairn was turning away two customers, stating that Morris had been taken ill and the family was at the hospital. Murdoch overheard one of the women say she'd go and call on Golda right away. He thought the real story would be revealed very soon.

When they walked away, Fairbairn acknowledged Murdoch.

"I believe I've found the weapon, sir."

He lifted a piece of tarpaulin that was underneath one of the vegetable bins. It was covering a bloodstained brick.

"It was used as a block for the barrow. The attacker must have grabbed it when he approached Morris Swartz. Then he discarded it. It was lying just over there by the curb."

Murdoch crouched down and studied the brick. "I'll send a constable to relieve you. I'd appreciate it if you'd bring this to headquarters and we can have it examined for fingerprints. It's not likely to yield much evidence, given the rough surface, but we'll try. Wrap it in the tarpaulin. Anything else?"

"No, sir. The young lad hadn't had time to unlock the front door but it has not been tampered with."

"So everything happened out here."

"I'd say so. There are no further blood stains on the pavement. Morris didn't move after he was struck down."

Murdoch looked around. The houses were close together but the street itself was wider than many of those in the Ward. Where had the attacker come from? Morris Swartz had been walking north along Centre Avenue. The street would have been dark but it would also have been quiet. Surely Morris would have heard or at least sensed somebody was following him. Had the attacker been in hiding, waiting for him? There was only one place that Murdoch could see where that might be possible.

"Constable, would you mind going to that entry? There, between numbers 73 and 71. Hide yourself for a minute. I'm going to stand in this doorway. See if you can sneak up on me."

They took up their positions. Murdoch pretended to fiddle with the lock on the door. Suddenly there was a tap on his shoulder. Murdoch hadn't heard Fairbairn at all.

"That seems to suggest the attacker was already lying in wait, wouldn't you say, Constable?"

"I agree, sir. But why was young Morris his target? This has been my beat for a long time. I've seen the young fellow grow up, as it were. They are a decent, hard-working family. I don't know why somebody wanted to do him in."

"Thank you, Constable. You've been very helpful."

"I'll drop off the brick as soon as I'm relieved, sir." Another woman was approaching. "I'll just head off this lady."

Murdoch left him to deal with her and rode off.

CHAPTER THIRTY-TWO

MURDOCH CHECKED IN WITH WALLACE AT THE FRONT desk.

"I could only round up six of the detectives, sir. Mr. Archibald and Mr. Rawlings have both come down with the flu. 'Laid flat' was the term Mrs. Rawlings used when she rang in."

Murdoch knew who was going to be blamed for that.

"Inspector Kennedy is also a goner." The clerk looked anxious. "Hope I'm not going to catch it."

"Hold your breath at all times, Wallace. It's the only safeguard. Is Constable Curnoe here?"

"Yes, sir. She's in the duty room with the others."

Murdoch divested himself of his hat and overcoat and

hurried down the hall. He never liked his detectives to feel they had to wait at his convenience if it wasn't necessary.

When he entered the room he was met with the usual fug. All of the detectives were smoking, either a pipe or a cigarette. Madge was sitting by the front desk, notebook open. He wouldn't blame her if she took up smoking in self-defence.

He went straight to the chalkboard.

"Morning, Miss Curnoe. Morning, gentlemen. Thank you for gathering at such short notice. We have another serious case on our hands and I didn't want to waste time getting on it."

He took the chalk and drew three vertical lines on the blackboard. At the top of the columns he wrote "AGGETT," "SWARTZ," and "SAMUELS?"

They all knew the details of Aggett's murder, and he filled them in on the death of Daniel Samuels, and also the events of the past night and the attack on Morris Swartz.

"Let's see if there are any points of comparison. Although Samuels was a suicide, I've included him. I'd like to find out more about him and his state of mind."

He drew more lines, this time horizontal, and labelled them: LOCATION; TIME OF DAY; AGE; PHYSICAL ATTRIBUTES; RELIGION; OCCUPATION; MARITAL STATUS; KNOWN ENEMIES; WEAPON.

Madge was copying this down in her notepad.

Fenwell was the first to speak. "The most obvious similarity to me is the timing and the location of the two attacks. Both took place in the Ward, and Centre Avenue and Chestnut

Street are only one block apart. Both happened in the early hours of the morning."

Murdoch wrote that on the board. "I'll put a checkmark for Samuels. He died at the City Baths, also within easy walking distance of Centre Avenue. A different time of day, however. Mid-afternoon. Age and physical attributes? Arthur Aggett was twenty-three years old, a big fellow. About six feet, strong build. Fair-haired. Moustache. Daniel was twenty. Morris Swartz is slight of build. About five-foot nine. Twenty-one. Dark-haired. Clean-shaven. So there are some common denominators, some differences."

"Would religion be a factor? The unfortunate suicide was Jewish," interjected Mitchell. He was undeniably the most devout on the squad. A Baptist, he tended to judge all occurrences on a moral scale.

Murdoch wrote "Jewish" beside both Daniel's name and Morris's. Aggett was Christian.

"Next. Occupation? Aggett was a teamster with the Dominion Brewery. Swartz worked at his father's grocer's shop. Samuels was a clerk for a company that makes monuments, but he had recently been fired. No obvious connection among the three of them there."

"How long had Aggett worked for the brewery?" asked Charles Croome, an ardent teetotaller. "The reason I'm asking is that, with the Temperance Act, he might have been expecting to find himself out of work soon."

Rubridge gave a derisive snort. "Surely that is more

significant with the suicide. Unless Aggett hired somebody to bash him on the head out of sheer despair. However, according to the post mortem, he did exit with a skinful, which must have made him happy, at least."

Croome's jaw tightened. There was no love lost between the two men and they had had some hot discussions about the value of the new law. Murdoch decided to slide over this flare-up.

"I believe Aggett had worked at the brewery for three years. I have not heard what Dominion is doing with their employees. They can still export what they make. Okay. Next. Marital status. Aggett was the only one married."

Guthrie grinned. "Then there's no reason to believe they were killed by a posse of disgruntled wives. You know how women can be when they feel hard done by. Right, Miss Curnoe?"

To Murdoch's relief, Madge didn't rise to the bait. "I certainly do know, Detective Guthrie. Thank goodness."

That last comment was ambiguous but Guthrie grinned again. He was the oldest member of the squad, white-haired and close to retirement. Murdoch had the feeling he wasn't looking forward to it. Not much to go home to. He had a tendency to hang around Madge and lob teasing comments at her.

"Next. Known enemies? None that we are aware of. None of them has been in trouble with the law, although Peter and I believe that Aggett was gambling the night he was killed. We have yet to identify the other players. Finally, we have the matter of a weapon."

Murdoch faced the men. "We have not yet located the weapon that was used to kill Arthur Aggett. The physician thought it was metal. Swartz was hit with a piece of brick. I can only assume that was opportunistic because the brick was being used to brake the barrow in front of the shop. In Aggett's case, because so far we have not found any traces, the killer may have both brought the weapon with him and carried it away. Interestingly, the attacks had similar features in that both came from behind, with great ferocity."

Roy Rubridge took a draw on his cigarette. "So it's hard to conclude at this point whether or not the attacks were premeditated and whether or not the targets were intended."

Murdoch sighed. "Certainly, they both took place in darkness and at an hour when most of the city was asleep, which might suggest planning."

"Maybe we're dealing with somebody who's insane," said Guthrie. "Anybody escaped from the lunatic asylum lately?" He made a chopping motion.

"A man-hating ex-wife, you mean?" said Madge, her voice sweet as honey.

"It's not completely out of the question," retorted Guthrie. "Look at the Jack the Ripper case."

"I thought that was a man murdering prostitutes," said Fenwell.

"I was simply using it as an example of a killer targeting a specific class of people."

Rubridge stabbed his cigarette in Guthrie's direction. "A far-fetched example, if I may say so. We've only got two attacks and a suicide. Hardly a pattern."

"Can I say something, sir?" Madge said.

Murdoch nodded. "Of course."

"Acts that are random or apparently unconnected might still be intended."

"You've lost me there, Miss Curnoe," said Guthrie. "The workings of the female mind do sometimes elude me."

"All right. Let me elucidate. I might, for instance, randomly choose a streetcar to go home. That one and not the next, for example. But that does not mean I have no intent. Clearly I do. My intention is to catch a streetcar to take me home. Which one I end up on is destiny."

"Meant for you, as it were?" chimed in Montgomery.

"Just like you and me," muttered Guthrie.

Madge ignored him.

"You make a good point, Miss Curnoe," said Murdoch. "Did the victims have the sheer bad luck simply to be out when our murderer wandered by?"

"We are looking at a madman, then," said Mitchell.

Fenwell shook his head. "If he's that insane he still has enough savvy to act when there is nobody else around. In both cases, the police constable on his beat had just passed by."

"I agree," said Murdoch. "It might be sheer animal cunning, or it might be careful planning."

"That would suggest he did know the lie of the land," continued Fenwell. "He is familiar with the area. All of our constables' movements are predictable. We've always considered that this provides a sense of security to the populace."

Madge spoke up again. "Excuse me, sir, but I can't let go of my theory. What is the intention? Is our attacker prowling around the city in search of a particular kind of victim? Back to Jack the Ripper. He didn't seem to care what prostitute he killed as long as she was a prostitute."

"I'm telling you, Miss Curnoe," said Guthrie, "it's a bitter woman we're after. She wants to destroy any young man she finds. Intention? To rid the world of bachelors. Think of Miss Havisham tenfold."

"Arthur Aggett had a young wife," said Madge.

Murdoch intervened. "There is something I haven't had a chance to tell you yet. It seems that the person who attacked Swartz chalked a yellow cross on his back."

"What do you mean, 'chalked'?" asked Croome.

"Exactly that. It was done with the kind of ordinary chalk you find in a tailor's shop, a schoolroom, a toy store. The cross is about six inches long. The arms are of equal length."

He drew a cross to illustrate. "I am assuming it was significant to the attacker."

He stepped back and surveyed the board. "What, then, do the three men have in common? Not marital status, not occupation, not religion, not physique."

"While you're doing the 'nots,'" said Rubridge, "you should add not soldiers. One was about to try for an exemption.

Swartz was already exempt on the basis of ill health. Even Samuels wasn't enlisted."

Suddenly, Montgomery blurted out, "I know what that cross stands for. I know exactly. My son mentioned it once. It's a mark the Germans put on gas canisters. It means they contain mustard gas."

The others all stared at him.

"Why go to the trouble of scrawling that on somebody's back?" asked Croome.

Rubridge drew on his cigarette. "Aren't we forgetting one important thing? Yellow is also the colour of cowardice."

CHAPTER THIRTY-THREE

JACK PICKED UP THE PACK OF CARDS, SHUFFLED THEM, and laid out six, face up on the kitchen table. The knave fell into the third spot. He scooped them up, reshuffled, and laid them out again. This time the knave was in the fifth spot. Another scoop, another shuffle, and the cards laid out. Knave was in the second spot. He did this another half a dozen times. In none of the layouts did the knave land on the first or sixth place.

The sergeant says it's random but it's not. They always put the blank in either the sixth or the first spot. Either end of the line. The central guns, directly facing, are most likely to be spot-on accurate so they are always loaded.

THE QUESTION

How will I die?
He asks the nurse who steps by his bed
Softly
As they do for the "soon-to-be-dead."
"I will bring the doctor," says she,
And subsequently
He arrives.
In white coat and stethoscope.
"I hear you have a question for me."
"I'd like to know how I will die,"
Is the reply.
"Chin up, there's a good chap.
That's a morbid thought.
You ought
To think of getting better.
You'll soon be just grand."
The boy sighs again.
Despair settles in.
"I want to know what to expect."
His voice is fading fast
And
At last, the doctor,
A good man, give or take,
Sees what's at stake.
"Well then, since you ask,
We can't fix you up,
But the opiate will increase

And you will fall asleep."
"Never to awake again," adds the boy.
"That's right.
There will be no more pain."
"Thank you, sir, that's all I need to know.
Let's hope my dreams are sweet."

CHAPTER THIRTY-FOUR

MURDOCH CONCLUDED THE MEETING SOON afterward. He thought it had been very productive. There had ensued a lively discussion about whether or not to put out a warning that there might be a madman roaming the streets who was attacking young men who weren't soldiers. Croome and Montgomery were all for notifying the newspapers, but Murdoch decided against it. He didn't want to alarm a city that was already filled with anxiety. And they didn't know for sure if that really was the link between Arthur Aggett's attacker and Morris Swartz's. He promised to notify all beat constables, especially in the Ward, to be extra vigilant. He sent the detectives to follow up with their own specialties and assigned Watson and Young to step in for the ill Archibald and Rawlings.

"Let's pay a visit to all establishments that we suspect might be gambling dens. Rattle them."

As everybody was gathering up his belongings—tobacco pouches, cigarette cases, and so forth—Murdoch added one more instruction. "For God's sake, don't get the flu. We can't afford to be even more short-handed."

He returned to his office, pausing to study the chess board. The little knight was pawing impatiently, eager to go in for the kill. The two queens were long retired but were trying to manipulate moves from the sidelines. His rook seemed impregnable.

It was funny how chess was all about capture and conquer. He wondered if the generals had ever studied the game and if it affected the moves of battle. Probably not. Here on the chess board there was no cold, teeming rain, no glue-like mud, no rotting bodies clogging up the trenches. All calm, orderly moves with no bloodshed. Interestingly, the king himself was pretty feeble; it was the queen who had all the power. Mind you, those bishops could be pretty nifty, dashing across great distances. Never straightforward, always slipping sideways. As for the poor pawns, what a dull life they had. Usually sacrificed early, there were no swift moves for them. Unless they got promoted, which didn't happen often. A promoted pawn could be ruthless. Reminded him of a constable's life.

The telephone on his desk rang, startling him out of his thoughts.

"Sir, there's a lady here says she needs to speak to you at once. It's concerning Miss Curnoe."

"Really? What's it about?"

"She wouldn't say. Said she could only speak to the chief officer and the lady herself. I told her you, as senior detective, were the only one available at the moment. She said you would do."

"Will I, indeed?"

"Sorry to put it that way, sir, but those were her words."

"How very mysterious. All right. Bring the woman down and see if Miss Curnoe can join us. Give me a chance to get the lie of the land before you do that. I'll buzz."

After a moment, there was a tap on the door. Wallace ushered in a woman who walked with the help of a cane.

"Mrs. Flynn, sir."

Murdoch stood up and came around the desk.

"Good day, madam. Please have a seat."

He'd seen her initially as middle-aged but now he wasn't so sure. Her clothes were shabby and worn and her lined face showed evidence of a difficult life, but she was neatly dressed, and he thought he could see evidence of rouge on her cheeks. She could have been any age.

Murdoch returned to his place behind the desk.

"I was hoping I could speak to the lady police officer." There was the faint suggestion of an accent to her speech. Murdoch guessed she was originally from Ireland.

"May I ask what it is in connection with?"

"I live at number 45 Louisa Street and I wish to report that my neighbour, Mrs. Payne, is conducting an illegal operation."

Fully expecting she was going to report a violation of the Temperance Act, Murdoch couldn't help but frown.

"What does this have to do with our officer?"

"She came to investigate. Now mind you I didn't twig as to how she was the police at first. She was wearing very nobby clothes, you see." She nodded somewhat apologetically at Murdoch. "I suffers bad from rheumatics. If my husband hadn't left me with insurance benefits I would be in the workhouse because I can't get around much at all. So I sits in my window most of the day. It passes the time."

"And one of the things you see is what occurs at Mrs. Payne's house?"

"That's right, sir. After a while, I saw the lady leave. I needed my constitutional anyways so I decided to follow her." She indicated her cane. "Like I said, I've got rheumatics and I don't walk too fast so I never caught up. But I was close enough to observe her come in here." She clapped herself on the forehead. "I thought to myself, I thought, Bertha Flynn, you've just run into one of those lady policemen. She must have been in disguise."

"I see. And you wanted to talk to her about the illegal selling of liquor?"

Mrs. Flynn stared at him. "What in the Lord's name gave you that idea? What I have to report is much more serious than that. My neighbour, Mrs. Payne, is selling something all right, but it's not liquor, it's babies."

Murdoch buzzed the front desk to send for Madge.

As soon as she entered the office, Mrs. Flynn exclaimed, "Yes, that's her. That's the lady was at Mrs. Payne's."

Murdoch addressed Madge. "Miss Curnoe, Mrs. Flynn just made the rather startling assertion that Mrs. Payne is, as she put it, 'selling babies.'"

Mrs. Flynn ducked her head. "It's true. I'm not making it up." She glanced at Madge. "That's why you was there, ma'am, wasn't it? You come to investigate her."

"I was following up on an advertisement she had placed in the *Star*. A child was being offered for adoption. I went to see if all was above board."

"I'll bet my boots she wanted money for the little one."

Murdoch looked to Madge for confirmation.

"It wasn't quite that direct. She said she needed money to cover her expenses. Medical bills and so forth."

"How much did she request?" Murdoch asked.

"Seventy dollars."

Murdoch whistled between his teeth. "Steep."

"I knew it would be," said Mrs. Flynn. "And that's not the first one, either." She paused, waiting to see the effect of her words.

"Would you elaborate, madam?"

"Winnie Payne is older than she looks. They like to keep her looking young so they can put the screws to any gentleman foolish enough to fall for it. You know, charge him with seduction. She had a bebbe last summer. I'll guess come spring she'll be with child again."

"What happened to the other infant?" asked Madge.

"Same thing. They puts an advertisement in the paper and along comes a couple of swells and off they go with the infant. That was a girl, that one."

Madge frowned. "You are making serious allegations, Mrs. Flynn. Winnie told me that she had met a soldier who then went overseas. Her mother felt he had taken advantage of the girl."

"Did she now? I wonder which soldier she was referring to. There's been so many trooping up to their door it's a wonder she can tell them apart." Mrs. Flynn shifted in the chair. "Don't think I enjoy telling you all of this because I don't, but it's time somebody put a stop to it. There are three other kiddies in that house. God knows what they will grow up like seeing their sister selling herself to the highest bidder."

"Are you saying that the children are present when these, er, these men come?"

"Oh yes. They're shoved outside no matter what the weather when their sister has, shall we call it, a visitor? But they know what it's all about. Mrs. Payne takes herself off for a walk. Used to be she went to the tavern but now she can't. At least, she can't legally, but we all know there's lots of places willing to flout the law."

Murdoch and Madge exchanged glances.

"I'm surprised she hasn't been charged before now," Mrs. Flynn continued. "One of your officers comes regular."

"One of my officers?"

"That's right. I wondered who he was at first. He wasn't in no uniform, but he must have seen me, because when Winnie answered the door he flashed his badge. I guessed he was a detective like you."

As far as Murdoch knew, nobody in the department had been on this case before Madge.

"He was a stout fellow. Ruddy face. One of those big moustaches you see on generals."

"And when was this exactly?"

"He came first off just before Christmas of last year. He's been another couple of times since then. Last time was after the babe was borned. Must have been October." The woman regarded Murdoch. "Something should be done is all I can say."

"Thank you, Mrs. Flynn. We will certainly pursue this matter further."

She struggled to her feet. "Well, I've done my duty. I'd best be off. It'll be dark soon and I don't like walking the streets by myself."

"I can have a constable escort you home."

Mrs. Flynn actually shivered. "You're not thinking straight. If I was to show up holding onto a policeman I'd never live it down. My name would be mud. Or worse."

Murdoch went to open the door for her. "Thank you for coming in."

At the door Mrs. Flynn paused. "Winnie told you she had been took by a soldier, did she? Might be the only true thing she did say. There was a couple of young fellows come to the house just yesterday."

"Soldiers?"

"They weren't in uniform but I could tell they was soldiers. I saw her open the door and she looked pretty pleased. They was returning soldiers, if you ask me. One of them had his arm in a sling, the other had a cane like me. He had an awful disfigurement, too. On his face. Like a V it was."

CHAPTER THIRTY-FIVE

MURDOCH TALKED MRS. FLYNN INTO ACCEPTING AN escort as far as the end of her street. After she had gone, he turned to Madge.

"What the heck do you make of this, Madge?"

"It's probably what Mrs. Flynn suggested. Prostitution. Then if Winnie gets in the family way, they can extort money from her seducer or prevail on a willing adopter for funds, the way they did with me. I'm saying 'they,' but essentially Mrs. Payne is the one running the show. God knows Winnie's still a child, whatever her exact age. We need to step in."

"We do, or the Children's Aid."

"I've been in touch with them already."

Murdoch rested his head in his hands. "Madge, there's no doubt the recent visitors were Jack and his pal, Percy. What the hell was he doing? Surely he wouldn't be mixed up with a girl who's prostituting herself?"

Madge stood up and leaned on the desk in front of him.

"William Murdoch, you have raised a good and honourable young man. You have to trust in that."

"Madge, this war has changed everything. I fear it has pushed even good young men to the breaking point."

"Well we can't stick our heads in the sand. I suggest we pay a visit to Mrs. Payne."

There was a dim light shining in the Paynes' window and Murdoch could see, across the street, an even dimmer light revealing the shadowy figure of Mrs. Flynn at her vigil. He and Madge had discussed the situation and, rather reluctantly, she had agreed that he should go by himself. She might be needed at a future time to go under cover in this neighbourhood.

He knocked on the door, and after a long time it was opened by a raggedly dressed young boy. His expression was wary.

"Hello, young fella. My name is Detective Murdoch. Can I have a word with your mother?"

"She ain't in."

"Is your sister Winnie at home?"

The boy shook his head emphatically. "Not any more. She's done a bunk."

"What do you mean?"

"She's done a bunk."

"Why is that?"

"She said she didn't want to live here no more."

"When did she leave?"

"Last night. Her sweetheart came for her. He's a soldier."

"Did you see him?"

"No, I didn't. She left him here. She says she don't want him."

"By *him* do you mean her baby?"

"That's right."

From the room behind, Murdoch heard a baby break into wails.

"Who's taking care of the baby?" he asked the boy.

"My mam."

"You said she's not here."

"That's right. Cissy's looking after him until she gets back."

"How old is Cissy?"

"She's older than me."

"And how old are you?"

"Dunno exactly. Nine most like."

Murdoch felt a flush of anger but he tried to hide it from the boy. The child was looking more and more nervous as the conversation went on. The sound of a deeply distressed baby continued.

"What is your name, young man?"

"Sidney."

"Sidney. Where would I find your mother?"

"I dunno."

"Didn't she say where she was going?"

"No, sir."

"Did she say when she'd be back?"

"No, sir."

"All right, Sidney. This is what I'm going to do. I'm going to get in touch with some people who will take care of the baby so you children don't have to worry about him. I'll tell them to bring some supper for you as well. They should be coming by sometime this evening."

"Ma won't like that."

"I'm afraid she won't have any say in the matter."

The boy shrugged but didn't answer.

The baby's crying was starting to subside. Cissy was obviously doing something right. She'd probably had plenty of practice.

"Get inside now, son. It's cold."

"What shall I tell my mam?"

"Tell her a police officer came by. Tell her not to worry. We are here to help."

Cynicism in such a young boy didn't seem possible but Murdoch thought he glimpsed such an expression flit across Sidney's face. He felt cold with anger. This was no way for a police force to be perceived. *Damn it. Damn it.* What the hell was the point of working to bring justice to bear if the very people you were trying to help mistrusted and hated you?

Murdoch went straight back to headquarters and found Madge. She was conferring with Peter Fenwell. He related the results of his visit.

"We've got to get the Children's Aid workers to the Paynes' immediately. All of those children must be removed. If they don't do something, I'm going to take them out myself."

"I'll call them again."

"Say it's an emergency."

She got up at once and hurried out.

Fenwell waved at Murdoch. "Will, sit down. Get it off your chest before you explode."

"Why do people have to live like that, Peter? What the hell are we doing prosecuting petty crimes about breaking Sunday observance laws, selling liquor when you're not permitted—" Murdoch slammed his fist on the desk. "It's a load of shit. There are serious and major crimes happening out there and we hardly make a dent. There are children without enough to eat, not enough warmth. They'll grow up to be criminals, sure as shooting, and we do nothing."

"What do you suggest?" Fenwell asked quietly.

"No landlords should be allowed to profit from the misfortune of others, for one thing. They should be made to clean up those bloody slums. Fix the goddamn roof when they need to. Build a proper privy. The city should cough up money to support women who have no means so they don't have to resort to selling babies." Murdoch aimed his finger at his friend. "There should not be anybody in this city who is in need. Poverty should not live side by side with wealth. It's wrong."

"Will, ever since I've known you, this has irked you. You should apply for the job of chief constable. You might have more heft."

"Oh sure. I'm still a Catholic, Peter. I would never get a promotion like that, even if I wanted it, which I don't."

"So what's going to ease your conscience, Will? Tender as it is."

"Goddamn it. I wish I could answer that. The only thing I know is that I'm going to be the best goddamn detective I can be."

"Will, do you notice you're swearing a lot?"

Murdoch had been finishing his reports and was getting ready to take a break and have a bite to eat when he heard shouting outside in the hall. A woman's voice.

"You have no right. No frigging right."

He went to see what the fuss was about. A woman was being forcibly held back by one of the constables. She seemed intent on getting at Roy Rubridge, who was standing in front of her.

"Hey. What's going on?" Murdoch said loudly. "Madam, you're creating a disturbance."

She whirled around. "And I have every right."

Even from a few feet away, Murdoch could smell the liquor on her breath.

She pointed at Rubridge. "He's had my children taken from me. All my babies."

"I don't know what the hell you're talking about," said Rubridge angrily.

"Yes, you do. The social workers came and said they had had a warrant to remove my kiddies. That I wasn't a fit mother and they weren't being taken care of properly."

Murdoch interceded. "You must be Mrs. Payne."

"That's right. And who are you?"

"I'm Detective Murdoch. I was the one who ordered the Children's Aid to come to your house. There was an infant who was in distress and who had been left in the care of two children who were far too young to have that responsibility."

"Bloody rubbish. It wasn't for long."

"Perhaps so, but you yourself are clearly not in any condition to be responsible for these children. They will stay with the Children's Aid for the time being."

Mrs. Payne was too drunk to be cautious, and Murdoch's remarks incensed her further. She managed to grab Rubridge by the arm.

"Can't you do something? I need my children. I love my children."

Bubbles of mucous were coming from her nose. Rubridge tried to disentangle himself.

"They are in good hands."

She was purple in the face now. "You! After all we've done for you. You owe me, mister."

"Let go of me, woman."

He shrugged her off so roughly she staggered backwards and flopped to the ground like a rag doll. Madge had emerged from her office and went to help.

"Put her in one of the cells," said Murdoch. "When she's sober, we might have a rational talk. Until then it's a waste of breath."

"Come on, Mrs. Payne," said Madge. "Stand up."

The drunken woman looked up at her. "I know you. You came to adopt Baby. Well, he's gone now. You won't have him now."

In her besotted state it didn't seem to bother her that the woman she knew as Mrs. McIvor was currently in a police station trying to get her to stand up.

Then suddenly she vomited copiously on the floor.

"Beg pardon. Touch of indigestion."

"Miss Curnoe, get her out of here," said Murdoch.

"Baby's gone," wailed Mrs. Payne. "Winnie's gone. Gone forever. And all my children, gone forever." She was weeping alcohol-fuelled tears.

Murdoch couldn't stand it any more. He called to the desk clerk.

"Wallace, fetch a mop, if you please. Clean up that mess. Detective Rubridge, I'd like a word with you."

He wheeled around and went back to his office.

CHAPTER THIRTY-SIX

RUBRIDGE SAT DOWN ACROSS FROM MURDOCH AND immediately fished a cigarette out of his case.

"That was disgusting. Why we have to deal with such guttersnipes I don't know." He lit the cigarette and exhaled a long puff of smoke. "Did you want to talk to me about something? I've got a lot to do."

Murdoch felt like grabbing Rubridge by the collar and shaking him.

"Detective. What is your relationship with Mrs. Payne and her family?"

"Relationship? None."

"She seemed to know you."

"I don't think so. She was so drunk she would have claimed acquaintance with the Pope himself."

Murdoch clenched his teeth. "I don't feel like dancing around this, Rubridge. A neighbour claims to have seen a man fitting your description visiting the Payne house over the past months. She says he was a police officer."

Rubridge continued to draw on his cigarette.

"Wasn't me."

Murdoch leaned forward. "They live on Louisa Street, in case it has slipped your memory."

Rubridge looked up at the ceiling, still smoking. "Louisa? That does ring a bell. I might have been checking on a complaint that she was violating the liquor laws. It was last year."

"I suppose she had second sight, then."

"What do you mean?"

"The Temperance Act hadn't become law yet when Mrs. Flynn says she saw a man looking ever so much like you knocking on the door."

Rubridge was becoming decidedly uncomfortable. In between deep drags of his cigarette, he began twiddling with his moustache.

"They're all alike, those people. They get so drunk they can't tell a Monday from their rear ends. If I did go to Louisa Street, which I'm still not sure I did, it was recently."

"If you went to follow up on a complaint from a member of the public you would have made a report. And I presume I would be able to read it."

Rubridge's answer was a shrug. More fiddling.

Murdoch tapped his fingers on the desk. He'd known this detective ever since he'd taken over as senior of the department. He'd seemed a decent man, no more reliant on liquor than any of the others.

"Roy. You have a good record with the department. I'm going to ask you for the truth. Which can be verified without much difficulty."

"All right. What do you want to know?"

"Did you have carnal knowledge of Winnie Payne?"

Rubridge took a long time to stub out his cigarette.

"No, I did not, and that's the truth."

"Is that what she'll say if she's under oath?"

"Yes, that's what she'll say. I went to that vixen's den because there'd been rumours that a girl was available. At a price. Frankly, I was, shall we say, hungry? In case you're wondering, my wife has gone to live with her parents in Manitoba. It will probably be an indefinite stay. I wish I could say we were happily married before that but, unfortunately, that is not the case. Probably Dick was the only thing keeping us together. His death dissolved that tie."

"I'm sorry," said Murdoch.

Rubridge shrugged. "*Say la vee.* So yes, I went to Louisa Street to see what I could get." He stared at the floor. "Winnie was available all right. She invited me in, discussed terms like she was a shopkeeper . . . then she removed her clothes." He put his hand to his eyes. "God, Murdoch, she's a child. Naked she looked about twelve years old. I couldn't stomach it. I told her to get dressed, paid the agreed amount, and left."

Murdoch looked at the man sitting in front of him.

"You could be dismissed, you know that, don't you?"

"Of course I know it. And right now, I don't give a fart."

Murdoch leaned back in his chair and laced his fingers behind his head. The silence was heavy between them. Then he straightened up.

"Roy, I'm going to order you to take a short leave of absence. You need to get yourself together. We'll say it's a medical leave. You can make up the reason. I want you to take a month off."

Rubridge took another cigarette from his case and lit it. "I hope you don't want thanks. I have no desire to be the subject of office tittle-tattle."

"Nonsense. Everybody knows you've been under strain since Dick was killed."

There was an odd expression on Rubridge's face.

"You don't need to feel sorry for me, Murdoch. It's not sorrow that's rotting out my guts, it's shame."

"What do you mean?"

"The War Office is circumspect in the telegram. 'We regret to say that your son has died.' Not killed in action, notice; not died a hero's death. No phrases like that. I insisted on more information. Perhaps I should have left it and retained my illusions." Rubridge's voice became choked. "You see, Murdoch, my son died at the hands of a firing squad."

"Good God!"

"He was court martialled for deserting his post and thereby contributing to the deaths of several of his fellow soldiers."

"I'm so sorry, Roy."

The detective smiled a chill, bitter smile. "You have no idea what it's like. Your son is a hero. Honoured for his bravery. My son was yellow-bellied. And I have to live with that for the rest of my life."

FROM THE HISTORY OF THE PRINCESS
PATRICIA'S CANADIAN LIGHT INFANTRY

THE ROADS WERE IMPASSABLE AND THE TWO BATTALIONS went forward in single file along a duckboard track traversing a sea of liquid mud. As they passed Wieltje both units ran into heavy German artillery fire, and the 49th began to lose men. To leave the wounded to shift for themselves in the slime would have condemned them to death. Yet every minute of delay meant more casualties, as the Patricias, who had started 1000 yards in the rear, were soon on top of the 49th and in the danger zone. With the finest spirit of inter-regimental chivalry the Commanding Officer of the 49th Battalion gave orders that every wounded man of his unit was at once to be lifted off the duckboards and supported in the mud by two of his comrades until the Patricias were safely past.

CHAPTER THIRTY-SEVEN

Two further telephone calls had gone unanswered, and Murdoch was not surprised that Jack wasn't home when he returned later that night. As before, there was a note propped up on the kitchen table.

Pa,

I seem to be having trouble knitting the ravelled sleeve of care with some solid shut-eye. It seems better when I'm with Percy. Fellow brother in arms, I suppose. Don't worry. This will settle down soon. We're going to Shea's for a show tomorrow evening so I won't see you until Saturday.

Jack

Leaving his door ajar in order to hear anything, Murdoch finally went to bed.

Murdoch awoke at dawn, unrefreshed, and got up right away. Jack's bed had not been slept in.

He made himself a pot of tea and sliced off a couple of pieces of bread. At half past seven, he rang headquarters. Detective Baldy Watson answered.

"Watson, Murdoch here. Is Young on duty with you?"

"Yes, sir."

"As soon as Wallace comes in, which should be in half an hour, I want you and Young to fetch Bessie Schumacher. I don't care if you have to carry her. Take the Ford. She can come in style."

"Yes, sir."

"Has Constable Curnoe come in yet, by any chance?"

"Yes, sir. She just arrived."

"Excellent. Put me through."

Madge answered right away.

"Listen, Madge, I want you to go and see Mrs. Aggett and Mrs. Samuels. I need photographs of their sons. Assure them they will be returned. Be as fast as you can. We're bringing in Bessie Schumacher and I want her to have a look at those pictures."

"What shall I do if the daughter-in-law is back?"

"Let's hope she's not an early riser. If she is up, dampen the fire as much as you can."

"Right away. Oh, are you planning to bicycle here?"

"Yes, of course. Why?"

"Nothing. It's cold out. Bundle up."

"Madge!"

"I know, I know. You're quite capable of looking after yourself but . . ."

"That is true. Don't fret."

But secretly Murdoch was pleased that it mattered to her.

He went out to the back shed and wheeled out the bicycle. It seemed all right. No nicks or dents that hadn't been there before. Wrapping his scarf tight around his face, he set off.

Light was just creeping over the edge of the city; early workers, muffled against the cold, were making their way to their jobs. Murdoch felt a sharp pang of loneliness. He had frequently experienced this many years ago, in the empty hours of the early morning. At times, the pain was as sharp as a physical pain. Amy had entered into that lonely place and, for the most part, she had healed it with her love. The hurt only came back to visit him on occasion, the way a bad bout of rheumatic fever might come back on chilly days and remind the sufferer of its presence.

He increased his speed. He had just rounded the corner onto Albert Street when suddenly he lost his momentum and was forced to stop. His chain had snapped and was dragging on the ground.

Damn. Damn. Damn.

Do you notice you're swearing a lot lately?

CHAPTER THIRTY-EIGHT

For the first time since he could remember, Murdoch was actually late for work. He'd been forced to walk his bicycle the rest of the way. He left it in the courtyard. He'd have to fix it when he had time.

Watson and Young had acted promptly and Bessie Schumacher was already sitting in the room they used for questioning when Murdoch arrived upstairs. Beyond a perfunctory greeting, he didn't pay her any attention, which he knew she was keenly aware of. She remained motionless, however, hands clasped in her lap, back straight against the chair.

Murdoch went into his own office. He'd brought a framed

photograph of Jack and he placed it face up on the desk. He sat still for a few minutes trying to gather his thoughts. He was heartily glad when Madge knocked on the door and came in.

"I've got photographs from both families." She took them out of her briefcase. "Only the older Mrs. Aggett was present."

"Good. Put them on the desk," said Murdoch.

She did so, and gave him a startled look when she saw he'd added the picture of Jack.

"I can't stick my head in the sand, Madge. Let's see what Mrs. Schumacher has to say."

"Shall I bring her in now?"

"If you please. And I'd like you to stay. Take notes."

She left, and Murdoch arranged the three photographs: Arthur Aggett on the left, Jack in the middle, Daniel Samuels on the right. In his photo, Aggett appeared smartly dressed, but at first Murdoch didn't realize the photo must have been taken on his wedding day because the bride at his side had been cut out of the picture. But Arthur was smiling and he looked happy. Damn. He should not have come to such an end. Neither should Daniel. Mrs. Samuels had given them a formal picture obviously taken in a studio. Daniel was holding a scroll in his hand. He, too, looked happy and proud. There was an inscription on a board beside him: "MISS WILDIN'S SECRETARIAL COLLEGE FOR YOUNG LADIES AND GENTLEMEN." This was his graduation picture.

Jack's portrait had been taken a year ago, shortly before

he enlisted, and Murdoch himself had snapped it. It was a sunny day, the lake placid in the background, the trees lush. Jack was perched on his bicycle. Studying the picture more closely, Murdoch was appalled to see how much healthier Jack had looked then. More muscle. Trim, not gaunt. Happy, not haunted.

Damn.

Madge returned with Mrs. Schumacher. Murdoch stood and gestured to the chair opposite.

"Please have a seat, madam."

She did so, and in her unsmiling way she regarded him. She seemed wary but not intimidated.

"May I ask why you have brought me here at such an early hour?"

"Our investigation is not yet finished, Mrs. Schumacher. I was hoping you would be able to help us further."

"I've already given you a complete account."

"Why do I doubt that, madam?"

"I beg your pardon, I don't know what you mean."

"As well as the two men who lied to the constable, I believe there were others at your house on the night Arthur Aggett was killed. You tell me you have a poor memory. I thought if I showed you these photographs, it might help you to recollect who else was there." Murdoch pushed the photographs close to the edge of the desk. "I wonder if you can identify any of the men."

Mrs. Schumacher fished in a beaded reticule and took

out a pair of steel-rimmed spectacles, which she perched on her prominent nose.

"Please take your time, madam. We can take all day if we have to."

His implication was obvious and she flashed him an angry look.

She picked up the photograph of Daniel Samuels first and brought it close to her eyes.

"Yes, I recognize this man. But don't expect me to name him. As I told you, I don't ask names."

"Was he at your establishment on Tuesday night?"

"Yes. He was."

"Did he gamble?"

"As I said, we play whist. No gambling allowed."

Murdoch frowned. She was going to be hard to budge from that position. Too much was at stake for her.

"Was he involved in the argument?"

For the first time she hesitated. "It is possible. I don't recall. He left before the other men."

She studied the photograph again, and for the first time a softer expression crossed her face. "He never appears to be this happy. He is always despondent. He was eager to enlist but I believe he wasn't allowed to because of a dependent mother."

"Did he tell you that?"

"No, it came out when he was, er, discussing the issue of conscription with the others."

"Mrs. Schumacher, I regret to tell you that Daniel Samuels has taken his own life."

She looked shocked, and Murdoch liked her better for it.

"He drowned himself in the City Baths on Wednesday afternoon."

"Why would he do such a thing?"

"We don't know precisely. He didn't leave a note. But he had recently lost his job. Apparently, he was afraid to tell his mother. And, as you say, he seemed to be distressed that he was not able to enlist."

"Yes, he was."

"We found a white feather among his possessions. As you are no doubt aware, these feathers have been handed to young men who have not enlisted. It is an accusation of cowardice. Did one of the others give it to him?"

"Not that I saw. Besides, Detective, I would not have allowed it. I prefer to keep the war out of my house."

This time Murdoch believed she was telling the truth.

He tapped his finger on Arthur Aggett's picture.

"Do you recognize him? Was he playing, er, cards at your house?"

Again she made the gesture of bringing the photograph close to her face.

"It is possible he was. He does look a little familiar, but I wouldn't swear to it."

"We found some foreign coins on his person."

"Foreign?"

"French and English. Do you know how this money came into his possession?"

"Of course not. Why should I?"

Murdoch pushed Jack's photograph closer to her. "Have you seen *this* man before?"

She studied the picture briefly, then a tightening of her lips suggested a smile.

"The young man looks like you, Detective. There is a strong family resemblance. You're playing a little trick on me, aren't you? No, I have not seen him before."

Given how different Jack looked now, Murdoch couldn't totally disbelieve her. He leaned back in his chair.

"It would be a great help to us if we could speak to the two men who were still in your house when the police constable came to investigate. Although they gave false names and false addresses, I assume they live in the vicinity. You would recognize them, I'm sure, if you were to see them again."

She looked uneasy. "I might. As you can see, my eyesight isn't the best."

"Let's put it this way, Mrs. Schumacher. You are a vital witness. Constable Curnoe will accompany you in a search of the area. You will knock on every door on every street in the Ward until we locate these men."

"That is preposterous. I am not a young woman. My legs are bad. It might take hours to do that."

"Yes, it might. But I think you are forgetting that you are in fact facing serious charges. Running a gambling den and selling liquor, both illegal activities, are relatively minor compared to the fact that we are investigating a major crime of homicide—perhaps more than one—and I could have you charged with obstructing justice. You are not telling the truth, and you are making our task much more difficult. I am sure you are the kind of woman who is aware of absolutely everything that happens under your roof. If a fly moves you would see it, however poor your eyesight. I believe you could find those two men without much problem. Your bad legs won't suffer in the least. If they do, we will happily commandeer an invalid chair and push you."

Murdoch tented his fingers. "So, what do you say, Mrs. Schumacher? Is your memory improving, by any chance?"

If looks could kill, he would certainly have been dead several times over. She returned the spectacles to her reticule.

"Very well. I believe I know where they can be found."

"And the other men so far unaccounted for? The ones Mr. Odacre heard involved in an argument?"

"I do remember now. There were two of them. Both returning soldiers. Frankly, I thought they were inebriated. One in particular was belligerent, wanting to pick a fight. It was because of him that the game ended and they all went outside. To brawl."

"Can you describe these two men?"

"Dark-haired, both of them. Thin. Above medium height."

"Did one of them have a scar on his forehead?"

"I don't know. The provoking one was wearing a wool hat

that covered most of his face. Very strange-looking."

"And the other?"

She pointed at the photograph. "That is he. Are you related, Detective, or does this man simply resemble you?"

CHAPTER THIRTY-NINE

Murdoch sent Frank Ashbourne to accompany Mrs. Schumacher and Madge Curnoe. Frank was tall and solidly built. He had the kind of presence that would make troublemakers think twice before getting out of line.

Bessie Schumacher had no trouble finding the house where she "thought" one of her guests lived. He was at home, and seeing his erstwhile hostess with a police officer, he knew enough not to fob them off. His real name was Howard Wasman, and yes, there was a second man, his cousin, Richard Golden. He was at work right now, and they could find him at the Distillery on Parliament Street.

Madge accompanied Mrs. Schumacher home, and Frank

brought Wasman into the station.

Murdoch put him in the room and showed no mercy.

"Name?"

"Howard Wasman."

"Age?"

"Twenty-three."

"Married?"

"No, betrothed though."

"I pity the girl. Where do you work?"

"Gooderham and Worts. I fill fuses."

"Were you at Bessie Schumacher's on Tuesday night?"

"Yes, sir."

"You were gambling and drinking?"

"I . . . er . . ."

Murdoch looked at him sternly. "Don't bother lying to me. You're in enough trouble as it is. If I catch you in a lie your sentence will double."

"My sentence, sir? I didn't know as I was being sentenced."

Wasman had a round, chubby face, curly hair, and dark brown eyes. He didn't seem the least bit vicious. At the moment he was truly scared.

"You had a barney with a young man who was later found stabbed to death. Why did you give a false name to the constable?"

"Just a bit of a joke, sir. And I didn't want my mother to know."

"If you tell me exactly what happened, no lies, no evasions, I will consider staying the charge of homicide."

"Sweet Jesus, sir. I swear I didn't lay a hand on the fellow. It wasn't even him I was arguing with. It was the other two chaps, the soldier and his chum."

"Go on. Start at the beginning."

"Well, the four of us was playing a game of Crown and Anchor. Peaceable as a church picnic."

"What four?"

"Rich and myself, the Jewish lad who goes there regular, and another fellow who's been there a few times."

"Names?"

"Bessie doesn't encourage us to exchange last names. Just first. The Hebrew was Daniel. Other fellow was Arthur. Lucky at the game, he was, I can tell you that. Anyways, we'd been playing about an hour when in comes these two new fellows. They was in civvies but I knew they was soldiers. They was already tanked up, and they downed two cups of Bessie's home brew right off. That stuff will take the paint off your walls so you can imagine what it was doing to them two."

"Hold on," Murdoch interrupted him. "Did these two new men introduce themselves?"

"One said his name was Legion, the other said he was Faust." Wasman tapped his finger to the side of his nose. "They were phony names. They thought we were ignorant most likely. I know that Legion is a name given to the devil and Faust is one of our generals. It didn't matter to me what they called themselves. As long as their money was good, I didn't care."

"And was it? Was the money good, I mean?"

"Yes and no. We played a few rounds, and one of them put some Limey money and Frog money on the board. I didn't want to accept it but Arthur said it was all right, he would. It was as good as Canadian currency these days, said he. He was the one winning so it wasn't no skin off my back. I think he could see they was spoiling for a fight, and if he said no, they would have used that as an excuse."

Wasman glanced at Murdoch to see how his story was going down.

Murdoch simply nodded. "Continue."

"We kept on playing for mebbe another hour. Truth is we were all throwing back Bessie's shots. Oh, not the Hebrew lad. He's teetotal. Then the soldiers started to ride us on account of we weren't enlisted." Wasman's shoulders slumped. "I'm getting mighty sick of this being thrown in my face all the time. Rich and me was given exemptions. We ain't cowards, nor slackers neither, but if you aren't allowed to go because you're doing war work what can you do? You've got to do your bit on this side of the pond. We ain't no conchies or Frenchies. We would have signed up right away if we could have."

"You said that to the men, I presume?"

"Oh yes. We said it more than once, truth be told. But it didn't satisfy them. 'The country needs every man to do his duty. Good men and true are dying by the dozens for want of relief.'" Wasman lowered his head. "We knows that, sir. What are we supposed to do about it?"

"You keep referring to 'they,' in the plural. Were both men

involved in this argument?" Murdoch avoided looking at Madge. "The man calling himself Faust, for instance, what did he have to say for himself?"

Wasman chewed on his lip. "He was more like a *rah, rah* man. The other chap would start up as how conscription was vital and he would say something like 'Go, pal! Tell them. We hates slackers.'"

"Was he also inebriated?"

"Yeah, he was glassy-eyed. But Legion, he was really knocking it back. And it wasn't long before he accuses Rich and me of cheating, which we weren't. Rich didn't like it. Me, I wanted to shake it off. They was mad drunk. But no, 'Let's take this outside,' says Legion. My cousin is slow to rile up, sir, but when he does, you can't pull him back. So Rich won't let that go by and he says, 'Sure thing . . .' At that point the young Jewish lad says he's going home. He don't want no part in it. So off he trots, but not before Legion starts jeering at him. Calls him nasty names." Wasman paused. "Now I must admit, in all fairness, his chum did try to shut him up, but he was too hot by then. Even Arthur was steaming. He didn't like being called a yellow-belly. So outside we all go and there we were shouting and shoving at each other." Wasman actually gave a little grin. "Who knows how far it would have gone, when Bessie came out. She had a bucket of cold water ready to throw over us like we was dogs." He shuddered at the memory. "She ain't a woman you give grief to. Rich, Arthur, and me all quieted down real fast. She told the two soldiers to leave or she'd do worse. So they did. The three of us went back inside. Bessie made us some proper tea this time and made us sit there and drink it."

He halted and ran his hand through his hair. "That's it, sir. I'm terrible sorry Arthur has got himself killed but I swear it wasn't me."

"If not you, who, then? Golden?"

"Oh Lord no. Not Rich. We went home shortly after. He stayed at my house because we weren't in great condition by then, and it's closer. My mother will tell you we was both there."

"You could have gone out again. How would she know?"

Wasman rubbed his head again. His expression was that of a small boy.

"You don't know my ma, sir. She locked up the house and sat in the chair by the front door. She wasn't letting us out for one minute. We had to show up for work the next day and that was all there was to it. Besides, we had no reason to kill that fella, Arthur. Only met him three or four times and he seemed like a straight-ahead chap."

"One more question, Mr. Wasman. Did anybody by the name of Morris Swartz join you at any of Mrs. Schumacher's evenings?"

"Not that I recall. The group don't change that much, truth to tell. Is he in trouble?"

"He was attacked yesterday morning. He is critically injured."

Wasman looked even more frightened. "Do you know who did it?"

"Not yet. I'm hoping that when, or if, he regains consciousness, he'll be able to identify his attacker."

"If you're looking for a suspect, sir," said Wasman, lowering his voice, "I'd say take a gander at them two soldiers. They was real riled up. In a killing frame of mind, if you ask me."

Murdoch couldn't help himself. "Both of them?"

"Well, more the scarred up one, mostly, but yes, both."

"The scarred up one?"

"Mr. Legion. He was wearing this funny hat thing covering his face but it came off in the pushing. He has a nasty scar on his forehead. Shaped like a V."

Murdoch had been intending to keep young Wasman in the cells for the night to scare him into honesty, but after this interview he knew he didn't need to. He sent him home and directed Ashbourne to bring in Rich Golden. He'd made sure Bessie Schumacher had been kept in the station, and now he brought her back into his office. He asked Madge to be present. This time, Mrs. Schumacher offered little resistance, and after a few preliminary skirmishes, she admitted to everything, including selling liquor.

"So you were lying to me the whole time? I could charge you with trying to pervert the course of justice."

"Yes, you could," she said, unfazed. "But that would mean a trial, and if I have to be on the stand a lot of muck might come out. Muck involving the Toronto constabulary."

Murdoch was furious. "You're trying to threaten me, Mrs. Schumacher, and I won't have it. I am going to charge you. I don't care what *muck*, as you call it, will come out. You will receive a summons, and your establishment will be closed until such time as the government of this province sees fit to rescind the temperance laws. Is that clear?"

She shrugged. "Doesn't really matter to me. I was considering joining my sister-in-law in Alberta anyway. There's more opportunity there."

"I'd wait to make your plans if I were you. You don't know how long you will be in the Mercer Reformatory."

When Madge came back into his office, Murdoch was standing over the chess board. At least he could see this next move clearly. He was about to checkmate his opponent.

"Do you want a cup of tea?" Madge asked.

Murdoch turned around and went back to his desk.

"No. No thanks."

Madge hesitated. "Will, I've never seen you this impatient. Not even with a tough piece of work such as Bessie Schumacher."

Murdoch sighed. "You're right. I let her get to me, didn't I. Essentially she was trying to blackmail me, and I can't stand that. Where is she?"

"She's left."

"I'm sorry, Madge. It's just that I'm . . ."

"I know what you are," she said. "You're worried sick about your son. But I already told you what I thought about that. He's a good lad, I'm sure of it."

"I'd feel a lot better if we had a chance to have a good chinwag, but so far, we've been reduced to writing notes."

"Do you want somebody else to take over the case?"

"Good God, no, Madge. At least, not yet. I don't want any surprises." He smiled at her. "But thanks. What would I do without you?"

She shrugged. "Suffer?"

CHAPTER FORTY

MURDOCH'S DESK PHONE RANG. IT WAS CONSTABLE Wallace.

"Sir, there's a Captain Runcie on the telephone. He wonders if you could drop by the Armouries at your convenience."

"Why?"

"He didn't say exactly. Just that there is something he'd like to discuss with you."

"Ring him back, then. Tell him I'll be over at two o'clock. Oh, Constable, a couple more things. If there is any word from the hospital about Morris Swartz, let me know at once. And will you keep trying to ring my house? If my son answers, put him through right away."

"Yes, sir. And I almost forgot, sir. Sergeant Allen telegraphed. He wondered if you had made your next move."

"I have. Do you want me to write it down?"

"No, I'll remember. I've been following quite avidly, if I might put it that way, sir."

"You may. I'm happy to hear it matters to somebody. All right, here's the move. Knight to c 5. Check."

"And checkmate, unless I'm mistaken, sir."

"Well done, Wallace. You should be promoted."

"Thank you, sir."

Murdoch would have to say that the remainder of the day didn't feel very productive. The weapon used to kill Arthur Aggett had not been found. The police laboratory had not been able to get any clear fingerprint from the brick used to batter Morris Swartz, and it wasn't likely they would, given the rough surface. Morris himself was still unconscious. Jack was still not answering the telephone, and Murdoch had no idea how to locate his friend. It took him a long time to fix his bicycle, although it shouldn't have.

Detective Lennox seemed to be coughing and sneezing over every surface, and by a quarter to two Murdoch was glad to have a change of scene. He set off to meet Captain Runcie.

When the Armouries had opened, there had been a hullabaloo about how grand they were, what a jewel in the city's crown, but Murdoch had never liked them. The castellated towers, poor imitations of a medieval castle, aggravated him.

Surely the architects could have come up with something more contemporary. He found the squat main building with its enormous drill hall and steel girders ugly and without grace. When he had fumed about it to Amy she had laughed at him.

"What do you expect from a fortification? You can't look as if a strong breeze could blow you away. If you don't puff yourself up, how are your enemies going to be intimidated?"

"What enemies? We are not going to be besieged, surely? We're all chummy with the Yanks now, and the natives don't seem ready to throw us out."

The building was twenty-three years old now, but on this damp, grey afternoon the smooth sandstone facade gleamed as red and raw as the day it was built. Time could never soften it. Only the greying trim looked as if it were succumbing to age, and that was more shabby than enhancing.

The main entrance was arched, wide enough to admit a marching band, and would have gone nicely with a portcullis and drawbridge.

Murdoch approached the pedestrian door tucked into the niche of the tower. A uniformed soldier stepped out of a sentry box.

"Please state your business, sir."

"I'm Detective William Murdoch from the Toronto police department. Captain Runcie has expressed a desire to see me."

"One moment."

The soldier turned smartly and re-entered the box. It meant he had his back to Murdoch, which confirmed his opinion that the whole damn contraption was for show. A huge toy manned by toy soldiers. If he had been a serious malcontent, he could easily have jumped on the sentry and disarmed him. Didn't he know the basic rules of engagement? Never turn your back to a stranger.

The sentry consulted a piece of paper and came back out.

"Yes, sir. Captain Runcie is expecting you. Go through the door. Down the hall. Turn left. The captain's office is the third one down." He saluted smartly. Not quite sure what sort of return was called for, Murdoch simply nodded and headed for the door.

The hallway was rather dark but he could see it was lined with framed photographs. Important military men, by the looks of them.

He followed instructions, and as he turned into the next hall a door opened and a man that had to be Captain Runcie stepped out. He wore a beautifully tailored uniform and sported a thick moustache waxed into points at the ends. He was younger than Murdoch had expected and, despite the military moustache, not particularly soldierly in bearing, being rather stoop-shouldered. He immediately stretched out his hand.

"Detective Murdoch, thank you for coming. Please enter."

The office was small with spartan furnishings. A large map pinned to one wall dominated the room. Murdoch recognized it immediately: the Western Front, heavily marked with the lines of battle of the Canadian troops. He'd spent many hours himself poring over such a map.

"I know your time is valuable, Detective, so I'll get right to the point." He went behind his desk.

"How can I be of service, Captain?"

Runcie plopped down in his chair and started to fidget with a paper knife.

"I think we have had a robbery."

"You *think*, sir? You mean you're not sure?"

"Precisely." Briefly, his eyes met Murdoch's. "What has happened is this. We have a store of ammunition in the basement. Rifles, bullets, and so forth. When the troops were training here we would use it for certain drills. Lately, of course, all that is taking place over the pond, so we have less call on our supplies. They are used mostly for special occasions when we call up our reserve militia. We fire off some rifles or cannons in a salute. We intend to do that at the medal presentation ceremony on Saturday, for instance."

He halted and his gaze drifted over to the wall map. He seemed so lost in thought that Murdoch wondered if he were ever coming back to the point.

"You were saying, sir?"

"Ah yes. Beg your pardon, Detective Murdoch. Got a bit distracted there. My brother has earned himself a medal at Vimy. Lucky fellow, to be able to do his bit. Me, I'm waiting for my call-up but so far no luck. Tricky knee. Looks like I might be stuck here until the end of the war."

"Let's hope that isn't too far off."

"Quite so. Just hope I don't miss it. Anyway, as I was saying …

this morning I had a telephone call from the munitions depot in Ottawa. There appears to be a discrepancy in our accounts. It has specifically to do with the amount of gun cotton explosive we ordered. According to Ottawa, they sent nineteen boxes. Our quartermaster, Sergeant Campbell, says we received only eighteen, and that's what he paid for." Runcie gave Murdoch a wry smile. "I know what you're thinking. These are likely small errors in bookkeeping." He tapped the knife on the desk. "To tell you the truth, this puts me in an awkward position. Sergeant Campbell is a good man, very good. He went through the Boer War and all that. But . . ." Runcie tapped his head with his forefinger. "Unfortunately, mental complexity isn't what he's good at. Generally speaking he does a capable job with keeping account of the supplies and so forth, but sometimes there have been errors. Easily corrected, mind you, but he always takes umbrage at any suggestion he's not up to the job."

"Wouldn't you be better off consulting a bookkeeper, Captain?"

Runcie flashed a smile. "I see your point, Detective, but I thought it best to begin by speaking with a member of our police force. Hence my telephone call."

"But if I understand correctly, Captain, you don't know if there's even been a crime committed."

"Quite so. Better safe than sorry, that's my motto."

"There are no other discrepancies? All other supplies are accounted for?"

"Quite so."

"Just one box of gun cotton that *might* be missing."

"I know it all sounds frightfully trivial, tempest in a teapot sort of thing, but Sergeant Campbell would be much eased if he knew we were doing a thorough investigation. Matter of pride for him."

Murdoch could see what was happening. An old-timer, lots of bristle and indignation if impugned. A young captain, already feeling insecure about his own capabilities. Bring in a detective. He might as well have been mediating between Lottie and Arthur Aggett.

Something must have been showing on Murdoch's face, because the captain became flustered and he got to his feet abruptly. "Tell you what, better if you hear from the man himself. I'll take you to Sergeant Campbell and he'll apprise you of the details. He said he'd be in the guard room. I have a meeting to go to, can't avoid it, otherwise I'd sit in."

Captain Runcie escorted Murdoch to the guard room and introduced him to the quartermaster before scuttling away. Campbell, a big-boned, kilted Scotsman, turned to Murdoch.

"I certainly hope we can get to the bottom of this, Detective. I don't like it being implied that I'm not properly taking care of things."

Murdoch almost said "Quite so," but he stopped himself just in time. He took out his notebook.

"Will you give me more details about the missing item, Sergeant?"

"The delivery arrived yesterday. I ordered an extra supply

because of the coming medal ceremony. We are going to give a demonstration." Campbell rolled his *r*s to the point of unintelligibility.

Murdoch raised his eyebrows. "With live ammunition?"

"It's *verrry* safe, don't worry. We just discharge a few cannons. People enjoy it." He chuckled. "That is, as long as they're standing on a dry platform, not in several inches of cold mud in a trench."

"Who checked the delivery?"

Campbell swelled his chest a little. "Why, it was myself, of course. I always do it myself. And I assure you, what was delivered matched what was on the tally sheet."

"And that was checked again when the boxes were stored?"

"*Corrrect*. Everything is transferred from the delivery wagon to the storage area in the basement. The tally is checked again."

"And they matched?"

"Aye. I have done a recount since the captain told me about this telephone call. The tally is exactly the same as at delivery. Nothing is missing."

Murdoch sighed. "Let me get this straight, Quartermaster. One box of gun cotton seems to be unaccounted for. If the delivery was correct and checked in as you say it was, that must mean it went missing somewhere in the transport from the depot in Ottawa to here. Unless it was taken from the Armouries since yesterday."

Murdoch had barely got his words out when the sergeant interjected. Definitely bristling.

"That is quite impossible, sir. As I have just said, the tallies were totally in order from arrival to storage. And nobody could steal from the basement. There is a guard there at all times."

"Do you have an explanation, Sergeant?"

"In my opinion, sir, those Ottawa folks couldn't count their own toes and get it right. I'm catching mistakes all the time. They just want to shift the blame onto somebody else."

"Can I take a look at the tally sheet, Sergeant?"

"I have it right here, sir."

Campbell removed a sheet of paper from his jacket and handed it to Murdoch.

"We had several items delivered." He pointed. "They are listed on the left with the number of said item. This first column is ticked by the Ottawa depot. This second column I mark myself. This third column is ticked by the guard in the storage area after he does his count."

Murdoch surveyed a rather untidy-looking sheet. The writer had been having trouble with his inkwell and there were a few scattered blots.

"You're *correct*, sir," said Campbell, even though Murdoch hadn't spoken. "I've complained several times about the scrawl they send me. Them Frenchies don't speak proper English is the problem. But that's where they've written gun cotton boxes and the number. See, it says eighteen."

He was right about the scrawl but the number did seem to match.

"Could you describe for me what the box of gun cotton looks like, Sergeant?"

"The boxes themselves are not large, about the size of a child's pencil box."

"My knowledge of explosives is a little limited, Sergeant, but as I understand it, gun cotton must be ignited to be effective. It will not be activated simply by impact, for instance."

"That is *corrrect*."

"Would there be sufficient gun cotton in each box to create an explosion?"

"Aye."

"How big an explosion would you say?" Murdoch asked.

"It would be sufficient to kill or seriously injure anybody within three or four feet."

There was a note of pride in his voice. "Very useful to our lads, this. Earlier in the war, it saved a lot of lives, destroyed a lot of Huns. You see, if supplies of explosives ran out, the men would improvise their own bombs."

Murdoch murmured encouragement. "That so?"

"Aye. They called them jam-tin bombs." Campbell chuckled. "Sounds funny, I know, but the reason is they made use of discarded jam or beef tins, you see. And there are lots of those in the trenches." He began to explain, using his hands to mime each step of the process. "First off, they stuff a tin with gun cotton. Then they put that tin inside a second one. This tin contains nails, the sharper and rustier the better. Next they light a fuse—ordinary string will do—and then they chuck the whole thing into the enemy line." He pretended to make the throw. "*Poof.* Lots of dead Huns."

This time Murdoch did say "Quite so." He closed his notebook. "You've been most helpful, Sergeant. I wonder if you wouldn't mind showing me the delivery and storage areas before we wrap this up."

As Campbell had claimed, the basement looked impregnable. A guard was stationed outside. Inside, there were only two narrow windows, both heavily barred. The door was solid steel. Murdoch didn't think anything could have been stolen from there once it was stored. Rows of boxes containing various munitions were labelled and neatly stacked on shelves. The gun cotton was indeed packed in a container small enough to be a pencil box. Campbell immediately insisted on re-counting. Eighteen it was.

The sergeant escorted him by way of a narrow corridor around to the rear of the building, where there was a small courtyard. He pointed to a steel trap door close to the building.

"That opens onto the stairs to the basement. As soon as we've unloaded, the trap door is barred on both sides. Nobody can get in, nobody can get out."

"Was yesterday's a smooth delivery?" Murdoch asked.

For the first time, the sergeant hesitated.

"Truth is, sir, lately, they're never smooth. I've been asking Captain Runcie to give us a barrier across the road in, but so far he hasna done so. There's a group of agitators and anarchists who have a bee in their bonnets that this war mustn't continue. They do everything they can to disrupt normal operations. On the last two deliveries they blocked the steps to the basement so we couldn't unload. I don't know what good they think that will do."

"Really? I hadn't heard about this. Did you call the police?"

"Nay need. We deal with it ourselves. There's only a handful of them. Mostly lassies. I ask them to move aside, politely, and if they refuse I just call up my guards and get them out of the way."

"By force."

"Aye. Sometimes my men get overly excited and some of the lassies have fallen to the ground. It's nothing we like to have happen, but it has."

"And this is what happened yesterday?"

"It did. Shameful. There was a banquet going on in the hall. Sir Harry Lauder was present. These lassies were an embarrassment to our city."

"How long did all this take?"

"Longer than usual. In this case, they did appear to be particularly determined. It took us a good three quarters of an hour to get them to disperse."

"Where was the delivery wagon?"

Campbell walked away to the other side of the courtyard. "He had to pull up over here. Usually he can be right near the stairs."

"You then began to check the tally?"

"Aye."

"Where was the sheet?"

"It's kept on a hook in the back of the wagon."

"And if I know the protesters, they were probably shouting, waving placards, and so on?"

"Aye, that they were."

"Could this have distracted you? Forced you to make an error in the count?" Murdoch knew he was likely putting his hand in the lion's mouth with this question.

The sergeant flushed. "Let me put it this way. I've done my service in the Boer War. Believe me, a group of lassies has nothing on a group of commandos if distraction is what they're after. I could concentrate standing in the flames of Hell if I had to."

"When your guards came to deal with these women, did you go over to help them?"

"Yes, I did. I dinna know what the world's coming to, sir. A young lassie had got one of my men by the nose. I swear she would not have hesitated to break it if she could have. And she was a wee slip of a thing."

"And that's when you went to intervene?"

"Aye. Me and the driver both did. He took her arm and I gave her a slap. That made her let go in a hurry."

"Did you take the tally sheet with you?"

Campbell paused. "No, I believe I left it in the wagon."

"Did you close the rear doors of the wagon?"

Another pause, then Campbell said, with less confidence, "I canna remember exactly. I may have."

"I quite understand, Sergeant. What was happening in the melee must have been compelling your attention."

"Aye, it was."

"Did you notice anybody standing near the wagon?"

"No."

As they were on the exact spot where all this had taken place, Murdoch could see that if somebody had got to the wagon he would have been shielded from view, especially if the rear doors were open.

The sergeant shook his head. "I dinna understand it, sir. All at once they all started to shove toward the wagon. I don't know what they were thinking of doing, but I couldn't have them destroying government property. One of them was pushing a perambulator and she actually used it like it was a battering ram. We had an awful struggle to get them out of the courtyard."

"Were they all women who were demonstrating?"

"Mostly. I did see a couple of men. Two, mebbe three. God forbid. One of them took a hold of the lassie with the perambulator and steered her away. I am just hoping he gave her what for and a smack or two."

"Could you describe him?"

"I must say I wasn't giving him much mind given what was happening all round. But I suppose he was about as tall as me. He was wearing a cap, dark coat. That's all I can tell you, really. If he's connected with a harridan like that lassie, I do sincerely have pity for the man." He frowned. "If you can do anything to control these rabble-rousers, sir, me and my men would most appreciate it. They don't like having to lay hands on lassies in anger any more than I do."

There seemed no more to be gleaned, and Murdoch left him to go back to his duties.

Captain Runcie was not to be found. He'd have to telephone him later with his conclusions. The whole situation was very troubling. It was hard to be sure if, in fact, a theft had taken place, but it was not impossible. A small box was easily removed, and the demonstrators had provided a nice diversion. Intended or coincidental? But if intended, to what purpose? Sergeant Campbell's description of the jam-tin bombs was disturbing. Easy to make and capable of causing serious damage. Murdoch hoped he wasn't dealing with an anarchist.

But that wasn't the only thing that bothered him. There was that detail Campbell had mentioned about the man pulling the demonstrator away from the scene. And yet there were probably dozens of young men walking about the city who were tall and who wore caps and dark overcoats. And to Murdoch's knowledge, Jack had no relationship with any young lady who would be pushing a perambulator.

But one more check was in order. He mounted his bicycle and headed for Oak Street. When he had last visited the home of the Williams family, Fiona had been a child. She was all grown up now. And did not hesitate to make her anti-war sentiments known.

CHAPTER FORTY-ONE

JACK NEEDED TO WALK. HE WAS COLD BUT HE DIDN'T care. This time, he welcomed the feeling.

Shortly before he was shipped out to Halifax, he'd gone to Mass at his old church and found some comfort in the familiar rituals. But once at the Front, he hadn't had much to do with the army chaplains. They had come in search of him, though— one of the flock, as one priest had said. Initially, he'd made his confession, taken the wafer and the penance, never a stringent one. No priest wanted to add to the hardships so many of the men were already suffering.

Today he was approaching St. Paul's once again. Against the grey clouds and gathering gloom, the elegant shape of the cupola was comfortingly familiar. As he drew closer, he found himself singing softly.

> O little town of Bethlehem
> How still we see thee lie!
> Above thy deep and dreamless sleep
> The silent stars go by.

It was his favourite carol.

Were the people truly dreamless? What did that mean? He could barely recall a time when he'd had no dreams, although they seemed more like memories than dreams.

He sang, *"O little town of Ontario, how still we see thee lie."*

A few people were scurrying into the church, and as the doors opened, a pungent waft of incense drifted out. Slight as it was, it made him cough. He'd always liked the smell of the incense when he was serving as an altar boy. He'd admired the priest, Father McKenna, too. They'd exchanged letters while Jack was in France, and the priest was aware he'd been wounded and was returning to Canada. He would be expecting to see him. He'd be expecting to celebrate Mass with him. But Jack couldn't participate in the Mass without going first to confession.

He turned on his heel and left.

THE CHOSEN

I don't understand why I was the one got
    through
And not you.
As far as vice and virtue go
We were about the same.
Although I thought you had the edge
In the goodness game.
You sent away for improving books.
You were the first to pet
The bone-thin dogs
Left behind in the villages we passed on the
    way.
"Is there anything you can say?"
I asked the padre.
"An explanation of some kind?
You supposedly being in the know."
"We cannot see what's in God's mind,"
He replied.
"You must trust in the Divine Plan."
A lot of blokes believe the shell's got your
    name on it
Or it doesn't.
If it's your time, so be it.
I've seen men with their number
On so many bullets.
They ended up in pieces.
I suppose that's considered certainty.

So if I go over the top will my fate find me?
Or if I stay here
At the bottom of this stinking pit,
Will the artillery do it?
"You're being stupid," says my pal.
"You can't think like that.
Just keep your head down,
Dive low when you have to
And kill all the Krauts you can."
"Is that considered a plan?"
I asked.

CHAPTER FORTY-TWO

MOLLY WILLIAMS HERSELF ANSWERED THE DOOR. FOR A moment she looked at Murdoch in bewilderment, then she broke into a smile.

"As I live and breathe, it's Will Murdoch. I can't believe it's been such a long time since we saw you. Come in, come in."

"I'm sorry, I can't stay, Molly. I wonder if Fiona is at home."

"Oh no. She's at work. She's a telephone operator at Eaton's."

"Was she at work yesterday?"

Molly frowned. "She was."

"What time does she get off?"

"Six o'clock. Now, Will, you can't come dropping in like this after so much time and start asking questions about my

301

daughter. I do know you're a detective, after all. Has Fiona done something wrong?"

Murdoch was still standing on the doorstep. Molly hadn't changed much since he'd seen her last. A little stouter perhaps, her hair a little grey, but she had the same brown eyes her daughter had. He remembered how much he'd always liked her.

"Molly, I do apologize. I ran into Fiona at the train station recently. I wanted to follow up on some incidents that have occurred."

"To do with the war, I imagine? She's got strong opinions has that daughter of mine."

"Precisely. I can come back later."

"She won't be home this evening. She's participating in a Red Cross fundraising event at Shea's Theatre." Molly smiled. "Would you believe she's a ventriloquist? The only girl in the country, more than likely."

"Will you tell her I'll come by another time?"

"Only if you promise to stay longer."

"I promise."

He left. In spite of the circumstances, he felt warmed by the encounter.

CHAPTER FORTY-THREE

In spite of the best efforts of both Ruth and Peter Fenwell, Murdoch thought the dinner party was a dismal failure. There were just the four of them: Murdoch, the Fenwells, and a Miss Grace Cotterill. She was a friend of Ruth's, and Peter had mentioned her before: "A nice woman, very devout." As his intention to matchmake was pretty obvious, Murdoch was not surprised that Miss Cotterill had also been invited to dinner. She was middle-aged, neatly dressed and coiffed, and by no means unattractive. She appeared, however, to have only one interest in life, other than the Church itself, and that was the priest she tended to. She introduced his name at every opportunity.

"Father Philip gave a wonderful homily on just that subject," she said after Fenwell had (ill-advisedly) raised the issue of conscription.

"Is he for or against?" Fenwell asked.

"Most definitely for," said Miss Cotterill, emphatically. "He considers it the sacred duty of our young men to take up arms against those devils incarnate."

"Are the Germans truly devils?" Murdoch said. "I am sure many of those young Germans dying in the trenches are devout Catholics, not to mention true patriots. Their priests are probably exhorting them to kill as many of us as they can. Aren't we all brothers in Christ?"

Miss Cotterill shook her head. "Father Philip thinks not. The Huns do not deserve our charity. They are barbarians. The barbarians were the ones who killed our Lord. We must root them out."

Murdoch saw a look of dismay pass between Peter and his wife. Miss Cotterill's pale skin was pink and blotchy with the intensity of her fervour.

"More custard, Will?" piped up Ruth. "There's plenty left."

Miss Cotterill beamed. "Father Philip adores vanilla custard. He says it's his one vice."

Murdoch couldn't resist. "Lucky him."

She blinked. "I beg your pardon?"

"To have merely one vice."

Fenwell chuckled falsely. "Speaking of vices, I'd rather like to indulge in a pipe. Care to join me, Will? I usually smoke on the front porch. Ruth doesn't care for tobacco that much."

Murdoch laid his napkin on the table. "Thanks, Peter, but I must confess I'm ready to call it a day. I should be getting home."

"I should go too," said Miss Cotterill. "The day starts early for Father Philip, and I like to be ready with some tasty breakfast for after his Mass."

"I'm sure William will escort you home, Grace," said Ruth.

"Of course," said Murdoch with a smile, but he groaned inwardly. How the heck was he going to get this woman to her house without offending her, or worse, murdering her on the way?

The Fenwells lived in a modest row house on Duke Street near Jarvis. The most direct route to the rectory was to walk up Jarvis and turn onto Shuter. Murdoch offered Miss Cotterill his arm and they proceeded in silence for a while. He couldn't call it a companionable silence.

The night was overcast and cold. Not many people were out and about, although lights shone in many of the houses they passed. Jarvis Street north of Queen was often referred to as "the widow's walk," as so many wealthy widows had taken up residence there. Many of them had settled into the grand apartments that lined each side of the street. He thought of asking Miss Cotterill why she thought the apartments were named "Royal" and "King" and "Marlborough," but he wasn't sure if she'd understand his little joke. Amy would have been the first to comment on it, of course. Feeling he was being discourteous, he searched for a neutral topic of conversation.

"That was a delicious meal Ruth served, wasn't it?"

"It most certainly was. Roast pork is Father Philip's favourite dish. He will be pleased to know I was able to partake of it."

Murdoch already knew that the absent priest favoured parsnip soup and cornbread, and that he liked vanilla custard, but he didn't feel like enumerating the vegetables to determine how the man of God felt about roast potatoes and buttered carrots. Another silence fell.

As they approached the rectory, Miss Cotterill said, "Father Philip kindly allows me the use of the parlour once a week if I wish to entertain guests." She had turned a little pink. "I wonder if I might have the temerity to invite you for tea tomorrow afternoon. I usually serve at four o'clock."

"Thank you so much, Miss Cotterill. Unfortunately, I'll have to keep the day clear. My son Jack is to be honoured at Queen's Park. He has been awarded the Military Medal."

"Oh my. That is wonderful. Was there a particular battle? Was it at Passchendaele?"

"No. He was wounded shortly before that."

"My, my. You must be so proud of him. How was he injured?"

Murdoch groaned to himself. "To tell you the truth, Miss Cotterill, I don't know. He's only been home since Tuesday and we haven't had a chance to talk about anything. He has a ruddy deep scar on his arm but I've yet to be informed as to how he acquired it."

"I see . . . Is he recovered, would you say?"

"Not completely. It will take time."

"I shall ask Father Philip to say a special novena for him."

"Thank you. That is very kind."

They arrived at the door and she turned to look at him. "Perhaps the week following might be more suitable for tea?"

"Thank you, Miss Cotterill. Would you mind if I don't make any definite plans at the moment? It's hard for me to foresee what is happening more than one day ahead."

"Of course, Mr. Murdoch. I quite understand."

He could see the wistfulness of her expression. She held out her hand.

"That was a most pleasant evening. I do hope our paths will cross again before too long."

"I'm sure they will."

He shook hands, tipped his hat, and stood back while she let herself in.

When he'd determined she was safely inside he turned to head for home. He knew he'd hurt her feelings, and he felt like a cad. Nevertheless, he'd have to tell Peter that under no circumstances should he and Ruth play matchmaker again.

That is, unless they were able to link Murdoch up with some exotic pagan who wasn't in love with her priest.

CHAPTER FORTY-FOUR

MURDOCH LOOKED AT HIS WATCH. NOT YET NINE o'clock. On impulse he decided to head for Shea's Theatre. If the mountain wouldn't come to Muhammad, maybe Muhammad could go to the mountain. Or something to that effect. If he had to handcuff his son to a chair, he was determined to spend more than ten minutes with him.

When he got to the theatre the show was well underway, but he insisted on being admitted, muttering vaguely about being a police officer. An elderly usher, clucking his tongue, showed him to the back row. He shuffled past the somewhat disgruntled patrons to the one empty seat.

The theatre was packed. All around him Murdoch could

make out well-dressed men and beautifully coiffed women in formidable hats. He had the sense of much velvet and silk. The air had never smelled so pleasant and flowery.

There was a considerable sprinkling of young men in uniform. Many of the civilians were wearing black armbands.

He had come in during one of the acts. On stage, a young girl with golden ringlets and a huge pink bow in her hair was singing "Keep the Home Fires Burning." For a child she had an astonishingly big voice, and she sang the lyrics in such a heartfelt way that Murdoch actually felt a lump in his throat. The woman directly in front of him was crying, wiping at her eyes with a lacy handkerchief. In vaudeville style, a board at the side of the stage announced the girl was "EVANGELINE, The Singing Sensation with the Voice of an Angel." She finished the last lines, her voice soaring to rival that of John McCormack.

> Turn the dark cloud inside out
> 'Til the boys come home.

There was tumultuous applause.

"That was wonderful," whispered the woman beside Murdoch as she, too, dabbed at her eyes.

A portly man came on stage and stood beside the girl. He was dressed in a khaki outfit that suggested an officer's uniform without actually being one. He held up his hands for silence.

Somebody in the audience shouted, "Encore!"

"She'll be back, ladies and gentlemen."

The call was taken up by others. "Encore! Bravo! Bravo!"

Miss Evangeline gave a little curtsey. The man had a whispered consultation with her, then nodded at the pianist, who was obviously expecting this. The audience fell silent.

Before Evangeline could burst forth again, a man near the front shouted, "How about 'Tipperary'? Army version." He started to sing, "*It's a long way to tickle Mary.*"

There was a palpable ripple of shock through the audience. Murdoch realized that the young man was sitting next to Jack. It was his friend Percy. There was a hiss of disapproval directed at him, and Murdoch could see that Jack was trying to keep Percy quiet. Fortunately, the portly man on stage was an experienced and consummate master of ceremonies.

"Must be one of our gallant lads. He might have a bit of shell shock, folks, so let's not take him too seriously. Maybe, given the circumstances, Evangeline will take a break."

"Shame," called Murdoch's neighbour, stirred to make a public display.

The MC held up his hands again. "Don't fret, you'll hear her again. In the meantime, feast your eyes, gentlemen . . . and ladies, I know you will enjoy this too. The Five Fabulous Fantastic Farmerettes will do their dance number, and then we will have Miss Fiona Williams with her extraordinary ventriloquism act. So, on with the show. Let's not forget why we're here tonight. When Miss Williams concludes her act, we will ask you to remain in the theatre and the Farmerettes will come around with their buckets. They will encourage you to give as generously as I know you can."

Murdoch scanned the rest of the audience and was surprised to see that Roy Rubridge was seated in an aisle seat about six rows from the front. He was looking unusually nobby in a dark suit and white cravat but appeared to be alone.

"Ladies and gentlemen," the MC continued, "the Farmerettes are going to give you their very own version of a well-known song." He put his finger to his lips. "It's a tiny bit naughty but we don't mind, do we? They will return and sing 'Pack Up Your Troubles,' and, by popular request, will conclude our evening with another round of 'Keep the Home Fires Burning.' I know you're going to love them. Ladies and gentlemen, put your hands together and give a hearty welcome to these splendid young ladies."

More piano music and loud applause.

The MC offered his hand to little Evangeline and escorted her off the stage to much enthusiastic clapping. From the other side of the stage the Five Farmerettes marched out. Now Jack and Percy were half standing, twisting around, apparently engaged in an argument with a white-haired man behind them. That is to say Percy was, while Jack was clearly trying to appease him. Murdoch wondered if he should go and intervene but was saved by the entrance of the dancing girls. The two boys resumed their seats, as did the man behind, whose wife seemed to be importuning him.

Unsettled, Murdoch turned his attention back to the stage.

The Farmerettes were certainly a showy bunch. They wore

blue, loose-fitting tunics over short white skirts and dark stockings. Each wore a straw sun hat pinned at an impossible angle to the back of her head. They were carrying buckets and pitchforks which they wielded in unison as they stamped in a line, singing "Mademoiselle from Armentières." The young women who'd volunteered to help with the hard work of food production during the war had been given the name of "farmerettes," but there was something about this five— the shortness of their skirts, their gestures, and the way they responded to the audience—that made Murdoch doubt they had seen much, if anything, of genuine country life. Everything about them said burlesque, not berry picking.

> She had four chins, her knees would knock,
> And her face would stop a cuckoo clock.

They gesticulated with great animation to the audience, encouraging them to join in. Everybody responded willingly, if not with great musicality.

> Hinky, dinky, parley-voo.

The Farmerettes did a few high kicks in unison.

> You might forget the gas and shells, parley-voo,
> You might forget the gas and shells, parley-voo,
> You might forget the groans and yells

But you'll never forget the mademoiselles.
Hinky, dinky, parley-voo.

Percy leaped to his feet. "Hear, hear!"

He sat back down heavily. Murdoch couldn't say whether Jack had pulled him or he fell back. He was certainly acting like somebody who was thoroughly inebriated.

The Farmerettes turned their backs to the audience and waggled their comely rear ends. Big laughter at that. Then, still singing, they marched off stage.

Hinky, dinky, parley-voo.

The MC bounced back onto the stage, clapping.

"Give a big hand, ladies and gentlemen, for our gallant young women. They are doing vital work for the war effort."

When the applause had died down the MC waved his arm to the wings.

"They will be back. In the meantime, here is a show you are going to enjoy. Miss Fiona Williams and her companion, the chatty Miss Happ."

There was more applause, and Fiona walked onto the stage carrying her dummy in one hand and a stool in the other. She sat down and placed the dummy in her lap.

"Ladies and gentlemen, allow me to introduce Miss Happ, whom you probably know from her ever-popular column, "Don't Worry," appearing in the *Toronto Daily Star*, wherein she replies to letters from both men and women who are in need of answers."

Fiona turned her head in the direction of the dummy. "Miss Happ, say hello to the audience."

She manoeuvred the lever in the dummy's back that manipulated the arm and Miss Happ waved. Many in the audience waved back.

"Miss Happ, you kindly said you were going to give us some examples of the letters you receive. Did you bring them?"

"I did, but ye'll have ta read them. You canna move my jaw and have me hold them at the same time."

That got a laugh.

Murdoch thought Fiona was doing an excellent job of hiding any lip movements. And the dummy's Scottish accent was funny. He could hear echoes of Molly Williams.

Fiona had brought a satchel with her and she reached into it with her free hand and pulled out a sheet of paper.

"How about this one? It's from a K.W."

Fiona rolled the dummy's eyes from side to side. It was actually comical and there was some laughter. She manipulated the jaw.

"Oh, aye. K.W. I remember that one. At first I thought it might be from Kaiser Wilhelm himself. After all, my column is called 'Don't Worry.' I thought he might be in need of an answer."

Percy whistled shrilly.

Fiona had Miss Happ face the audience.

"Wha' should I tell him, ladies and gentlemen? Should the Kaiser wurry?"

A few bolder people shouted out, "Yes!" There was more applause. So far so good. Fiona was certainly winning them over.

"All right. Let's go on." Fiona fished out another piece of paper from the satchel.

"*Dear Miss Happ, I am engaged to a wonderful young woman. However, since I have been over here, I find more and more that I have become reliant on our daily rum ration that the captain doles out in the morning. It cheers me up enormously. Same with the other chaps. My question is this. My fiancée is strict temperance, as was I before I came overseas. Should I tell her about my secret vice or let sleeping dogs lie? Yours, B.D., Corporal.*"

"What was your answer?" Fiona asked Miss Happ.

More head-turning and eye-rolling. "I said, *Dear B.D., You have absolutely no reason to wurry. When you come back you won't be able to get rum anywhere in Ontario.*"

The woman seated beside Murdoch muttered, "Good thing too."

Most of the audience, however, laughed.

Fiona took out a third sheet.

"Here's another letter, from a woman. Do you get many letters from women, Miss Happ?"

"Oh yes. Lots."

"Here we go. B.J. writes, *Dear Miss Happ, Every month I send my husband a comfort box and I always include a homemade fruitcake. Recently he wrote to me and said would I please not send him any more fruitcake even if it was homemade. It gives* him a stomach ache. He shared it with some of his chums and they all got stomach aches as well. My dilemma is this. Should I fire my cook?"

"And what did you advise?" Fiona asked.

"I said, *Under no circumstances should you fire your cook. Good help is impossible to get these days. You'd be better off to get another husband.*"

That got a huge bellow of laughter. The difficulty of maintaining servants was an issue many in this audience seemed to be familiar with.

Fiona replaced that letter in the satchel and picked out another. "This is also from a woman. *Dear Miss Happ, I am writing about a delicate matter concerning my fiancé. Recently he was asked to join the Comedy Company, which is part of the Princess Pats regiment. They perform a very important role in entertaining the troops. Kevin likes this very much and has been most successful in the roles of Desdemona, Lady Macbeth, and other comic characters. He says he likes playing female parts.*"

Fiona paused and gave an ostentatious sigh as if the letter were sort of boring. Miss Happ waved her hand. "Keep going. The guid part is coming up."

"*I have received a letter from him. He wondered if, when he returns, I might be so kind as to lend him some of my frocks to go about in. He particularly likes my polka-dot afternoon dress.*"

There was more laughter, although Murdoch thought some of the audience seemed uncomfortable. Fiona waited until it had subsided.

"Miss Happ, can you advise me? Should I worry?"

"And what did you say?"

"I told her there is no cause for concern. Polka dots are most becoming, especially in the afternoon."

Surprised laughter. They hadn't seen that coming.

Fiona fished in the satchel, making a big production of sorting out another letter. "All right. Here's one from a man. He says, *Dear Miss Happ, I have been called up and I'm expecting to leave soon. My problem is this. I would like to have more cuddles from my sweetheart as you never know if I will return alive. She is a loving girl but she has always been on the stiff side.*"

Fiona moved the dummy's arm so she patted herself.

"Sounds like me."

Fiona continued. "*Will her attitude change when we are married? Should I worry? Yours, P.O.* What did you tell him?"

"I gave him a properly sensible answer. *Dear P.O., Don't worry about what your fiancée will be like when she's your wife. I suggest you be grateful for what she gives you now. Don't forget, very soon, the only thing you will be embracing is a wet sandbag that probably smells like dead men. A little stiffness is preferable.*"

Percy again shouted out "Hear, hear!" But the response from the rest of the audience was less enthusiastic. Fiona was edging into darker territory. Murdoch hoped she would not go too far.

Miss Happ surveyed the theatre. "My, my, this is a well-heeled group, isn't it? I'm sure they'll cough up a lot of money tonight."

Fiona spoke to the dummy in a stage whisper. "*Cough up*

isn't a very polite expression, Miss Happ. You promised you would be on your best behaviour."

"What should I have said? Is 'expectorate' better? They will *expectorate* a lot of money?"

A more subdued response at that one.

"No, of course that's not better." Fiona frowned.

She swivelled Miss Happ's head so they were looking at each other.

"Miss Williams, I have a wee problem."

"What is it?"

"We're supposed to make the people laugh, are we not? Give them a good time."

"That's the intention."

"We were told that if they are happy, they will be more likely to 'spit out,' sorry, I mean *donate* money."

"I suppose you could put it that way. So what is the problem, Miss Happ?"

"There is nothing funny about this war. I can't find much to joke about when healthy young men are being maimed or killed on a daily basis."

Silence in the audience, then Percy yelled, "Right! Hear, hear."

Fiona looked over at him. She made Miss Happ wave her hand.

"Thank you, laddie. It's always guid to speak to like minds."

There was a muttering and shuffling among the audience. The MC stepped out from the wings.

She's skating too close to the edge, thought Murdoch. He could feel himself growing tense.

Fiona, however, didn't seem daunted. "We have time for one more letter. This one is from H.T. *Dear Miss Happ, I am engaged to a wonderful girl and we have set the date but I don't know how to tell her I won't be able to attend.*"

Fiona pretended to drop the letter so she could emphasize the punch line. She picked it up.

"Sorry. Where was I? . . . *I won't be able to attend. The problem is I am to be shot at dawn in two days' time.*"

There was a gasp from the audience. Definitely not funny.

Fiona kept on. "*In a moment of weakness, I fell asleep at my post. I hadn't had any sleep for three days but I know that is no excuse. Should I tell my girl the truth? I don't want her to think I am a deserter.*"

There was utter silence in the theatre. The MC was clearly unable to decide what to do.

Fiona raised her voice. "That's a tough one. How did you answer?"

"I said as follows. *Dear H.T., A wedding is much more fun than a funeral. Run away when you can and marry the girl. Don't worry. The firing squad will soon find a replacement for you.*"

From the second row, a man called out loudly, "Get her off!"

"Hurrah! Hurrah!" Percy was on his feet. Jack seemed to be trying to get him to sit down once more.

The man behind him also stood up and tried to catch hold

of his arm. Percy shook him off. Two soldiers sitting nearby also jumped up.

"Are you a conchie, woman?" yelled one of them. "We don't want your sort here."

"That's right," yelled Percy. "Tell 'em, chaps. Tell them conchies. We're the ones doing your dirty work for you."

The MC rushed on stage pulling little Evangeline by the hand.

"Ladies and gentlemen. Let's have some order, please. I'm sure Miss Williams didn't mean to give offence."

"Yes, she did," called the soldier. "She's a disgrace to our noble women. They're who we're fighting for."

A couple of women in front of Murdoch waved.

"Never mind her. Let's get on to the slackers," shouted another soldier a few rows down from Murdoch.

"I'm with you," called out Percy. "Yellow-bellies all of them. They need a taste of the real thing."

"There's some of them over there," shouted the soldier who'd started things.

Indeed there was a trio of natty-looking young men seated near the stage.

"I'd go overseas if I was allowed," returned one of them, angrily, but the other two looked frightened.

Percy had managed to shake off Jack's restraint and started to cross the aisle to the men. The first two soldiers soon joined him.

"Sure you would," spat out one. "Words are cheap. You could sign up if you wanted to."

Murdoch got to his feet but he was stuck in the middle of the row of seats and hampered by unyielding legs. The situation seemed to get out of hand with incredible rapidity. One of the soldiers lunged over the seats and grabbed a man by the lapels.

"Why aren't you in uniform? What are you, a Frenchie? A conchie? A lousy coward?"

Suddenly other men were on their feet, shouting, waving their fists. All of the front rows got involved, a couple of civilians siding with the first trio against the soldiers. Percy was still yelling and waving his arms, but Jack was nowhere to be seen. Even older men were getting mixed up in the fray, not to mention a few straitlaced matrons. There was so much chaos it was hard to determine who was with whom.

Murdoch finally pushed past his neighbours and started toward the stage but got stuck between the patrons who were already trying to leave and the others who were moving in the direction of the melee. It was impossible to make any headway. He could see Fiona abruptly pick up the dummy and walk off the stage. Her head was high. She was singing at the top of her voice, another popular song, "*Don't take my darling boy away …*"

The MC gestured into the wings and the piano player came on stage, sat down, and began to play loudly. The MC called out, "Order, please. Order!"

He waved frantically in the other direction and the Five Farmerettes marched back onto the stage. The piano player thumped out "Mademoiselle from Armentières" again.

Murdoch shoved harder. "I'm a police officer. Make way. Make way."

The patrons yielded reluctantly, and finally he reached the front. Percy and the two soldiers were trading punches with the trio they had challenged. Jack had joined them but was still trying to play the role of peacemaker. Murdoch yelled, "Police. Desist!" It didn't make any difference. Too much blood was up. Men were falling over the seats and continuing the fight in the aisles.

He grabbed the nearest soldier by his belt, hauled him out of the circle, and shoved him to the ground. "I'm a police officer. Stop this."

The soldier's eyes were literally red with rage. Murdoch was having trouble holding him down. Nothing was going to stop him inflicting as much damage as he could. A big, tough-looking fellow had grabbed Jack, who was trying to hold him off. Murdoch saw Percy dragged down to the floor, a man pummelling him. Murdoch had no idea how this uneven fight was going to conclude; he was about to let go of his soldier and go to Jack when help came from an unexpected quarter. Rubridge elbowed his way through and was able to get the attackers out of the way. It might still have gone badly for Jack and Percy, not to mention Murdoch himself, but just then the rear doors burst open and a half dozen constables came racing in, blowing their whistles and swinging their batons indiscriminately. Some women were now screaming. The Farmerettes bellowed out their song to deaf ears.

Murdoch felt rather than saw Jack slide to the ground

behind him. A man in an evening suit had come around to the side and punched him in the head. Murdoch could feel his own blood fired. He took a swing at the assailant and caught him so hard on the jaw that his own knuckles stung. The man dropped like a felled ox. Then it was all wild swings and shoving as two of the constables came to his aid.

Finally the exhausted fighters started to slow down. Bodies were lying on the floor, including an inert Percy. Murdoch struggled to get his breath. Space opened up around him as the constables asserted themselves. He was relieved to see that Jack was sitting up, although he was holding a handkerchief to his nose, which was bleeding profusely.

"Are you all right?" Murdoch called to him.

"I'm all right. Where's Percy?"

"He's over there."

Percy was lying across the aisle, not moving. The man Murdoch had knocked down was struggling to sit up, and Rubridge pounced on him. Hauling him to his feet, he twisted the man's arms behind his back.

"Constable, cuff him," he called to one of the officers.

The constable snapped on a pair of handcuffs.

Murdoch was in no mood to be sympathetic to Jack's assailant. "Lock him in the cell."

"I'll go with him," said Rubridge. The two of them half led, half dragged the dazed man away.

Murdoch went over to Jack, who was wincing as he tried to stand.

"Stay where you are," said Murdoch.

"No, Pa, I've got to see how Percy is," said Jack, and Murdoch had no choice but to help him.

They edged closer to the prone body. Percy's head was turned to one side and his eyes were open. For a minute, Murdoch thought he was dead, but then he saw him take a big, shuddering breath. Jack dropped to his knees beside his friend.

"Percy. Percy. Are you all right?" Although he was trying to stem the flow with the sodden handkerchief, Jack was dripping blood all over him.

Murdoch knelt down on the other side. He could see no visible injury. He felt for Percy's pulse; it was thumping strong and fast.

He called to a constable he recognized. "Clark, over here." Murdoch indicated Jack. "I want you to escort this man to the hospital. He has probably suffered a broken nose. Did the police ambulance come with you?"

"They're on their way, sir."

"Good." Murdoch addressed his son now. "I want you to go with this constable. I don't think Percy is seriously hurt. I will deal with him."

Jack was about to protest and Murdoch raised his hand to stop him. "I'm not giving you an option. When you've got fixed up, go straight home. I'm going to be here for a while dealing with this lot. You'll get a report on Percy then."

"But—"

"You heard me. See, he's breathing normally. His pulse is elevated but not alarmingly so."

Jack touched his friend's head gently. "It's all right, Perce. My pa will look after you. We're at home now."

Percy's eyes fluttered, and Murdoch assumed he'd heard what Jack said.

Jack got to his feet. Murdoch did likewise. He was relieved to see that the nosebleed seemed to be slowing down.

"He's probably gone into shock," said Jack. He turned to his father. "It's important that he's not left alone. He needs to be reassured he's here, not over there, and that he's safe. He can get confused."

At that moment, Fiona Williams reappeared in front of the stage. When she saw Murdoch and Jack, she picked her way toward them, looking pale and frightened.

"Jack, are you all right?"

"Right as rain," answered Jack. "Just a little nosebleed."

"This is awful. I feel so responsible," she said.

"Don't be silly," said Jack. "Some things have to be said."

"Maybe," snapped Murdoch, "but you were very foolish, young lady, to do what you did under these circumstances. This is a fundraiser. People are here because they want to help our soldiers. Many of them have lost loved ones."

"If people don't want to hear the truth about things that's their problem, not Fiona's," said his son.

"There's a right time and a wrong time to say the truth. Nobody wants it rammed down their throats."

Jack was looking angry. "There's a talk we need to have, Pa."

Murdoch snapped back, "I'm ready when you are."

Constable Clark came forward. "The ambulance has arrived, sir. Shall I escort this gentleman now?"

"Yes. Jack, go with him." Murdoch turned to the constable. "He's my son. He's not under arrest so you don't need to lock him up. Just get a doctor to have a look at him."

"Yes, sir."

"Jack, I'll come and see you later," said Fiona. "And I truly am sorry. I'll do whatever I can to set things right."

Before Jack could answer, Murdoch said, "What you can do is sit beside the young man who's lying on the floor. He's in a state of shock. Jack here thinks he needs to be talked to in a gentle, reassuring way until he recovers his wits. Can you do that? Gentle and reassuring, mind."

"Yes, of course. What's his name?"

"Percy McKinnon," answered Jack. "Thank you, Fiona. Oh, by the way, when he's in one of his states, he sometimes babbles nonsense. Don't take it seriously."

Murdoch interrupted. "Jack. You heard me. Go and get yourself looked after."

Jack allowed himself to be led away by the constable. Fiona crouched down beside Percy.

"It's all right," she said softly. "You're safe now."

"I've got work to do," said Murdoch. "Fetch me when he comes to completely."

He left her to it and went over to where Rubridge was

addressing a group of smartly dressed men and women whom he had ordered to remain in their seats. Another constable was collecting names and addresses. Murdoch could see that most of them were looking either bewildered or indignant. They were not accustomed to riots coming into their orbit.

RULES OF OFFICER'S MESS

4. The Mess Committee have the right to strike off the name of any member whose behaviour is prejudicial to the welfare of the Mess and/or the comfort of other members.

. . .

9. No ladies will be permitted to the Mess.

. . .

23. Discussions on religion and politics are strictly barred.

CHAPTER FORTY-FIVE

JACK TOUCHED HIS SWOLLEN NOSE GINGERLY. THE physician at the hospital had said it wasn't broken and had given him a couple of aspirin powders to take.

"Apply cold compresses until the swelling has gone down." He'd smiled at Jack. "I hope you gave as good as you got. I probably shouldn't say this, but I've got a lad at the Front and I despise slackers as much as any man. You returning boys have paid your dues as far as I'm concerned."

Jack simply shrugged. He'd not had a chance to do anything, the other man had leaped on him so fast. In addition, both he and Percy had been feeling the effects of the three or four glasses of *baijiu* they'd tossed back at Ghong Lee's house.

Jack's reactions had been slow and his recollections of what happened were rather hazy. He had been felled by a hard blow to the nose, he knew that, and his father, who had come out of nowhere, had knocked the assailant to the ground. Percy had caught one too, but Jack had been in no condition to go to his aid. Thank God his father had taken care of things. And Fiona, bless her.

As soon as he was patched up, Jack checked the base hospital on College Street, where he knew all the soldiers would have been taken.

A very pretty young nurse met him on the ward. He asked for Percy.

"Your friend left not too long ago. His sister came for him."

"He doesn't have a sister."

The nurse looked a little discomfited. "She said she was. The family has come in from out of town and she came to get him."

"Did she say where they were staying?"

"A hotel, but I'm afraid I don't know which one."

"How did Percy seem?"

"He was quite shaken but physically he's fine." She gave Jack another sweet smile. "He just needs a lot of tender care right now, wouldn't you say? I'm sure it will be good for him to have his family around him."

Jack left and went home.

CHAPTER FORTY-SIX

JACK DREW DEEPLY ON HIS CIGARETTE. HE'D ALREADY gone through five, lighting each one from the tip of the other. By now they had lost their taste and were making him cough. He stubbed out the last one.

He'd pulled the armchair as close to the blazing fire as he could. Since he'd returned from the Front, he'd found it hard to feel warm, and violent shivers periodically racked his body.

His gaze wandered to the mantelpiece. The shelf was cluttered with odd bits of bric-a-brac interspersed with some framed photographs. At the far end was a picture of his father in bicycling garb standing in front of his wheel. He was holding a trophy that he'd just won at the Police Games and he looked strong and fit.

His father was one of those men who hardly seem to age. His wavy dark hair was still thick, even if nowadays it was streaked with grey. He'd added a little more girth but otherwise he hadn't changed much since that photograph was taken. Next to that was a larger picture of his father and mother on their wedding day. They looked so happy, and as always Jack was struck by how attractive his mother had been. He'd always thought she was one of the prettiest mothers on the street.

Jack stood up and took another framed picture off the mantel. It had been taken in a studio a few days after Murdoch's triumph at the annual Police Games. The win had shot number four station into first place over all the others in Toronto. Jack smiled at the vivid recollection of a jubilant Constable Crabtree, who'd lifted his father off his feet in a bear hug then collapsed in a fit of embarrassment at his own presumption.

This was Jack's favourite picture. At that time he'd been just four years old, and he was sitting on his father's lap. Murdoch had let Jack hold the trophy and he was gripping it with as much pride as if he'd won it himself. His mother was standing beside them, her hand on Murdoch's shoulder. This was the last photograph taken when they were intact as a family.

Jack replaced the picture on the mantel. He took the playing cards from his pocket and dealt them out one by one on the couch. On the third layout, the knave fell into the first position.

He was staring at it when the sound of urgent knocking registered. He quickly gathered up the cards, put them away, and hurried to answer the door.

Fiona Williams was standing on the threshold. She stared at him in dismay, holding what appeared to be a bundle of rags in her arms.

"My God, Jack, you look awful."

"Sorry. It'll fade."

"Don't apologize. It's me who is sorry."

"Come inside. We can argue about it in more comfort."

She lifted her arms. "Somebody destroyed Miss Happ."

Jack could now see that she was actually carrying her ventriloquist's doll. The elaborate hat was smashed and the papier mâché head was caved in, the features completely destroyed. It looked as if one of the arms had been ripped off. He took the doll from her and nodded in the direction of the sitting room.

"Let's go in here."

She followed him.

Holding the doll as tenderly as if it were a child, Jack laid it on a chair.

"What happened?"

"I found her when I went to collect my things from the dressing room." Fiona ducked her head. "I really did offend people, didn't I, Jack? That wasn't my intent. I just wanted to draw attention to what is happening. I was so frightened when I saw what had been done to Miss Happ. It seems so violent. Look what's been done to her face."

Jack wasn't about to tell her that he'd seen men torn apart like that. Limbs blown off, skulls caved in.

"Did you report this to my father?"

"No, I didn't. For one thing he was too busy sorting out the melee . . . And frankly, I felt the attack might be deserved."

"Nonsense. It's vandalism, pure and simple. If people aren't allowed to express contrary opinions, what the devil are we fighting for? I don't suppose you noticed anybody going to the dressing room?"

"No, I didn't. I was concentrating on looking after Percy. I didn't go back until he was taken to the ambulance. Have you heard how he is, by the way?"

Jack didn't feel like explaining the appearance of a never-before-acknowledged sister, or that Percy had vanished with her, supposedly to be reunited with the rest of his never-before-acknowledged family.

"According to the hospital, he'll be all right."

"I'm glad to hear it. I was worried."

"Did he start babbling?"

"No. He was quiet."

"Good. I'm grateful to you for taking care of him. He's my pal and I'd hate anything to happen to him. He's had more than his share of trouble."

"Jack?" He became aware that Fiona was regarding him with concern. "Are you all right?"

He managed to smile at her. "'Course I am."

"You sort of went away, if you know what I mean."

"I'm fine. I just get sudden return of memories. Lots of soldiers experience it when they come home."

"I gather they are not pleasant memories?"

"Not most of them."

"You take very good care of your friend."

Jack shrugged. "Contrary to how it may appear, I need him just as much as he needs me." Abruptly, he stood up. "Let's take a look at Miss Happ and see what we can do."

He picked up the dummy and laid it across his lap. The damage was even worse than it had first appeared. As well as the smashed head, one of the arms had been torn off and the neatly stitched jacket and skirt were shredded.

"I'm sorry, Fiona, but I think it's beyond repair."

"Oh no. Can we at least keep the eyes and the hair? I had to save up for six months to pay for those."

"The hair you'll be able to reuse. And one of the eyes. The right one has had it." He grinned. "Maybe Miss Happ can become a pirate. Or a returning soldier, for that matter."

Fiona scowled at him. "Not funny."

She came over to where he was sitting.

"Poor, poor Miss Happ. What a dreadful thing to happen to you."

Jack was suddenly very aware that Fiona was only inches away from him. She smelled like fresh, cold air. He focused on the dummy.

"Can you mend the clothes?" he asked.

"Yes. That won't be so hard. But I don't know where I'm going to get another arm. I don't even know where the missing one is."

"Make a sleeve and I'll build a wire frame that you can sew

to the body. You can slip on the sleeve. Be good as new. Can you get another head?"

"I made this one myself. Took forever."

"When's your next booking?"

"Soon. I volunteered to be part of a Boxing Day concert for the Alexandra Industrial School. No fundraising for that. I just have to make the girls laugh and forget their circumstances for a little while."

"Miss Happ will be ready by then. I'll help you however I can."

"Give her to me."

He handed her the doll. Miss Happ, even damaged, retained such a personality that it felt like dealing with a human being, and the exchange was careful.

Fiona returned to her chair.

"Oh, Jack. I don't know what to do. Obviously my jokes won't be suitable for the residents of the school, but I haven't worked up another routine yet."

"I think they will be glad to see you no matter what you do. I can't imagine they get much in the way of entertainment."

She regarded him doubtfully. "I should tell you I don't completely approve of industrial schools. Girls are incarcerated there for paltry reasons. They are trained to be servants. No other options. Keeping them in their place at all times."

"Fiona. You need a rest from trying to change the world."

"Do I now? Well, don't hold your breath waiting."

* * *

The men were leaning against the side of the trench, waiting for the signal to go over the top. Jack was at the end of the line, Percy beside him. He heard a gasp and turned. Blood was streaming down Percy's face. What the hell? There had been no barrage for a few minutes. Then Jack saw the blood on a sliver of shrapnel at his feet.

Percy grinned at him, his eyes wild.

"See, Jack? I've got my Blighty. This is V for victory. Maybe they'll send me home now."

He'd carved the letter on his own forehead with the hot piece of metal.

"You idiot. You'll get yourself court-martialled."

The sound of the captain's whistle rang out. Jack grabbed Percy by his coat.

"Get over."

"I can't, Jack."

"Yes, you can. I'm going with you."

Several of the men had already clambered up the side of the trench. The sharp rattle of German machine guns greeted them. Jack saw the man directly to his left collapse. His skull was spurting blood like a colander.

"Come on, quick," Jack said to Percy.

One tug on the corpse's feet and he pulled him from the top of the trench. He was a man that Jack had liked, but there was no time to mourn.

"Percy, get up. I'm right behind you."

His chum wiped away some of the blood from his face with

his sleeve and, gripping his rifle, he climbed up the trench wall.

"Duck to the left," shouted Jack.

He gave Percy a boost and they both made it to the top, rolling away to the side.

"Run!"

Through the smoke of the guns they glimpsed the surviving members of their battalion running toward the enemy trenches. Many of them were dropping.

Jack and Percy advanced a few yards. Bullets hissed around them, kicking up the mud. "Drop."

There was a shallow declivity just in front of them and they dived into it, pressing themselves as flat to the ground as they could.

The bottom of the shell hole was filled with muddy water and, half in, half out, was lying a German soldier. He was bleeding from a wound at his neck, and he turned his head in their direction. His rifle was at his side and, seeing them, he reached for it and held it up as high as he could.

"Kamerad," he whispered.

Percy struggled to his feet.

"Kamerad," the man whispered again as he tried to lift his rifle, where he'd tied his handkerchief, his white flag of surrender.

CHAPTER FORTY-SEVEN

It was close to midnight before Murdoch could finally leave for home. As he cycled down Ontario Street he felt like a horse that smells the stable, and his pace quickened even though he was dead tired.

There must have been about two dozen people left in the theatre after things had calmed down, and he'd had to make sure all of them gave statements about what they had seen. Many of them were critical of the soldiers, who they thought had started the brawl. Almost all of them, however, blamed what happened on Fiona's act and her provocative so-called jokes. Not to mention the young man in the front row who had made such a spectacle of himself by shouting out like that. He'd thrown oil on the fire. "If I didn't know better, I'd say he was drunk," remarked one debonair man, his voice as smooth as his top hat. "I expect you will pursue that, won't you, Detective?" Murdoch had assured him he would do just that.

There were very few lights showing in the dark houses on the street, and none at all at number 222. He felt a pang of disappointment. It was late, after all. On the one hand, he hoped Jack was already in bed; on the other, he had been looking forward to his being there waiting in the sitting room, ready for a chinwag.

Like he and Amy used to do.

He stowed his bicycle and entered the house. He snapped on the overhead light and almost jumped out of his skin. What looked like a child was sitting slumped on the chair in the hall.

Whew. He realized it was in fact the ventriloquist's dummy that Fiona had used in her disastrous act. There was a note propped up beside it.

Pa. Fiona came by and I've taken her home. You can see what has happened to the dummy. It was done at the theatre. She doesn't know who did it. We should investigate the matter. Entirely not fair. After taking her home, I'll look in on Percy. Make sure he's all right. Don't wait up. I shall see you in the morning.

Thanks for looking out for me the way you did. Hope that fellow has a headache. A <u>bad</u> headache. My nose isn't broken, by the way. Just bruised.

JACK

Murdoch had to smile at the suggestion that "we" should investigate the matter. But he liked the fact that his son was linking them together that way. He liked it a lot.

He took a closer look at the doll. Papier mâché wasn't particularly sturdy but nevertheless somebody had given the head a blow severe enough to shatter the entire front of the face. He could see that the clothes had been ripped, not cut, the tears were ragged. One of the arms was missing and looked as if it had been twisted off. He thought the doll had been swung by its arm and the head bashed against a hard surface. It wouldn't have taken long to inflict the damage. Fiona had certainly stirred up a hornet's nest.

Well, there wasn't much he could do tonight. It would have to wait until morning. Yawning, Murdoch decided to head upstairs. The house felt cold but there was no point in building up the fire at this hour. He'd better take out an extra blanket for Jack. He'd noticed his son was often shivering.

He got a blanket from the airing cupboard in the bathroom and went into Jack's room. The first thing that hit him was how little evidence there was of his son's presence. The bed was made; haversack and uniform were nowhere in sight. Nothing seemed to have been moved since the first night. It bothered him, although he was at a loss to say why. Was this merely a sign that army discipline had been well learned?

He placed the blanket across the foot of the bed and turned to leave. Wait. On the dressing table was a notebook, which

Murdoch recognized as one Jack had used in school. He'd obviously been writing in it recently, because he'd left a pencil inside it.

The notebook was the one Jack referred to as his diary. He'd begun it when he was twelve. "Everybody should keep a record of what happens in their lives," he'd told his father. "Look at Samuel Pepys, for instance." Murdoch wasn't sure a twelve-year-old boy had a lot to record but he'd promised not to look at it unless Jack wanted to share something. As far as Murdoch knew, his son had made entries intermittently over the ensuing years. He'd never broken his promise about reading them. Until now.

He hovered for a moment over the book, but his need to understand what Jack was thinking and feeling was too strong. Turning the pages as gingerly as if they were red hot, he opened it to where the pencil protruded.

There was a sheaf of papers slipped inside. They appeared to be poems, ones that presumably Jack himself had written. All were dated 1917. Murdoch put them aside and began to read the diary itself.

Just before he died the boy called out for his mother. (I say "boy" because to all intents and purposes he was a boy.) The sergeant said I could not possibly have heard anything given the heavy canvas hood. "I was imagining it," said he. But I wasn't. Just as I didn't imagine the bright red blood that spurted from the boy's chest. Just as I didn't imagine the violent spasms that racked his body as the bullets thudded into the white circle pinned above his heart.

Murdoch closed the book.

"There's a talk we need to have," Jack had said.

CHAPTER FORTY-EIGHT

In spite of his exhaustion, Murdoch did not fall asleep for a long time, his thoughts moiling around in his head.

Jack had been born a little prematurely, and he was small. The midwife had put him in the warming cupboard where they kept the towels and sheets, but Amy soon demanded he be brought to her, even though she'd gone through a difficult labour and, according to the midwife, should be getting her rest. Murdoch sat beside the bed and watched his wife fall asleep with the naked infant lying on her chest. Not wanting to disturb her, he gently lifted the baby and wrapped him in a blanket. When he made sleepy sucking motions, he put the tip of his finger in the infant's mouth to soothe him. What a strong pull from such a tiny creature, Murdoch marvelled, and he thought that he had never known such joy. He could never have imagined the fierce feelings this scrap of humanity had aroused in him.

For those first four years, he'd spent as much time with his son as his work would allow. There were the three of them. Forever, as he'd thought.

Then Amy and the new baby had died.

Murdoch had asked his former landlady, Mrs. Kitchen, now a widow, to come and help look after him and Jack, which she'd done willingly. Overwhelmed by his own grief, Murdoch had retreated from family life. Over the following years, a distance had developed between him and his son that he didn't know how to bridge. How deeply he regretted that now.

So here they were, and it was obvious Jack was intent on keeping him at arm's length. People kept saying time would change that. Would it? What was the meaning of his diary entry? What had Jack gone through that he was so reluctant to share?

Eventually, Murdoch fell into a restless sleep.

He was awakened by a violent knocking on the front door. His heart leapt into his throat, alarm flooding his body. Grabbing his dressing gown, he hurried downstairs. A constable, not familiar to him, was standing in his cape, gleaming in the lightly falling snow.

"Sorry to pound like that, sir, but the sergeant didn't trust the telephone so he sent me round in person. Sergeant Caulback is the name. I work out of number two station."

"Yes. What is it, man?"

"I have to report that there's been a homicide. Young man has been found dead on Agnes Street."

"Do we know who he is?"

The constable was a big man, grey-haired, and well into middle age. He began to fish in his pocket for his notebook. To Murdoch he seemed to move with appalling slowness.

"Sergeant? Please answer me, do we know the identity of this young man?"

"Yes, sir." He flipped open the notebook. "Here it is. His name is Antonio Carella. He worked at the Italian consulate as a night manager."

Murdoch felt such a wave of relief that he could hardly speak for a moment. He was sorry a young man had died, but all he could think was *Thank God it wasn't Jack*.

"Step inside. I'll get dressed."

He soon joined the constable and they set off at a brisk walk.

"Do we know what happened?" Murdoch asked.

"The constable on his beat found the body about an hour ago. He was lying directly in front of the Italian consulate. The constable knew the young man to be an employee there so he went to rouse the consul, or rather, the deputy who is in charge at the moment. He was the one rang the station. I went over right away. It was obvious it was a job for headquarters."

"Is there any indication of a reason for the killing?"

"Nothing immediate. There was no apparent fight. The young man was clearing snow from the steps of the consulate. It would seem that the killer came from behind him, seized the shovel, and used it to overcome him."

"I assume there was no sign of the assailant?"

"None at all."

For reasons of war economy, the city was keeping wattage on all electric lights to a minimum. The dusting of snow brightened the surroundings somewhat but the streets were dark, the houses silhouettes. All was deadly quiet. A constable was stationed by the steps that led up to the entrance of the consulate. He came smartly to attention.

"Constable Harrar, sir. Number two station."

"You're the one who discovered the body?"

"I am, yes, sir."

Caulback held up his lantern and the beam shone on the body sprawled on the sidewalk. The dead man was lying on his back. He might have been peacefully sleeping, his arms at his side, his legs only slightly bent, but in the lamplight Murdoch could see that his eyes were bulging, his tongue was protruding, and his face was suffused with blood.

He gently moved the dead man's hand. Rigor mortis had not set in and there was a faint warmth to the body. He leaned closer.

There was a yellow cross on the victim's coat. He touched it gingerly and a little powder came off on his fingers. Chalk.

It looked exactly the same as the cross that had marked Morris Swartz's jacket. The German sign for mustard gas.

Murdoch looked at the steps. The snow had been cleared recently. There was a shovel lying on the sidewalk.

"I believe it's the young man's job to keep the steps clear," said Harrar. "I've seen him so occupied on previous occasions."

"Do you know when it started to snow?"

"It was just after midnight, sir. I came upon the body at half past one. I checked right away to see if there were any footprints. There were none. Snow undinted."

"So we can assume the assault occurred close to twelve."

"I'd say so, yes, sir. I was on my second tour and he certainly wasn't here when I came past at eleven."

"I'm guessing his assailant snuck up behind him, grabbed that shovel, and choked him by pulling the handle across his throat. Please remove it. We'll have it brought to headquarters for examination. I'll ring for the coroner. Until he gets here, make sure nobody interferes. If anybody does come by, take their name and address. It might be useful later. I'll go and have a talk with the deputy consul." Murdoch now addressed Caulback. "Come with me, Sergeant. We should get something to cover the body before the world wakes up."

Murdoch looked back at the corpse. He made the sign of the cross for the soul of the departed.

CHAPTER FORTY-NINE

THE DEPUTY CONSUL HIMSELF OPENED THE DOOR. HE was a striking-looking man, with a strong, hooked nose and sharp chin. His skin was olive and his dark, wavy hair fell from a centre parting. Murdoch thought his profile could have graced coins of the Roman Empire.

"Please come in, Officer," he said, offering his hand. He had only a trace of an Italian accent. "I'm Giovanni Furturo." He stepped back so that Murdoch could enter the narrow foyer.

Furturo was still in his night clothes, scarlet pyjamas topped by a wine-coloured silk brocade dressing gown. For a moment, Murdoch couldn't help but compare them to his own plain flannel robe and cotton pyjamas. They may have started out as navy but were now pale bluish grey. He brought his attention back to the matter in hand.

"I'd like to cover up the body, sir. Do you have something we can use?"

Furturo surveyed the wall where a large Italian flag hung from a rod. "This should do it. Antonio Carella was a loyal Italian and he should be accorded a patriot's respect in death." Furturo removed the flag and handed it to Sergeant Caulback, who took it and headed back downstairs.

"Let us go into my study," said the deputy consul, and he led the way down the hall.

The room was small and cozy, with plush burgundy wall coverings and several framed oil paintings that suggested Italian pastoral views. A couple of big armchairs sat in front of the hearth, while a desk in the corner sat next to a glass-fronted bookcase.

Furturo went over to the desk. "This has been a dreadful shock. You don't mind if I smoke, do you, Detective?"

"Not at all."

The deputy consul took an ornately carved wooden cigar box from the desk, removed one of the cigars, snipped the end, and lit it from an expensive-looking lighter. He drew in a deep lungful of smoke and exhaled slowly. The tobacco was highly aromatic. Definitely not the local kind, Murdoch thought.

Furturo held out the box. "May I offer you one?"

Murdoch would have liked to try the unfamiliar cigar, but not while he was on duty. He shook his head, contenting himself with breathing in the smoke.

"What can you tell me about the dead man, Mr. Furturo?"

Furturo scrutinized the glowing end of his cigar. "Not much, I'm afraid. He's worked here since the summer. He has always been absolutely reliable. He speaks English well, and Italian, of course."

"What was the nature of his work?"

"General caretaking. Keeping the premises tidy both inside and out. He has the night shift. He also answers any calls that come in after midnight. Just to take messages, naturally, but if he feels it necessary he will wake the consul or myself."

"Are there many such calls?"

"Not many, thank goodness. Immigration has slowed down considerably since the war. Most of our flock are well settled."

"I'll need the young man's address."

"He shared a lodging house with some other Calabrians. It's just up the street. Number 135."

Signor Furturo tapped the ash from his cigar into a brass dish. "It's so dreadful what has happened. Such a young man. Why, just yesterday he received an exemption from his tribunal. I had pleaded his case, of course. The consul and I both thought it would be hard to replace him here at the consulate given that he was fluent in both languages. The tribunal board agreed and he was granted an exemption from conscription for a year."

Another streetcar.

The deputy let out a long puff of smoke. "He might as well have gone to the front line after all."

CHAPTER FIFTY

LEAVING FURTURO TO CONTACT HEADQUARTERS SO THEY could arrange for a coroner to come, Murdoch went directly to question the other lodgers at Antonio Carella's boarding house. It was still the middle of the night and it took a while to rouse them. Sergeant Caulback came with him, and after a lot of thumping on the door, it was opened a crack by a young man in his nightshirt. He didn't seem to understand English at all but he understood the uniform. He ushered them into the cold house and rushed upstairs to wake up the others. Finally, in various states of undress and sleepiness, they all gathered in the tiny kitchen. There were four of them, all young, olive-skinned, and black-haired. To Murdoch's mind, more Romans.

There weren't enough chairs for everybody; one of the younger men offered Murdoch a place at the table and leaned against the wall on the other side of the doorway from Caulback. The sergeant looked uncomfortable at this unexpected proximity. The room felt very crowded. Anxiety drenched the air.

"Do any of you speak English?" asked Murdoch.

The man across from Murdoch, who had wrapped himself in a crocheted shawl, answered.

"I do, sir. A little."

"What is your name?"

Sergeant Caulback flipped open his notebook.

"Vincenzo Petrozzi."

He immediately began to spell it, and Murdoch had the impression this was not the first time the young Italian had been questioned by authorities.

One of the others said something sharply to Petrozzi. Murdoch didn't understand the words but the man's agitation and anger were apparent. His compatriot nodded and addressed Murdoch.

"May I inquire, sir, why you visiting us at this hour of the night? In this house, we have all registered with the military board. Three has already attended the tribunals and has exemption. Other two will meet tribunals in the upcoming week. Do you desire to see our papers?"

"No, that's not why I am here."

He waited while Petrozzi translated to the others. There was no putting it off.

"I regret to tell you that Antonio Carella has been found dead. I understand from the deputy consul that he lived here."

Petrozzi stared at Murdoch in disbelief.

"Antonio dead? How is that to be? What has happened?"

"It appears that he was attacked while he was at the consulate."

"Who? Who has done this thing?"

"We don't know yet. We are investigating."

Seeing Petrozzi's reaction, the man who had first spoken said something in Italian to him.

"Shall I speak what has happened?" Petrozzi asked Murdoch.

"Please tell them that your friend is dead. He was undoubtedly murdered. Anything they can tell me about him would be most helpful. Did he quarrel with anybody, for instance? Did he have any enemies that you know of? It is possible that the murderer was motivated by hatred."

"Hatred of foreigners?"

"Perhaps. Nothing is certain as yet."

"I will speak that, but I will tell you myself, officer, Antonio was of offence to no one. He was, what you say, our mascot. Like a little brother to one and all." He rubbed hard at his eyes. "It will be most hard to share this news."

The others were watching him anxiously. When he had finished his translation, they broke into voluble exclamations. One man put his arm around the shoulders of the man next to him, who began to cry. The exchange went on for several minutes until finally Petrozzi held up his hand for silence. As one, the young men turned to look at Murdoch.

"Did you ask about any enemies?" he asked Petrozzi, who nodded emphatically.

"It was as I said. Nobody has any idea who would this thing do. Perhaps it was somebody who did not know Antonio. A stranger. A robber?"

"We have not ruled that out. Do you know if he would have been carrying money on his person?"

The Italian shook his head. "Most unlikely. Just yesterday, he came to me to request a small loan until he had his wages. He desired to buy cigarettes. I handed him two dollars from our fund." Petrozzi shrugged. "We are not of the wealthy class, sir. Everybody has used their savings to come to this country."

Murdoch recalled that there was a steamship booking agency on the lower floor of the consulate building. They had probably arranged passage for the immigrants.

"Thank you for your co-operation, Mr. Petrozzi. I just have a few more general questions. According to the deputy consul, Mr. Carella had received an exemption from the tribunal. Did you know about this?"

"*Sì*. He was not happy with decision which it came about because the consulate pleaded his case. They said he could not be replaced. Antonio would like to have signed up for the war." He indicated the other men. "We all feel the same way."

"But you say three of you have been exempted. One was Mr. Carella. Are you also exempt?"

"*Sì*. I am hired by Reynolds Automobile livery. I fix their cars. They considered I too am not to be replaced."

"Are you happy about that?"

Petrozzi shrugged. "How could I be happy? Yes, I am safe from the fight, but people dislike me. I am considered slacker, or worse, a coward."

"Your employer cannot prevent you if you are determined to join up."

"Of that I am knowing but my *madre*, who remains in Calabria, does depend on me for money, and Reynolds pays well." He sighed. "We are hoping that the war will be over soon and we can be united."

"And the other exemption?"

"Angelo."

"Why was that granted?"

"He work for Mr. Gooderham and Mr. Worts." He allowed himself the smallest of smiles. "Because of the law, they can no longer distill the whisky and now produce acetone and cordite ketone to blow people to pieces. Very essential. The board agree. Angelo cannot be released." He pointed at the man standing at the wall. "The job of Franco is to help those who have, alas, been blown up by that same cordite. He makes, how you say? *Artificiale* legs and arms for soldiers. The tribunal board will surely agree."

Murdoch indicated the remaining man. "And him?"

"That is Zacchario. He is intending to sign up as soon as his name is called."

"There was a yellow chalk mark on Antonio's clothing. Does that mean anything to you?"

The Italian frowned. "The mark of a coward, perhaps? But Antonio was not coward. He was not permitted to go to war."

"It's possible his killer didn't know that. Or didn't care. Will you ask the others if they have heard of anybody accusing Antonio of cowardice?"

He did so, and again there was a lively exchange.

"They say no. Antonio wasn't happy with the exemption. He made that clear."

Murdoch stood up. There didn't seem much more to be gleaned at the moment. Again Angelo spoke to Vincenzo, who turned back to Murdoch.

"We wish to know when can we bury our friend, sir?"

"There will be a post mortem within the next two days and then his body will be released. Did he have any family in Canada?"

"Not at all. We are all the family we have." He lowered his head.

Murdoch reached over and touched him on the shoulder. The man was shaking beneath his hand.

"I am sorry. I will, of course, keep you up to date on the investigation. In the meantime, Sergeant Caulback will need to take down everybody's full name."

The Italians began to talk softly, their heads leaning in to each other. A family indeed.

DREAMS GONE

I had dreams once,
Love, family, a future.
All gone.
Broken like the bodies
Strewn on this grey wasteland.
No growing old for them:
No shared memories with friends
At gatherings
Where others look at us askance.
"Those men laugh.
Have they no reverence
For the fallen?"
They see not the truth.
We cradle each other in our arms
So we can press to our hearts
Our dead comrades
Who had dreams once.

CHAPTER FIFTY-ONE

THE AEROPLANE CIRCLED ABOVE THE TRENCHES IN THE soft morning light. The first bombs looked almost like bits of wood, twisting and turning as they fell to earth. Jack saw clouds of mud flung into the air as they hit the trenches several hundred feet down the line. No significant damage, he thought with relief.

Another aeroplane joined the first one; it too looked casual, in no hurry. Then it too released a clutch of bombs. By good luck or good planning, he'd never know, these bombs landed on the ammunition dump situated behind the lines. There was a ferocious bang as the dump exploded. The ground beneath him shook so violently he was almost knocked off balance. He knew that this time there would be casualties and, without thinking, he jumped up and ran along the trench in the direction of the dump.

Sergeant Bailey, already up in front of him, ran up the fire-step into No Man's Land. Another tremendous explosion and the sergeant was tossed into the air like a rag doll. He landed hard only a few feet from Jack, who could see him writhing. He was still alive. A rush of strength surged through Jack's body and he managed to drag the sergeant up onto his own back. It was like carrying a sack of potatoes.

"Hold on, Sarge. Hold on."

And he might have. Jack might have saved the man, except that the pilot of the low-flying aeroplane saw what Jack was doing. He banked steeply and, engine screaming, flew over them. Bullets began to rake the ground ahead. As best he could, Jack tried to zigzag, but he was hampered by the weight of the wounded man. They were almost safe when the pilot let loose another round. Jack could feel the impact as the bullets thudded into the man he was carrying. His own back was suddenly soaked with hot blood. He felt the sting in his shoulder and arm as one of the tracers passed through the other man's flesh into his.

He reached the trench, and willing hands reached out to take his burden. Then he dropped himself. Like a dog, he rolled in the clay as if he could wipe away the blood that had drenched him.

FAREWELLS

If you're lucky, really lucky,
You get to say goodbye properly
Before they die.
A smile, a touch, maybe
"See you soon," you say,
Expecting you will.
So when you don't,
When you won't ever,
It's a bit easier, the shock.
'Cos they left fondly.
But mostly
You don't get the chance to do it right.
You just hear
One night,
They copped it further up the line.
Could have been days ago
And you didn't know.
You recall that when they left,
You were sour and spent.
Your feet hurt,
You didn't care where they went.

You'll wish it had been different
Forever.

CHAPTER FIFTY-TWO

FIONA TOOK OFF HER HAT AND COAT, HUNG THEM IN THE anteroom, and hurried to her station. The other girls were already at their places. Always best to give the impression of diligence and responsibility. She was a little ashamed of the thought. Eaton's was a good place to work. A half day off every Saturday, natural light from the windows, a heater on cold days. Much better conditions than a lot of other places. She knew the other girls all wanted to keep the job. She did too.

She saw Miss Lindsay first. The manageress, tall and austere, was standing beside Fiona's chair in front of the switchboard. Uh oh. That did not bode well. Nor did the expression on Miss Lindsay's face. A list of her transgressions whipped through

Fiona's mind. Lateness had never been one of them, but today her mother hadn't been feeling well and Fiona had lingered to make her comfortable. Her bad spells had become more frequent lately.

"Good morning, Miss Lindsay," she said, trying to pitch her voice at exactly the right note of politeness and cheeriness. Mr. Eaton liked his girls to appear cheery. It showed they were well treated.

Miss Lindsay did not return her greeting. "Miss Williams, I would like to have a word with you. Will you please come into my office."

"I am due to start my shift in one minute, ma'am."

Wrong thing to say.

"Miss Costin will take your place."

A pretty, dark-haired young woman who had been hovering close to the manageress gave Fiona an apologetic smile and slipped into the chair.

"Come, Miss Williams," said Miss Lindsay, and Fiona had no choice but to follow her. None of the girls turned their heads, concentrating on plugging telephone lines into the correct extension.

The manageress ushered Fiona into her office. She took the chair behind the desk but she did not ask Fiona to sit down.

Fiona had not been called to the office before and she couldn't help but notice what a great view Miss Lindsay had of the girls through her windows. All goings-on were visible.

Fiona could feel butterflies acting up in her stomach. It

seemed obvious what was coming. At the very least a reprimand.

Miss Lindsay got to the point.

"Miss Williams, I have to inform you that your services are no longer required by the T. Eaton Company."

Fiona gaped at her. Worse, far worse than she had imagined.

"Why is that, ma'am? I had no idea my work was unsatisfactory."

Miss Lindsay threaded her fingers together rather as if she were praying.

"Your work is quite adequate. That is not the reason you are being dismissed."

Fiona could feel her face growing hot. She was beginning to suspect what the issue was.

"What is the reason then, ma'am?"

"It has come to our attention that you have been behaving in a way that is not fitting for a young woman in our employ. The good reputation of Eaton's cannot be sullied."

"Does this have to do with my sentiments about the war?"

"More than that. We are all entitled to our opinions. We just keep them to ourselves. What is unacceptable is that you have engaged in unseemly and provocative behaviour in front of some of Mr. Eaton's most valued customers."

Fiona took a deep breath. It was not going to help her cause to lose her temper.

"I would appreciate it if you would be specific, ma'am."

"Very well. I have been informed that yesterday evening you engaged in a form of entertainment during the course of which you made remarks that were deeply wounding to some people. And that as a result of this a near-riot ensued. People were injured, or at least seriously inconvenienced."

"You are referring to my ventriloquism act?"

"I am indeed."

"May I ask who gave you this information?"

"You may not. It is immaterial. What is important is whether or not it is true."

Fiona didn't answer right away, and Miss Lindsay regarded her with a frown.

"Well? Did you perform at Shea's Theatre last night? With a talking dummy?"

"Yes, I did."

"And did you so disturb the audience with your unfortunate remarks that the police had to be called?"

"I suppose, from certain vantage points, that is indeed true. I was attempting to draw attention to some of the dreadful tragedies of this killing we are engaged in."

Miss Lindsay lowered her hands.

"Miss Williams, my own nephew perished in the first month of this war. He was not yet twenty years old. I know how devastating such losses can be. But I also believe we cannot abandon honour and duty. If we do, we sink to the level of the savage."

"I'm sorry, ma'am. I cannot support murder, which is what it is."

The manageress frowned. The soft moment had gone.

"And neither can we continue to employ a woman who creates such upheaval. As of today, you are no longer employed by this company. You will go immediately."

"May I say goodbye to the others?"

"No, you may not. I will inform them of your leaving."

Fiona's anger drained away. She knew enough not to bother asking for a good character reference from Miss Lindsay. She wouldn't get it.

"Our bookkeeper will be at the door with your final day's wages," said Miss Lindsay. "As in fact you have not worked today, I consider this most generous on Mr. Eaton's part."

Most generous indeed.

THE DEPARTURE

I stayed with you while you died,
We lay side by side,
In the muddy hole
Pressed together like brothers.
Or lovers.
The guns wouldn't cease.
There was no peace
For dead or dying.
It seemed a long time
To be lying there.
Until night slid down the slope
And took over.
I wished you'd hurry up and die
So I could get back.
But you lingered
Until dawn fingered the dark sky
And you cried,
"God help me,"
You sighed once only,
So soft I almost missed it.
Did you see the Almighty?
Waiting with arms uplifted?
Was it joy upon your tongue?
Or was the sigh
Merely Death
That came at last
To seize your breath?

Frankly I was past
Caring by then,
Although I do admit
A certain curiosity.
Where do they go, the dead?
I'd rather like to know.

CHAPTER FIFTY-THREE

Dawn had hardly broken. Jack went to the wardrobe and rooted at the back for his old toy box. They had stashed it there when he was a young lad, and he knew his father wouldn't have disposed of it without telling him. Sure enough, there it was. He carried it over to his desk and opened it. What he wanted was still inside. Some pieces of cardboard, a pair of scissors, a pot of glue that had somehow survived the years of neglect. He removed those things, then was caught momentarily by the sight of a lead toy soldier wedged into the cup of the cup-and-ball game that he'd once played with by the hour.

He stood the soldier on the desk. His rifle was missing its tip and his red pantaloons had faded to a blotchy pink, but there he was, perpetually poised and ready to fight.

Jack went to the chest of drawers and took out a pair of socks. Basic army issue, khaki, rather rough. He put those too on the desk.

His hair was still short, army style, but he was able to snip a few strands from the top of his head. He placed them beside the socks.

The only other thing he needed was in the kitchen. Ever since he could remember there had been a tin box underneath the sink, supplied with the gauze and salves needed for the minor cuts that a young, energetic boy incurred regularly.

Again he paused. Still silence.

He looked at the shabby tin soldier. He gave it a flick with his finger and it fell over, lying stiff and immobile. He stood it back on its feet then flicked it again. And again.

He left his room quietly and went downstairs.

A SOLDIER'S DECLARATION

I am making this statement as an act of wilful defiance of military authority, because I believe that the War is being deliberately prolonged by those who have the power to end it. I am a soldier, convinced that I am acting on behalf of soldiers. I believe this War, upon which I entered as a war of defence and liberation, has now become a war of aggression and conquest. I believe that the purposes for which I and my fellow-soldiers entered upon this War should have been so clearly stated as to have made it impossible for them to be changed without our knowledge, and that, had this been done, the objects which actuated us would now be attainable by negotiation.

I have seen and endured the sufferings of the troops, and I can no longer be a party to prolonging those sufferings for ends I believe to be evil and unjust.

I am not protesting against the military conduct of the War, but against the political errors and insincerities for which the fighting men are being sacrificed.

On behalf of those who are suffering now, I make this protest against the deception which is being practiced on them. Also I believe that it may help to destroy the callous complacence with which the majority of those at home regard the continuance of agonies which they do not share, and which they have not sufficient imagination to realise.

Captain Siegfried Sassoon

CHAPTER FIFTY-FOUR

MURDOCH DEALT WITH THE ITALIAN SITUATION AS quickly as he could decently do, but he was all too aware that the hour of the medal ceremony was rushing toward him. He was sure now that the murders of Aggett and Carella, as well as the attack on Morris Swartz, were connected. Perhaps even the death of poor Daniel Samuels. The chalk mark on the clothing of two of the men pointed to somebody who had knowledge of the war. It might also have been an accusation of cowardice. Like a white feather. All four of the young men had been given exemptions from conscription. They were not soldiers.

Yesterday, when he had been at the Armouries, Murdoch had been skeptical that any theft had taken place. Now he was afraid that the explosives had, indeed, been stolen.

Soldiers knew how to build jam-tin bombs.

He got to his house as fast as he could, and just as he got to the door Jack emerged in his dress uniform. He was wearing the black sling.

"Pa. I was heading off for the ceremony."

"The one you didn't tell me about."

"Sorry. I was intending to, but we haven't seen each other."

"You seem able to write clear enough notes," said Murdoch. "You could at least have done that."

"Sorry," said Jack again. "Well, I'd better get to the end of the street. I'm being picked up."

"Hold on a minute. We've got to have a talk."

"Pa. I can't right now. The corporal is a stickler for punctuality."

He actually started to move off but Murdoch stopped him.

"Why are you wearing the sling?"

"My arm was sore this morning. I don't feel like aggravating it. We're marching from the Armouries to Queen's Park. Not far by infantry standards but far enough if you're out of shape like I am."

A motor car turned onto the street.

"There's my carriage," said Jack. "I'd better go."

"Wait. I'll come to the ceremony."

Jack's eyes met those of his father. "No need. Just a lot of dull speeches, more than likely."

Murdoch heard the telephone ringing inside the house.

"Damnation," said Murdoch. "Listen, son—"

"You've got that expression on your face, Pa. Try not to worry. We can talk later." The telephone continued to ring.

"You'd better answer it," said Jack.

The army car came to a halt in front of them. The driver gave a short blast of the horn and Jack turned and got in immediately. They drove off. Jack did not wave.

Damn. Damn.

Murdoch went to answer the persistent summons of the telephone.

It was Dr. Howitt calling from the hospital.

"Detective, I am glad to catch you. I am the deliverer of good news. Morris Swartz has turned a corner."

"Thank God for that."

"Not only is he conscious and asking for food, he has recalled a little more about the attack. He says he heard somebody across the road. It was a man coughing."

"Coughing?"

"That's right. He said it was most distinct. His attacker had a cough."

"Is he certain it was this man who attacked him?"

"Quite certain. He heard the cough and seconds later he was hit. Had to be the same person."

Murdoch wanted to sit down.

"Detective? That should be a big help to you in this investigation, shouldn't it?"

"Yes, indeed, Doctor. It should."

CHAPTER FIFTY-FIVE

THE CEREMONY HAD DRAWN A LARGE CROWD, AND Murdoch had to push his way through the throngs toward the flight of steps that swept down from the main entrance of Queen's Park. He used his police badge to gain access to a section of the risers just to the right of the assembled dignitaries.

"Are you one of the fathers?" asked an older woman as he squeezed in beside her.

"Yes, I am."

"You must be so proud. Your son is obviously a hero."

Murdoch fervently hoped that was true. He focused on the scene in front of him, searching for God knows what.

The gracious sandstone building was festooned with multi-coloured bunting, and stretched across the entrance was a large banner flapping in the gusty wind. "SIGN UP NOW. YOUR COUNTRY NEEDS YOU." The mayor and other dignitaries, in silk top hats and cashmere overcoats, were already gathered, their wives well bundled up in furs. At the head of the group was the lieutenant-governor, Sir John Hendrie. The crowd, many children among them, was contained behind a rope barrier across from the lieutenant-governor and his party. A few mounted police officers were waiting under the archway, their big horses standing stoic and steady.

Then Murdoch saw a young woman was waving at him from the bottom of the risers. It was Fiona Williams. Immediately, he gestured to her to join him. She stepped forward, but one of the aides stopped her. She pointed at Murdoch, who showed his badge again, and the aide let her through. She climbed up the riser and took the spot beside Murdoch.

"Thank you," she whispered.

"Not at all, Miss Williams."

She glanced at him mischievously. "Do you think you could call me Fiona? We've known each other since I was ten years old. I can't get used to you addressing me so formally."

"Of course." He glanced at her. "Did you get the morning off?"

She clenched her teeth. "You could say that."

Coming from across the park they heard the sound of the pipes and drums. The soldiers were arriving.

"I'll explain later," Fiona added.

The mounted officers moved forward with a jangling of bridles and snorts from the horses. Around the bend of the avenue came two landaus. A huge cheer went up from the crowd. The men waved their hats in the air, and some of the women twirled their boas and scarves. Following the carriages was a marching band, small in number but energetic enough.

Fiona squeezed Murdoch's arm. "Isn't it exciting?"

He nodded. He was sick with apprehension. All he wanted to see was Jack.

You have raised a good and honourable man.

The first carriage, drawn by two coal-black horses, was carrying seven women in mourning garb who were to accept the medals on behalf of the deceased soldiers who had earned them. Six mothers, one wife. The face of one was hidden by a long black widow's veil. Behind them came the carriage with the only two honourees who were alive, Corporal A.R. Mendizabal and Private Jack Murdoch.

"There he is," exclaimed Fiona.

The mounted guard wheeled around and divided to each side of the landaus, which had halted in front of the dignitaries. The horses tossed their heads.

The women alighted first and made their way, one by one, to the steps. There, at the direction of a uniformed officer, they lined up, quiet and dignified. At this the crowd fell silent.

Now it was the turn of the two men. Corporal Mendizabal

got out, moving somewhat stiffly. Jack followed.

"Oh dear. He's wearing a sling," said Fiona. "I thought his arm was better."

"He said it was sore this morning. He didn't want to aggravate it."

The soldiers who had marched up were now marking time.

A man in the regalia of a sergeant major stepped forward. He had a voice used to carry across parade grounds.

"Company. Halt."

There was a table behind the dignitaries where the medals were displayed. An aide picked one up and handed it to the lieutenant-governor.

The sergeant major bellowed, "Mrs. Brown. Step forward please."

She did so.

"Mrs. Brown is accepting on behalf of her son, Private Arthur Brown, who performed acts of great bravery while acting as a telephonist and signaller."

Sir John handed her the medal. Loud cheers from the crowd, more waving of hats and scarves. She gave a curtsey and returned to her place.

Murdoch was keeping his eyes on Jack, who had also got out of the landau and was standing quietly, waiting his turn to come forward.

One by one the women came up and accepted the medals Sir John handed to them. Each time, cheers resounded. There were many tears.

Suddenly Fiona pointed. "Look, Mr. Murdoch, there's Percy. There. Over on the other side behind the rope. I wonder why he's in a wheelchair."

Percy McKinnon was in his uniform, and his legs were covered with a tartan shawl. Behind him, her hands on the handles of the wheelchair, was a young woman, barely more than a girl.

Something about the sight made Murdoch go cold. He was about to climb down and go over to Percy when the sergeant major called out Jack's name.

"Private John Murdoch!"

Sir John stepped forward holding the medal.

"Congratulations."

Murdoch was close enough to hear the exchange that followed.

"My friend should be the one getting a medal, not me," said Jack. It was a declamation.

Sir John looked bewildered. This was not the typical response. "I'm sure many of our boys deserve medals, soldier. I wish I could hand out one to them all."

Before he could proceed, Jack suddenly slipped his arm out of his sling. At first, Murdoch didn't know what the hell it was. Then he realized Jack had a puppet on his arm. He must have made it from one of his army socks. It had tufts of hair, a wide mouth. There was a strip of bandage around the place where its eyes would be.

"This is TOM," said Jack loudly. "That stands for The One

Missing. TOM, show Sir John your tongue," said Jack, and he snapped open the puppet's mouth, revealing the green cloth inside. "His tongue is green because he was gassed. He was also blinded. TOM, tell Sir John how that felt."

At that, the aide, who had seemed frozen in horror, seized the medal from the lieutenant-governor's hand.

"We should move on, sir."

Nobody seemed to know what to do next. Those closest, who had heard what transpired, looked deeply uncomfortable. The sergeant major himself came forward.

"Private Murdoch, fall out."

Jack returned the puppet to its place in his sling. Smartly he stepped forward.

"Right turn," said the sergeant major. He was carrying a rifle and he slapped it against his shoulder. "After me. Quick march."

Jack did not hesitate to obey.

Most of the crowd had not caught on to what was happening.

Murdoch turned to Fiona. He was livid with anger. "Did you put him up to it?"

She looked at him in horror. "Oh no. I had absolutely no idea this was going to happen."

"I'd better go and see what I can do. The last thing he needs is to be cashiered."

Murdoch got down from the riser as fast as he could. The ceremony seemed to be continuing, with the lieutenant-governor getting ready to hand a medal to Corporal Mendizabal. Jack and the sergeant major were marching toward the entrance to the building.

Murdoch had almost reached them when, on some instinct, he turned and looked back at the group of spectators. Percy McKinnon had started to roll his wheelchair in the direction of the lieutenant-governor and the crowd of dignitaries. Murdoch could see Percy had a lit cigarette in his hand, and on his lap was a tin that had once contained jam. There was a string dangling from it. Even as Murdoch understood what he was about to do, Percy touched the lit end of his cigarette to the fuse. He raised his arm in the air.

Later, Murdoch thought he must have shouted but he couldn't be sure. Everything that followed happened so fast, it was a blur.

Jack turned and, apparently taking in the situation at once, he grabbed the rifle from the sergeant-major, raised it to his shoulder, and fired. He struck Percy in the forehead, right at the place where his V-shaped scar was most livid. As his friend dropped forward, Jack ran to him. He was not in time to deactivate the fuse, and the jam-tin bomb exploded on Percy's lap.

CHAPTER FIFTY-SIX

THE EXPLOSION RIPPED PERCY IN TWO. THE YOUNG GIRL behind him, who turned out to be Winnie Payne, was badly injured and died a few hours later. A few of the people nearby were also injured but all recovered. Some of the spectators on the risers were cut by flying glass from the shattered window of the nearby building.

Because Percy hadn't succeeded in tossing the bomb, the lieutenant-governor was not hurt, although he was knocked to the ground.

Jack was blown backwards. He lay there crumpled as Murdoch ran to him.

Bewildered, he looked up at his father.

"How can the Hun be shelling us over here, Pa?"

Murdoch crouched beside him. He put his arm around his shoulders.

"They can't be, Jack. There's no Hun here. You're safe, son. You're safe."

"Percy," whispered Jack. "I shouldn't have saved him."

HOMESICK

"I love my country," he whispered
As he drifted away on the raft of death.
"There are pine trees
That the big winds shape,
Blowing back their branches
Like hair from young girls' faces.
And along the edges of the lakes
Dance butterflies of summer light.
My heart aches that I might
See them all once more.
Promise me you'll take me home."
"Of course," I answered,
To soothe him.
The truth is
His bones will stay
In this foreign land
Mingled with those he killed
And those who murdered him.
So I pressed my lips against his dimming
    ear.
"Take comfort now, my dear.
Here is the home for which you yearn,
Here is the universal place
To which we all return.
Its name is Death."

AFTERMATH

GIVEN WHAT HE HAD DONE, THE MILITARY AUTHORITIES were prepared to overlook Jack's misdemeanour with the puppet. He was recognized as a hero who had saved many lives. However, after the incident Jack went into a state of deep depression. He refused to eat or speak. The doctor at the base hospital said they could try electrical stimulation, or they could brush him vigorously with a wire curry comb. Both treatments had shown some success with soldiers suffering from shell shock who had withdrawn from everyday life.

Murdoch refused to allow them to try either. He would later attribute his son's return to sanity to Fiona.

She showed up at the hospital with two hand puppets. Both

were dressed in army uniform. One she called Lieutenant Looz Bowells. The other she introduced as Corporal Con Shense. She plonked herself down at Jack's bedside, a puppet on each arm. He was utterly unresponsive. Taking each character in turn, she launched into a dialogue.

LIEUTENANT: So, Corporal, I know you'll help me out here. I'll be going overseas soon. What's the toughest thing about being in the trenches?

CORPORAL: Lice and rats.

LIEUTENANT: What? Not the endless noise of artillery? Not the snipers who'll get you if you move a muscle? Not the machine guns that mow down all your chums in one go? Surely that must be hard to bear?

CORPORAL: Not as bad as lice and rats.

LIEUTENANT: Come now. What about the shell holes filled with stinking mud and dead bodies? Horses, mules, men. Makes no difference. They're all in there. Isn't that tough?

CORPORAL: Not as tough as lice and rats.

LIEUTENANT: But what about the men whose heads are sliced off by a piece of shrapnel as they stand next to you? The ones who drown as their lungs fill up with fluid from gas poisoning? What about the constant fear that you could be next? That must be really difficult to withstand!

CORPORAL: Not as much as lice and rats.

LIEUTENANT: So you're telling me that if I am able to deal with the lice and rats, I won't find the other elements of war so difficult? Nothing to it, in fact? . . . Wait a minute—you look as if you don't agree. Is there something you'd like to say?

Jack's eyelids fluttered. "Fuck off, Fiona."

After that, Jack's recovery was quite rapid. He agreed to visits from Father McKenna, which seemed to ease his terrible guilt over killing his best friend. And once he was released from the hospital, he and Murdoch finally did have the "talk." Hours of it. Jack also gave his father a sheaf of papers. They were his poems; he said they would tell Murdoch what he needed to know about the war as Jack had experienced it.

It was much, much later that Jack told him about the man he had been ordered to kill. The deserter.

Mostly, in the beginning, he seemed to need to talk about Percy. Jack said that Percy had killed a German soldier who was about to surrender. This had seemed to send him over the edge, and his mental state had become more and more precarious. He had inflicted an injury on himself soon afterward. He'd lied about the cause, and their superior officers had assumed it was a result of enemy action. Jack felt that made him responsible for keeping Percy from harm.

"Looking after him kept me sane," he whispered to Murdoch one night.

Then Jack himself was injured as he was trying to rescue his sergeant from an exploding ammunition dump. Both he and Percy were invalided out and sent back to Canada. There, Jack had grown more and more worried that Percy had become totally unhinged. He raged about "slackers." He pushed for conscription. At the same time, Jack said, Percy was angry at the way the war was being conducted by the "brass," as he called them. War was something you could understand only if you experienced it, he said. His final act of self-immolation, Jack thought, was an attempt to bring attention to the terrible state of affairs.

Jack had made a puppet; Percy had made a bomb.

Murdoch knew there was no doubt that Percy had killed Antonio Carella. He had left clear fingerprints on the shovel handle. He was also sure it was Percy who had killed Arthur Aggett after they had argued at Mrs. Schumacher's, and Percy who had attacked Morris Swartz.

When Murdoch felt Jack was ready, he filled in the details.

When he attacked Arthur Aggett, Percy had likely used a pair of the large Chinese laundry tongs as his weapon. He had plunged the tongs into the boiler when he'd returned, which was how he'd scalded his hand. The size of the tongs, with their metal hinge at the end, fitted Dr. Vaux's description of what might have caused Arthur's injury.

If that attack had occurred in a fit of rage, the ones that followed seemed more premeditated. Morris and Antonio had both been given exemptions, and for that reason their names and addresses had been published in the *Toronto Daily Star*. Percy had tracked them down and waited for his chance to attack. Fired up by anger, not to mention *baijiu*, he might have tracked down more victims if he had lived longer.

One more thing had emerged during their investigations following Percy's death. Percy was the father of Winnie's baby. He had seduced her shortly before he was sent overseas. He had resumed contact when he'd returned and she had become his accomplice; whether she'd acted willingly or not, Murdoch would never know. According to the city's registry office, Winnie Payne was sixteen years old.

It was decided that Jack would be given work to do as a liaison officer for returning soldiers. Help them to readjust, and so on.

Jack said, "If Mother were still here, I think she'd like me to do that."

All Murdoch could say, softly and quietly to himself, was *Thank God*.

Madge Curnoe applied to adopt Winnie's baby once she learned what had happened to the girl. She and her grandmother would raise him. When she asked Murdoch if he would be a fatherly influence, he accepted.

Shortly after the beginning of the New Year, Murdoch invited Madge to accompany him to the theatre. There was a play on called *The Thirteenth Chair*, which featured a detective. Murdoch thought they would both have fun critiquing the depiction of police work.

Sergeant Allen from number four station sent a telegraph to say he had laid down his king and was surrendering.

LT.-GENERAL E.A.H. ALDERSON, C.B., COMMANDING THE CANADIAN CORPS

May 4, 1915

I tell you truly that my heart is so full that I hardly know how to speak to you. It is full of two feelings—the first being sorrow for the loss of those comrades of ours who have gone; and the second, pride in what the 1st Canadian Division has done.

As regards our comrades who have lost their lives— let us speak of them with our caps off—my faith in the Almighty is such that I am perfectly sure that when men die, as they have died, doing their duty and fighting for their country, for the Empire, and to save the situation for others—in fact, have *died for their friends*—no matter what their past lives have been, no matter what they have done . . . I am perfectly sure that the Almighty takes them and looks after them at once. Lads, we cannot leave them better than like that. . . .

I am now going to shake hands with your officers, and as I do so, I want you to feel that I am shaking hands with each one of you, as I would actually do if time permitted.

ACKNOWLEDGEMENTS

I'M SO LUCKY NOT TO WORK ALONE. MY GOOD FRIENDS are always ready to listen, which was especially appreciated in this case when I read the poems out loud. So, heartfelt thanks to: Brenda Doyle, June Handera, Julia Keeler, Sharon McIsaac, Lorna Milne, and Martha Pagel.

Because the book is set in Toronto, my English chums—Jessie Bailey, Enid (Molly) Harley, and Pam Rowan—weren't here to drive me around, find me material, and generally be helpful, but they were with me in spirit. My life would be considerably poorer without them.

Lynda Wilson and Lynette Dubois were enthusiastic about sharing past times with me.

The people who assured me I was on the right track by moving ahead to 1917 are too numerous to mention, but if I could shake hands with each of them I would. This applies especially to David and Ruth Onley, whom I am so fortunate to count as friends.

A special thanks to Marian Misters and J.D. Singh of Sleuth of Baker Street. Their contribution to the health and welfare of Canadian crime writers is impossible to measure.

Cheryl Freedman was her typical perspicacious self and read an early draft for me. I am most grateful.

Andrea de Shield at the City of Toronto Archives has always been a big help. Her cheerful encouragement is invaluable.

I owe an immense debt of gratitude to Christina Jennings of Shaftesbury Films. She has produced the *Murdoch Mysteries* television show, and because she had faith from the beginning and never gave up, she has opened so many doors for me.

And, of course, where would I be without my friends at McClelland & Stewart, especially my editor, Lara Hinchberger, whom I can only describe as long-suffering. And thanks also to Catherine Marjoribanks for being such a careful copyeditor. I'd be a mess without the two of you.

AUTHOR'S NOTE

THIS HAS BEEN ONE OF THE MOST FASCINATING OF THE explorations I have undertaken while attempting to create Detective William Murdoch's world. Threaded throughout the book are excerpts from various publications current during World War I, and I have used them to illustrate typical thinking. In some cases, they provide an unintended ironic comment; in others, they are moving accounts of a nobility and courage that should not be overlooked. You can judge for yourself.

HERE ARE THE BOOKS FROM WHICH I TOOK THE INSERTS (not necessarily in order)

S.J.C., *England's Welcome (On The Coronation of George V)*. London: Baines & Scarsbrook Printers & Publishers.

Dr. Stephen Bull, *An Officer's Manual Of The Western Front, 1914–1918*. London: Conway, 2008.

Sir Max Aitken, *Canada In Flanders*. London: Hodder and Stoughton, 1916. *This was a particularly extraordinary find. I came across it at a used book sale at the Canadian War Museum in Ottawa. There I discovered a strange and poignant note in the back of the book written in Pitman shorthand. It is as used in the novel.*

Ralph Hodder-Williams, *Princess Patricia's Canadian Light Infantry 1914–1919, Volume 1*. London: Hodder & Stoughton, 1923. *Not only is this a physically beautiful book, it is wonderful to read. One steps into another world.*

Siegfried Sassoon, "A Soldier's Declaration," written on June 15, 1917; read before the House of Commons July 30, 1917; published in *The Times* of London, July 31, 2017.

Memorandum on the Treatment Of Injuries In War, Based On Experience Of The Present Campaign. First published by the General Staff, War Office, 1915.

ABOUT THE AUTHOR

MAUREEN JENNINGS WAS BORN IN BIRMINGHAM, England and emigrated to Canada at the age of seventeen. Jennings's first novel in the Detective Murdoch series, *Except the Dying*, was published to rave reviews and shortlisted for both the Arthur Ellis and the Anthony first novel awards. The influential Drood Review picked *Poor Tom Is Cold* as one of its favourite mysteries of 2001. *Let Loose the Dogs* was shortlisted for the 2004 Anthony Award for best historical mystery. *Night's Child* was shortlisted for the Arthur Ellis Award, the Bruce Alexander Historical Mystery Award, the Barry Award, and the Macavity Historical Mystery Award. And *A Journeyman to Grief* was nominated for the Arthur Ellis Award. Three of the Detective Murdoch novels have been adapted for television, and a Granada International television series, *The Murdoch Mysteries*, based on the characters from the novels, is in its tenth season on CityTV and Alibi. She lives in Toronto, Canada, with her husband Iden Ford.

The Murdoch Mysteries
BY MAUREEN JENNINGS

Except the Dying

IN THE COLD WINTER OF 1895, THE NAKED BODY OF A servant girl is found frozen in a deserted laneway. The young victim was pregnant when she died. Detective William Murdoch soon discovers that many of those connected with the girl's life have secrets to hide. Was her death an attempt to cover up a scandal in one of the city's influential families?

Under the Dragon's Tail

DOLLY MERISHAW IS A MIDWIFE AND AN ABORTIONIST IN Victorian Toronto, and although she keeps quiet about her clients, her contempt and greed leaves them resentful and angry. It comes as no surprise to Detective William Murdoch when she is murdered, but when a young boy is found dead in Dolly's squalid kitchen a week later, Murdoch isn't sure if he's hunting one murderer – or two.

TITAN BOOKS

Poor Tom Is Cold

IN THE THIRD MURDOCH MYSTERY, THE DETECTIVE IS NOT convinced that Constable Oliver Wicken's death was suicide. When he begins to suspect the involvement of Wicken's neighbours, the Eakin family, Mrs. Eakin is committed to a lunatic asylum. Is she really insane, he wonders, or has she been deliberately driven over the edge?

Let Loose the Dogs

DETECTIVE MURDOCH'S LIFE AND WORK BECOME TRAGICALLY entwined when his sister, who long ago fled to a convent to escape their abusive father, is on her deathbed. Meanwhile, the same father has been charged with murder and calls on his estranged son to prove his innocence. But, knowing his father as he does, what is Murdoch to believe?

TITAN BOOKS

Night's Child

AFTER THIRTEEN-YEAR-OLD AGNES FISHER FAINTS AT school, her teacher is shocked to discover in the girl's desk two stereoscopic photographs. One is of a dead baby in its cradle and the other is of Agnes in a lewd pose. When Agnes fails to attend school the next day, her teacher takes the photographs to the police. Murdoch, furious at the sexual exploitation of such a young girl, resolves to find the photographer – and to put him behind bars.

Vices of My Blood

THE REVEREND CHARLES HOWARD SAT IN JUDGMENT ON THE poor, assessing their applications for the workhouse. But now he is dead, stabbed and brutally beaten in his office. Has some poor beggar he turned down taken his vengeance? Murdoch's investigation takes him into the world of the destitute who had nowhere else to turn when they knocked on the Reverend Howard's door.

A Journeyman to Grief

In 1858, a young woman on her honeymoon is abducted, taken across the border to the US and sold into slavery. Thirty-eight years later, the owner of one of Toronto's livery stables has been found dead, horsewhipped and hung from his wrists in his tack room. The investigation endangers Murdoch's own life – and reveals how harms committed in the past can erupt fatally in the present.

TITAN BOOKS